PRINCE OF SHADOWS

CROWN OF LIES™
BOOK TWO

RIVER TATUM

MICHAEL ANDERLE

DON'T MISS OUR NEW RELEASES

Join the Florid Romance email list to be notified of new releases and special promotions (which happen often) by following this link:

https://floridromance.lmbpn.com/about/sign-up-for-our-newsletter/

Published by Florid Romance
an imprint of LMBPN Publishing
2375 E. Tropicana Avenue, Suite 8-305
Las Vegas, Nevada 89119 USA

Version 1.00, January 2026
eBook ISBN: 979-8-89354-954-6
Print ISBN: 979-8-89354-955-3

CHAPTER

ONE

Morning light crept through the silk gauze curtains, pale threads slipping across the stone floor. Miera surfaced from sleep slowly, as she always did, suspended between waking and the shapeless dark where memory refused to live. For a heartbeat, hope flickered—thin, familiar, foolish. Maybe today she would remember something. Anything.

Then the jagged fragments returned, and she wondered if she were still dreaming or if the visions in her head were part of a memory. Or maybe part of a nightmare.

She saw steel flashing in torchlight. Heard a man's warning shout. Then there was a blow she never saw coming, but she flinched as though she'd actually felt the strike. And then there was darkness. Not the dark of closed eyes while resting, but a void that swallowed sound, shape, and her senses. It felt like a force capable of erasing the entire world.

Her body tightened as the vision repeated itself; her muscles felt locked into a defensive coil rooted in readiness to strike. Her breath came in sharp, ragged gasps until she focused on calming herself with steadier breaths. The scent of linen and dried lavender anchored her, a quiet tether to the present. A small mercy. Enough to keep her from tipping into panic.

The mind sometimes builds walls around what it cannot survive. The healers' voices echoed faintly—clinical, assured. A pragmatic defense, they'd said. Brutal, but effective. A way to survive what the mind could not bear.

She lay still until her pulse leveled. Then the room assembled itself around her in familiar shapes: Durevin Hold. Verthar's mountain fortress. The place Prince Jareth insisted would keep her safe.

That insistence had become its own kind of lifeline. Something to cling to when the alternative was a blank, formless void. Better a story—even one she hadn't chosen —than nothing at all. A role, even an invented one, was still armor.

But the nights betrayed her. Sleep never offered peace. Dreams came sharp and sensory, carrying scents and textures that did not belong to Verthar's dry cold. A sigil carved into weathered stone. The tang of salt spray. The warm, green-heavy air of a place her waking mind did not recognize. They struck with the clarity of touch. Too vivid to dismiss. Too real to accept.

Could they be memories? The thought sent her pulse climbing. To have a past meant having enemies. It meant the attack had not been random. It meant she had once stood on a gameboard—and someone had struck with purpose.

Yet the healers warned her, too: after trauma, the mind might invent phantoms. Echoes. Illusions.

Safer to believe the illusions. Necessary, even. Her hand went to the pendant she wore. The silver was cool beneath her fingers; the veilstone crystal pulsed faintly, a soft, deliberate rhythm to which she timed her breaths. Jareth had given it to her, clasped it in place himself. *A charm,* he'd said. Something to help quiet her mind so she could sleep. So the visions she had, whatever they were, would not drive her to madness.

Three days, the king had decreed. Three days for Jareth to produce answers. Yet here she remained, the deadline passed and her head still attached to her shoulders. Something had shifted in those final hours—some bargain struck or threat deflected. Jareth had not spoken of it, and she had not dared to ask. The reprieve felt borrowed, not earned. A stay of execution rather than a pardon.

She focused on the faint pulse of the pendant. Let it steady the edges of fear. Let it smooth the sharpness of the dreams into something harmless. *The dreams were only dreams.* Echoes. Residue.

She would not be a liability. The instinct sat deep, older than her memories. A liability was a weakness. A piece sacrificed first. Jareth had risked standing and reputation to bring her here. She would not repay that by collapsing under nightmares she could not even prove were real.

The garden attack had revealed something else—

something perhaps more terrifying than the nightmares. A capacity for violence that moved faster than thought. Her body remembered what her mind could not. She had broken a man's arm with techniques she couldn't name, had felt the precise angles of combat as naturally as breathing.

The veilstone had suppressed the memory of learning these skills, but it could not suppress the skills themselves. They lived in her muscles, her reflexes, waiting. She did not know if that made her safer or more dangerous.

If she could not remember who she had been, she would choose who she would be now: a woman recovering. Grateful. Composed. A guest worth the trouble of protecting.

The thought placed a thin, serviceable calm over the unease inside her. She was alive. Sheltered. Remembered by someone, even if she could not remember herself. That she could inhabit.

She pushed herself upright and glanced to the window. Beyond the glass, House Verthar's black banners hung motionless in the pale morning air, the falcon stark against grey sky. She'd learned the rhythm of the patrolling guards without meaning to—the fourth bell shift change, the footfalls that passed her door like a circling tide. Details her mind gathered automatically, as though pattern mattered even when she claimed it didn't.

Reassurance did not live in patterns. Containment did. The chamber wrapped that truth in contradiction. Soft linens. Hot meals delivered without a word. The hearth's steady ironwood fire. Enough comfort to dull discomfort

—yet the door had no lock on the inside. And the windows, though beautifully latticed, were reinforced. Decorative. Impassable.

A gilded cage remained a cage. She exhaled and pushed the thought aside. The cold bit at her ankles as she swung her legs over the bed. Sunlight spilled across the velvet coverlet, dissolving into motes of dust that drifted in the air. Chamomile and comfrey lingered faintly—someone had tended the room before dawn.

Simple goals. Rise. Dress. Find Jareth. Thank him.

She crossed to the washbasin. The linen of her nightgown whispered against the floor with each step. Her fingers closed around the silver pitcher that was heavy, and finely wrought. The Vertharian falcon crest gleamed near its base.

She lifted it. And froze. The polished basin reflected a face she knew was hers: dark hair, pale skin, a slim nose. But the eyes were all wrong. They were still the same color, but they looked clearer, stripped of confusion and doubt.

These eyes looked focused, calculating. Then the woman in the reflection turned and Miera could see the room behind her. Her mouth fell open when she realized the room in the water's reflection was the very same room where she stood now.

Miera was mesmerized. She could not look away, no matter how frightened and anxious the vision made her. She watched in stunned silence as the reflection swept the room with rapid, unnervingly precise attention. It marked the door, the iron-latticed windows, the hearth tools, the placement of the furniture, cataloguing the space as if assessing exits and options she herself would never have noticed.

How could this version of herself—it was herself, was it not? Whether a vision or a waking nightmare, it *was* her. But this version of herself was not frightened. Not lost. She looked...dangerous.

Miera's breath hitched. She blinked and the vision in the water's reflection vanished. Only her own shaken reflection stared back: wide-eyed, ordinary, throat tight.

The pendant pulsed once, a sharp jolt against her skin. Then the quiet rolled through her mind, sweeping everything else aside. It wasn't peace. Not exactly. It was more like a soft, unnatural blankness that rolled through her mind and smothered the rising terror before it could form any further.

The memory of the other face dissolved like salt in water, leaving only the faint sense that something important had slipped through her fingers. Her hands steadied. Her heart slowed. The unease thinned into a distant whisper.

She set the pitcher down with care. The morning light had brightened, pooling in the corners of the chamber. Tasks awaited. A day to face. She moved to her wardrobe, choosing one of the gowns Jareth's household had provided. She would dress. She would thank him. She would be the woman she needed to appear to be.

TWO

Jareth had spent the day barricaded behind the duties of his station, building walls of ink and parchment against his own conscience. Border correspondence. Army requisitions. Patrol reports tracking Avenali movements along the northern passes. Necessary work, to be sure, but today, none of it offered shelter.

Every crisp report on a skirmish only sharpened the blade he'd driven into himself. Every signature authorizing troop movements reminded him that he was waging a silent war inside these fortress walls, a war with one unknowing woman as its contested ground.

He'd orchestrated her captivity with military precision. Commissioned the veilstone. Crafted the fiction of her amnesia. Built a prison and draped it in gentleness. And she thanked him for it. The thought sat in his gut like spoiled wine.

The three-day ultimatum had been a blade at his

throat. He had bought time with a carefully constructed lie—a fabricated lead on her identity that required 'delicate investigation.' His father had granted a fortnight's extension before departing on his progress through the eastern lords. Fourteen days. It was not mercy; it was a longer leash on a shorter chain. The king's spies remained behind, watching, waiting for Jareth to fail.

When the summons for the evening meal arrived delivered by a page who bowed low enough to suggest he feared interrupting something important. Jareth almost welcomed it. A public performance gave him structure. Expected rules. Predictable patterns. Yet the knowledge that he would have to sit near her made the evening feel harder.

The Great Hall blazed with captured light. More than a thousand candles burned in iron candelabras, their glow reflecting across the gilded ceiling until the hall seemed to shimmer with its own fire. Below the dais, the long tables gleamed with wealth his grandfather had wrung from conquered provinces: polished pewter, fruit pyramids from the southern orchards, crystal goblets filled with wine from vineyards taken by force. The air pressed thick with roasting meat, mulled spices, beeswax, and the perfume of courtiers who bathed in oils more expensive than a farmer's yearly earnings.

From a gallery above, musicians played, strings threaded through with the low, mournful call of a Vertharian horn. Its tone tried for elegance but carried something older beneath it, a tension that radiated from the throne like heat from a forge.

And at the center of that stillness sat King Halric.

He occupied the high seat carved from a single petrified ironwood trunk, posture rigid, hands resting motionless on the chair's arms. His short-cropped grey hair caught the candlelight; his pale eyes swept the hall with methodical precision.

Missing nothing. Forgiving less. Jareth had spent twenty-eight years trying to read emotion in that face. He'd learned only that his father's stillness was more dangerous than most men's fury. A man could drown in the power Halric held over everyone at court.

Jareth's boots echoed across the polished marble as he descended into the hall. Courtiers bowed as he passed, their murmured greetings blending into a meaningless wash. His attention had already found her: Miera.

She sat at the far end of the dais, as distant from his father's scrutiny as the seating arrangement allowed. Halric had insisted she dine there—ostensibly for observation, though they both knew it served other purposes. Seating her at the high table told the court one thing unmistakably.

This woman mattered to the prince.

Which made her either valuable or vulnerable, depending on who noticed. She looked small in the vast hall, despite the rich gown his household had prepared, a deep blue silk that sharpened the grey of her eyes. Her dark hair had been arranged simply, revealing the elegant line of her throat.

And the veilstone pendant resting at its center. From here he couldn't see the crystal's faint pulse, but he knew its cadence. He'd chosen it. Specified the enchantment. Watched the court mages sketch sigils that hurt the eyes.

Subtle, he thought bitterly. Her focus was fixed on the tapestry behind the king—a depiction of the Siege of Corthen Harbor, his grandfather's most celebrated victory. She studied it with the earnest attention of someone trying to learn the history of a foreign land, unaware she was staring at her own kingdom's humiliation.

The cruelty of it struck sharper than he expected. Protocol dictated that Jareth take his place at Halric's right hand. Every dignitary watched that chair. Every ambitious noble read meaning into who occupied it.

But his feet shifted. Without permission from his reason. His steps carried him past the king's empty right-hand chair. Down the length of the dais. Toward her.

Conversations faltered. Heads turned. A ripple moved through the hall. Even the musicians missed a beat before recovering.

Everyone saw it: the Crown Prince bypassing his father to sit beside the mysterious woman. Jareth ignored the iron weight of Halric's gaze. Pulled out the chair beside Miera, then sat.

A small rebellion, but rebellion nonetheless. He offered his father a polite nod. Not defiant, not apologetic. Simply acknowledgment. The king's expression didn't shift, but the hall seemed to cool by several degrees.

You'll answer for this, Halric's stillness promised.

Jareth turned to Miera, keeping his voice quiet beneath the music. "You look well."

The words tasted false. Hollow. It had been days since

an assassin's blade—*his* assassin's blade—had nearly found her throat. The attack that let him "save" her. Bring her here. Lock her behind the veilstone.

She turned to him, and her face transformed. Her smile struck with a physical force. Bright. Unguarded. Free of the fear he'd seen when she first arrived. Free of the sharp, analytical intelligence he'd glimpsed before the veilstone had fully settled its influence.

Only soft, profound calm. A perfect success. The thought should have eased him. Instead it curdled in his chest.

"I am," she said, voice steady. "Thanks to you."

The words dropped like stones into deep water. Thanks to him, she remembered nothing. Thanks to him, Princess Seraya of Corthen—daughter of the king his grandfather had crushed, sister to the crown prince his father still plotted to eliminate—sat smiling at her captor as though he'd saved her life.

Thanks to him, one of the sharpest political minds in three kingdoms was reduced to a gentle conversationalist discussing poetry and library books.

Servants arrived with the first course—pastries filled with spiced lamb and pine nuts, silver plates stamped with the falcon crest. Pale wine poured into crystal goblets.

Jareth forced himself to speak about inane things: border envoys, minor lords with grand ambitions. Safe topics. Meaningless topics. Court noise.

She answered with equal ease about books she'd found, poetry she liked, gentle observations. She'd discovered a volume of Vertharian verse, she told him, and found the meter fascinating even when she missed the references.

No trace remained of the woman who'd debated treaty law with him during their journey. No hint of the strategist who'd once frustrated advisers across three realms.

That woman now lived behind stone and silver and spelled crystal. He had put her there.

"The poem about the ironwood forests," she said, eyes brightening. "How they endure harsh conditions? I found it beautiful."

Ironwood doesn't bend. It breaks, or it endures. His father had drilled that line into him at age seven—right after punishing him for crying over a horse that died.

Jareth lifted his goblet and drank. The wine tasted like ashes.

"I'm glad you're finding ways to pass the time," he said, keeping his tone neutral.

She studied him for a moment. For a terrible heartbeat, he thought something sharp and knowing flickered behind her gaze—Princess Seraya looking out from behind the quiet. But when she spoke, her voice held only gratitude.

"Truly, Jareth. I feel peaceful for the first time in a very long while. The charm you gave me..." Her fingers brushed the pendant unconsciously. "It's magic."

He remembered the court mages bowing their heads in the dim workshop, chalk sigils curling across the stone floor in tight, disciplined patterns. They mixed herbs and ground minerals into the markings, their hands moving with the calm certainty of men who had done this many times before. A thin plume of smoke rose as the symbols reacted, seeping toward the pendant on the table. The crystal took the change with a faint glow, then dimmed again, the enchantment settling like a weight inside it.

"Mind and magic spring from one root," the eldest mage had said. "Bind one, and the other quiets. She will remember only what we permit. Feel only what we allow."

"And if she resists?" Jareth had asked.

"The stone is stronger than her will. It will feel like peace to her. Like safety. She'll never know she's in a cage."

He'd told himself it was necessary. Mercy, even. Watching her thank him for it made the lie curdle in his stomach.

"I'm glad it helps," he managed.

For one unguarded instant, he forgot to maintain the mask. His hand twitched toward hers, impulse breaking through duty. He stopped himself just in time, thumb pressing against the sharp edge of his signet ring until pain grounded him.

Sentiment is weakness. Mercy is for those who can afford to lose. He reshaped his expression into composure, but not quickly enough.

"What is it?" she asked softly. Concern replaced her smile. "You seem troubled."

Everything, he nearly said. *Every lie. Every choice. Every stolen piece of you.*

Instead, he replied, "Only the burden of duty. And the memory of the attack."

It was true enough, and that was what mattered. Her eyes warmed with sympathy that cut him more deeply than accusation ever could.

"I wish I could ease your burdens as you eased mine," she whispered.

The blow landed cleanly. He had no defense against it.

Servants arrived with the next course—quail glazed with honey and pears. The scent turned Jareth's stomach, but he lifted his fork. Performance was expected. Performance was survival.

The musicians shifted into an old Vertharian waltz—beautiful, unless you knew it had been composed to celebrate a massacre.

Jareth nodded and answered as expected while Miera described the gardens she'd glimpsed from her window—the roses, the arbor, how it must look in summer. He told her his mother had planted them. Mentioned it lightly. Too lightly.

Halric's gaze pressed into the back of his neck. Cold. Inevitable.

We will discuss this.

Jareth took another sip of wine. Every comfort in this hall—from the goblets to the food to the woman beside him—had been paid for in blood.

He held his posture rigid, his expression calm. A prince performing strength. A man wearing a mask he could no longer take off.

He would endure. He always endured. But as she sat beside him, smiling with that terrible trust he had not earned, he no longer knew whether enduring meant strength—or surrender.

The meal dragged into the night, course after course, mask after mask. And through it all, the veilstone pulsed against her throat—steady, gentle, relentless as a door locking shut.

CHAPTER

THREE

The image of Jareth's face at the high table followed Miera from the cavernous warmth of the Great Hall, a splinter lodged in her thoughts that she could not quite shake free.

Not the composed mask he wore for the court, the expression carved by years in a world that prized strength before mercy. What troubled her was the moment that mask had cracked, the brief, unguarded instant when something beneath the surface had shown through. Weariness. Bone deep and unmistakable.

She had seen it in the taut line of his shoulders, tension that even the immaculate cut of his crimson coat could not hide. In the way his hand had started toward hers, then diverted to his signet ring, as if catching himself at the edge of an impulse he was not permitted to indulge.

Her quiet words, meant as sympathy, had not eased him. If anything, they had darkened his gaze. The look he had given her stayed with her now.

A man standing at the edge of a precipice. A man who did not yet know whether he would step back or fall. The memory tugged at something in her chest, a restless sympathy she could neither name nor dismiss. An unwelcome variable in the careful equation of her survival.

She needed distraction. She craved it, actually, as her chambers were lonely, filled with the echo of questions she could not yet answer. She needed an exercise for the mind, something solid and impersonal to anchor her before night settled fully and the specters of dream rose up again.

The library would do. Durevin Hold's library occupied three levels of the eastern tower, reached by a corridor lined with torches that never seemed to burn low. At her request, the guards outside her door had nodded, one offering to escort her.

She refused as politely as she dared. A small rebellion, perhaps, but she needed at least the shape of freedom, even if she knew the guards would note every step she took.

The library door stood open, twice her height and carved from single slabs of blackwood. The handles were wrought iron shaped like falcons in flight. She stepped inside and the world changed.

Silence here felt different than in her chamber. Not smothering, but intentional. The sort of quiet that settled over long hours of study, accumulating like dust on shelves. It wrapped around her shoulders with a weight that felt almost ceremonial.

The air was thick with layered scents that her mind

catalogued without effort: old parchment and cracked leather, wax and ink, the faint sweetness of lamp oil burning in bronze brackets along the walls.

Towering shelves of blackwood rose toward a vaulted ceiling lost in shadow, three stories of books disappearing into dimness overhead. Afternoon light spilled through tall, arched windows, the glass so old it had rippled and warped, casting a softened glow across worn flagstones.

It felt like ancient light. Ordered light. The sort that belonged in a place where history lived.

Miera's soft-soled slippers made little sound as she moved between the aisles. Her fingers skimmed along the spines of leather-bound volumes, noting the changes in texture. Some bindings were smooth from generations of hands. Others felt stiff and untouched.

The soft shift of parchment and the steady burn of the lamps were the only sounds besides her own breathing, which seemed too loud in the vastness.

One entire section held nothing but military histories. The Campaigns of Halric the First. Ironwood Economics: A Treatise on Resource Extraction. The Art of the Siege. Line after line of conquest, strategy, and the arithmetic of killing.

She was not looking for poems tonight, nor romances. She wanted facts. Clear narrative. Names and dates that belonged to this place, anchors to keep her mind from drifting into the unsettling currents of what she could not remember.

Her hand paused on a solid volume bound in dark

leather. Its spine was cracked yet strong, the gilt title faded but legible: *A History of Vertharian Court and Culture.*

Suitable reading for a guest of the court. A map to the world she now inhabited, whether she had chosen it or not.

She eased the book from the shelf. It had a reassuring weight in her hands. Dust motes wheeled lazily through a bar of light as she moved. The pages smelled of old glue and pressed flowers; someone had once used sprigs of lavender as markers, and a ghost of the scent lingered.

Back in her chamber, the fire laid earlier had burned down to a bed of coals. The embers cast a low, steady glow that sent shadows flickering across the tapestries on the walls. One showed the Battle of the Mourning Trail, according to the brass plate beneath it, Vertharian soldiers in black and crimson encircling an enemy force.

A constant reminder of the pride of her hosts. The wide stone room felt a little less empty with the book in her hands, but no less like a confined space.

She slipped out of her outer robe, the heavy silk catching faint light on its subtle embroidery, and folded it with care at the foot of the bed. The linen of her night-gown felt like a small indulgence by comparison, soft and light against her skin.

She settled into the high-backed chair near the hearth and drew a wool blanket over her legs against the evening chill. The solid weight of the book in her lap steadied her. Anticipation stirred, a quiet, almost forgotten pleasure at the thought of occupying her mind with something beyond its own circling fear.

She opened to a page at random, then another, letting the book reveal its scope: chronicles of kings, descriptions of court rituals, long passages on proper address. Then a chapter heading caught her eye.

The Treaty of Redmere.

Something tightened beneath her ribs. She could not say why. She turned to the beginning of the chapter and began to read. The vellum pages were thick and smooth beneath her fingers, the ink still dark despite the years. The text described a pivotal accord signed twenty-five years earlier, the treaty that had ended a generation of brutal conflict between Verthar, the island realms, and the kingdom of Corthen.

Corthen. The name sent a fine tremor through her, like a plucked string.

The writer's tone was reverent. Each paragraph praised the restraint and wisdom of Verthar's delegation. The envoys, the book claimed, had borne terrible provocation with patience, seeking only a just and lasting peace. Their enemies, by contrast, were described as erratic and cruel.

Something in the prose scraped her nerves raw. She could not have said exactly what was wrong, but dissonance hummed under the surface of the words, a sour note within the melody. Some deeper instinct in her recoiled.

Each line presented Verthar as slow to anger, reluctant to harsh action. Yet every sentence felt like a brick laid in a wall that hid more than it revealed. Her gut insisted Verthar had not been patient. Verthar had been hungry.

The version of events on the page tasted like a lie told by omission.

A thin, unfamiliar anger twisted through her. She read on, brows drawing tight.

The narrative shifted its focus to the Cortheni delegation. The king was called arrogant. The court was dismissed as vain, obsessed with display. The author mocked what he called their *theater of diplomacy.* He described layered silks and jeweled fans as tools of artifice. He framed their preference for subtle negotiation as cowardice wrapped in perfume.

Their refusal to surrender coastal lands their families had held for generations was not described as the defense of a border. It was sentimental pride. Weakness pretending to be principle.

Every line was a barb. Every phrase chipped away at the dignity of a people she was supposed to know nothing about.

The anger inside her coiled tighter, a serpent rousing from sleep. Her hands began to tremble. This was not neutral history. This was an indictment dressed as fact, a careful defamation written with the authority of a chronicle that would teach generations how to despise.

She turned the page, telling herself she should stop, unable to stop. The closing paragraph hit with the force of a blow. She read it once, twice, the words cutting deeper with each pass.

The unyielding arrogance of the Cortheni monarch, coupled with the decadent weakness of his court, left Verthar no choice but to enforce terms by strength rather than reason. That such a proud and foolish kingdom should have held power for so long stands as proof of the world's former disorder, a disorder Verthar's righteousness has corrected.

Something inside her broke. Tears rose without warning, hot and heavy, spilling over before she could summon the discipline to stop them. They burned tracks down her cheeks, carrying with them a grief that seemed far too large for the fact of a biased history.

This did not feel like general sorrow at injustice in the abstract. It felt specific. Personal. As if the author had insulted someone she loved. As if he had dragged the name of her own family through the mud.

The injustice lodged in her chest, sharp and choking. Her throat closed. The chamber blurred.

Why?

The question lodged like ice beneath her ribs.

Why should a history of a conquered rival, a kingdom she did not remember, tear at her like this?

She was Miera, a woman with no past, no family she knew, no loyalties beyond the practical need to survive in this fortress. Yet the slanders on the page felt like wounds carved directly into her.

She pressed a hand to her sternum, fingers digging through linen as if she could still the pounding of her heart. She groped for logic, the only shield she trusted.

Perhaps this had nothing to do with Corthen itself. Perhaps she simply despised injustice. Perhaps some temper of hers had always bristled at the deliberate twisting of truth, and this was that trait rising to the surface.

Yes. That could be true. It was safer to believe that.

She told herself she had always been that sort of person, someone who could not bear dishonesty, who felt others' slights as if they were her own. A strong sense of fairness, she decided, was a good thing to learn about herself. A virtue. Something she could claim as part of her identity. The thought steadied her slightly. She clung to it.

Yet even as she shaped that explanation, tears continued to fall. Her hands still shook. Deep inside, that wounded place kept crying out, as if the words in the book had trampled something sacred.

With a sharp crack that broke the room's quiet, she snapped the book shut. Her breath came in ragged pulls. The fire had settled lower, shadows climbing higher along the walls. She had no idea how long she had sat reading.

She pressed her palms over her eyes, as if she could push the tears back where they had come from.

Control. She needed control. Her gaze dropped. Silver glinted at her throat.

The pendant lay warm against her skin, the crystal catching the last of the firelight. As her panic crested, as grief and fury and confusion rose in a snarl that threatened to pull her under, she felt it: that familiar, quiet pulse against her collarbone. Steady. Insistent.

She wrapped her fingers around it, clinging to the cool metal and smooth stone with desperate focus. The charm's influence rolled outward, not gently but with clinical efficiency, the way a draught might calm a patient who struggled.

The sharp edges of grief dulled. Anger softened, pushed back until it felt distant and blurred. Thoughts that had started to form, questions that reached for shape in her mind, slid apart before she could hold them.

Why do I care. Why does this feel personal. What am I forgetting. The ideas dissolved, leaving only faint impressions.

Relief came with the quiet that followed. It felt like shelter from a storm she did not know how to weather. Yet somewhere under that relief, another awareness flickered. This was not true peace. Something had been cut away to make room for it. The notion lasted only a heartbeat. The veilstone's pulse smoothed it flat.

She drew a long breath. Then another. Her hands had stopped shaking. Her chest no longer ached as sharply. The calm she had hoped to find in the library had finally arrived, though it felt thinner than she had imagined, like borrowed cloth laid over a wound.

It would do. It had to. With careful movements, she rose and set the book on her bedside table, cover turned down as if she could quiet it. As if closing it could undo what she had read.

She needed sleep. Tomorrow she would think more clearly, when shadows seemed less menacing and history less like a personal accusation.

She climbed into the wide bed and slipped beneath the heavy coverlet, drawing it up as a barrier against the chill that lived in the stone and the colder thing that lived inside her.

The fire whispered softly. The chamber settled into stillness. The pendant rested against her throat, its pulse a patient metronome.

She closed her eyes and willed her mind to match the quiet around her.

Sleep crept in by degrees. Even as it did, a low ache throbbed beneath the veilstone's calm, a muted hum of feeling the magic could not quite erase. It spoke of loyalties unnamed and truths she did not yet know how to reach. It spoke of a kingdom she was meant to have forgotten.

Somewhere in the drifting space between waking and sleep, a name stirred. It rose like a bubble from deep water, carrying with it the sense of who she truly was.

The pendant pulsed once, firm and final. The name slipped away before it could reach her lips, leaving only the ache behind.

FOUR

The summons arrived after the evening meal, delivered by a guardsman whose face had been trained into perfect indifference. A single piece of folded parchment, sealed with black wax stamped with the royal falcon. Not a request. A command.

The King's Solar. Immediately.

Jareth had known this confrontation was inevitable. The chill that had settled over the high table during dinner, his father's silence more cutting than any verbal rebuke, had been the prelude to the storm he now walked toward.

His boots echoed against the stone floors with controlled precision. The tension coiling in his gut threatened to tighten his stride, but he forced each step to remain steady. The corridors of Durevin Hold stretched before him, lit by torches that cast restless shadows across walls carved with the victories of Vertharian conquest. Every surface in this fortress proclaimed the same truth: strength through brutality. Order through fear.

Two guards flanked the door to his father's solar. They stepped aside as he approached, pulling open the heavy ironwood doors.

The King's Solar was a chamber built to make lesser men crumble. Shadows gathered in its corners despite the lamps burning on the massive desk. The air hung heavy with the scent of hot lamp oil and stale smoke. A low fire burned in the hearth, though its warmth never seemed to reach the rest of the room. Cold radiated from the walls like a second presence.

Strategic maps covered every surface. Corthen. Avenal. The Shardspine passes. The world laid out as territories to dominate. Colored pins marked positions and projections. Lines of future violence.

Halric sat behind his monolithic desk, hands resting flat on the polished blackwood surface. His iron-grey hair caught the lamplight, but nothing softened his expression. He did not look up.

Jareth stood at attention three paces from the desk. The silence felt like a vise tightening around him. He had endured this tactic since childhood. He would endure it now.

Finally, Halric spoke without lifting his gaze. "Report."

Jareth began the recitation he had prepared. The coded correspondence to compromised contacts. The scouts sent with a uselessly broad description. The guild channels that would lead nowhere. He outlined every false avenue of investigation he had pursued to ensure nothing would be found.

When he finished, Halric finally looked up. "You have turned over stones in a desert and pretend surprise at finding only sand. There is nothing to find because you have not looked in the right places."

"The methods are sound," Jareth said, voice neutral. "Given sufficient time—"

"Time." Halric's voice sliced through his like a blade. "Time is a resource I do not grant to liabilities. She is most certainly an unknown. Unknowns are threats. And you have grown soft."

He leaned forward, features sharpening to a cruel edge. "Sentiment is rot. Mercy is a luxury reserved for lesser men. Neutralize the threat before it declares itself. A fall from the eastern tower. A fever. An accident in the training yard. Be creative."

Jareth felt his breath catch. Rage flared so violently it stole his equilibrium. His hands trembled before he forced them still.

"She is not a threat." He bit his lower lip. He hadn't intended to speak that thought aloud but yet, there it was. And he could not take it back.

Halric's eyes narrowed. "Indeed."

"She is a woman with no memory, alone in a foreign land. I am handling it."

"'Handling it.'" Halric repeated the phrase as if tasting something rancid. "Your judgment is compromised. Your priorities have shifted. Do not confuse the warmth of your bed with strategic clarity."

The blow landed as intended. Jareth felt the truth of the accusation like ice. His father knew. Of course he knew.

"You have your orders," Halric said. "I expect results within the fortnight. Dismissed."

Jareth bowed stiffly, turned, and walked out with mechanical precision. When the door closed behind him, he exhaled a harsh breath, almost staggered by the weight of what had just been demanded of him.

His father wanted her dead. And Jareth had already committed himself to defiance.

He paced the corridors, boots striking the stone in a rhythm that steadied him. He needed to think. Needed to plan. Needed to find a way to protect her without lighting a firestorm he could not control.

He stopped walking when he realized where his steps had taken him. Miera's chambers. Two guards stood at her door. They straightened as he approached.

"Leave us," he told them. "Your watch is ended for the night."

The guards exchanged a quick, uneasy glance. When they caught the sharp look Jareth leveled at them, their backs straightened at once.

"Your Highness," they said together, the words tight with restraint. They bowed and moved off down the corridor, boots fading into the distance.

When they had gone, Jareth let out a slow breath, lifted his hand, and knocked. Three firm, deliberate raps against the heavy door.

The door opened. Firelight spilled over Miera's face.

She wore a nightgown with a dark silk robe draped around her shoulders. Her hair fell loose down her back. The veil-stone rested against her throat, pulsing softly.

Relief softened her features. "Jareth. Is everything all right?"

No. Nothing was.

He swallowed hard. "I was concerned about you. May I come in?"

She stepped back. "Of course."

He closed the door behind him. The chamber felt smaller than usual, warmer, its shadows deeper. A book lay on the bedside table. *A History of Vertharian Court and Culture.* The reason her eyes had brimmed with tears earlier.

"Would you like to sit?" she asked, gesturing to the chair.

He shook his head. "I won't stay long. I just... needed to ensure that you are safe."

Her expression shifted, something tender rising in her gaze. "I am. Thanks to you."

His chest tightened. Why did her gratitude keep cutting him open? He gestured to the book on the table, an easy way to deflect the simmering unease in his gut.

"Are you enjoying the book?"

She let out a small, uneasy laugh, though nothing about it was amused. "Enjoy is not the right word," she said, voice softer now. "Some of what I read... it felt wrong in my bones."

Her hand rose unconsciously to her throat, fingertips brushing the pendant as if it might steady her. "The way the book spoke about Corthen. About its people. The contempt in it. It was like reading an insult I should have shrugged off, but... I cannot."

Jareth took a slow step closer. She did not retreat. "What did it make you feel?" he asked.

She drew in a shallow breath. "Anger. Sadness. Almost a sense of... loss. And none of those reactions make any sense." She drew a breath, then another, as if bracing herself.

"Do you think that means something?" she asked quietly. "My reaction, I mean. When you found me in the forest... you told me I had a Cortheni accent."

Her gaze searched his, earnest and troubled. "You said it without hesitation. Before I had spoken more than a single sentence. Why would I sound Cortheni if I am not from there?"

He forced his breath slow, steady. "Accents can be misleading."

"Can they?" she asked. "Or am I trying to avoid the obvious?"

She pressed a hand lightly to her sternum, as if trying to quiet something beneath her ribs. "If the book feels like an insult I cannot ignore... if my voice sounds like theirs... then perhaps I am Cortheni. Or was. Or..."

She shook her head, frustration flickering across her face. "I cannot make sense of any of it."

Her vulnerability hit him like a physical blow. She looked lost. Seeking truth he could not give her. Truth he had buried under silver and spell work.

"Miera," he said gently. "Your memories will return in time."

He stepped closer before he realized it. She tilted her face up to him. Something in the air changed, thickened, as if the room itself were holding its breath.

He lifted a hand, hesitated, then touched her cheek. Her breath hitched. Her eyes fluttered closed. "We will find your identity. That I promise." And he meant every word. He just couldn't let her find out before he did, in case she were a threat to his kingdom.

"Jareth," she whispered.

She leaned into his touch, just a fraction, the movement so slight he might have missed it if he had not been watching her so closely. Her lashes lowered, then lifted again, her gaze pulling to his with new intensity. Heat gathered beneath his palm where her skin warmed, her pulse beating softly at the edge of his thumb.

He should stop. He knew it. But her warmth tugged at every frayed piece of him. "Miera." His voice was raw. "I should not..."

She opened her eyes. Whatever she felt for him was there, unguarded. Trust. Need. Longing.

She reached up, fingers curling gently into the fabric of his shirt, drawing him closer.

"Then do not stop," she said softly.

The words undid him. He kissed her. The first touch of her mouth ignited him. Not gentle. Not restrained. Hunger broke through years of discipline. She gasped softly, then kissed him back with a need that stole his breath.

His hands framed her face, then slid to her waist,

pulling her against him. Her robe slipped from her shoulders. His fingers found the curve of her hips, caressed through linen. She parted her lips, inviting him deeper. The kiss grew heated, urgent.

"Jareth," she breathed against his mouth.

He pressed his forehead to hers. Their breaths tangled. Her hands slid up his chest, fingers finding the line of his jaw. Her touch felt like worship. He cupped the back of her neck, thumb stroking the soft skin beneath her ear. She shivered.

"You are..." His voice failed. He kissed the corner of her mouth, then her jaw, then lower, trailing heat along the delicate line of her throat. She made a quiet sound that shook him to his core.

He slowed, savoring the feel of her. The scent of her skin. The warmth of her body pressed fully against his.

"Miera, if I keep touching you like this..." His breath faltered. "I will not be able to stop."

She looked up at him, eyes dark with desire. "Do you want to stop?"

He shut his eyes. He wanted her more than he wanted the crown. More than he wanted his next breath. But he drew in a sharp breath and forced himself to step back. Only a few inches, but it felt like tearing free of a snare.

"I cannot," he whispered. "Not like this. I do not want to hurt you. I do not want to take more than I should."

Her expression softened. Pain, disappointment, but also understanding. "You aren't taking anything. I want..."

He pressed a finger lightly to her lips. "I know. And that is why I need to be the one who stops this."

She held his gaze. Vulnerable. Achingly beautiful. "Then stay with me. Just stay."

He hesitated, then nodded.

She climbed into the bed, curling beneath the quilts. He remained fully clothed, sitting on the edge for a moment, watching her breathe. She reached for his hand. He let her take it.

He lay down beside her on top of the covers. They faced each other in the dim firelight, her fingers brushing his knuckles.

"Thank you for coming," she whispered.

He swallowed hard. "I needed to make sure you were safe."

She inched closer. Her forehead touched his.

He exhaled slowly, fighting the ache in his chest. He wanted her. He wanted everything. But he would not cross the line that would make him unworthy of her trust.

They fell asleep like that. Fully clothed. Her hand warm in his. His heartbeat steady against the storm inside him.

And when dawn came, guilt would rise with it.

But for now, he held her in the quiet dark and let himself pretend that this, just this, was allowed.

CHAPTER
FIVE

Dawn crept through the silk-gauze curtains with the cold inevitability of an executioner, draining color from the chamber until only shades of grey remained. The fire that had burned with such fierce warmth through the night had consumed itself entirely, leaving nothing but a bed of fine white ash in the hearth. Cold air settled over the room like a shroud.

A verdict rendered in silence. Miera lay perfectly still, a habit ingrained so deeply she couldn't name its origin. Some part of her understood that stillness was survival, that drawing attention could mean danger. She listened to the rhythm of breathing beside her, cataloging what the sound told her.

Jareth was awake. She knew it with certainty, though he hadn't moved, hadn't shifted position, hadn't given any obvious sign. But the quality of his breathing had changed, no longer the deep, unguarded cadence of true sleep but the shallow, deliberate pattern of a man who was awake and thinking. A man who had already retreated into the fortress of his own mind.

A stark tension hummed in the space between them, displacing the warmth that had filled it mere hours ago. A cold front moving in to scour away the last traces of the night's consuming heat.

The memory of it lived in her body like a phantom. She recalled the surprising gentleness in his hands, the possessive strength in his arms that had somehow felt like safety rather than constraint. The way he'd whispered her name against the hollow of her throat, each syllable weighted with something that had felt dangerously close to reverence.

For those few stolen hours, the world had contracted to the confines of this room. To the tangled velvet of the coverlet and the press of his body against hers, skin against skin, breath mingling in the darkness. The relentless analysis in her mind, that constant questioning of who she was, where she belonged, what danger lurked around each corner, had finally, blessedly ceased.

She had felt anchored. Safe in a way the veilstone's artificial peace had never managed. Now, that safety revealed itself as the fragile construct it had always been, as lacking in substance as morning mist burned away by harsh light.

Jareth lay with his back to her, an unscalable rampart of muscle and bone. The intimacy they had shared felt like a state secret he already regretted divulging. Each centimeter of distance between them on the bed might as well have been leagues. Miles. An ocean of cold water she had no way to cross.

Part of her, the foolish part that had unfurled under his touch like a flower seeking sun, yearned to reach across that distance. To press her palm against the rigid line of his spine and feel the warmth of his skin. To reassure herself that the connection had been real, that she hadn't imagined the tenderness in his eyes when he'd looked at her in the firelight.

But a colder, more familiar instinct held her motionless. This silence was a language she was beginning to understand. It was freighted with unspoken calculations and strategic retreats. The texture of everything between them had changed, shifted like sand beneath her feet, and she didn't yet know how to find solid ground again.

She watched the pale morning light trace the contours of his shoulders, highlighting the taut muscles and the dark hair at the nape of his neck. A profound sense of loss settled in her chest, sharp and specific, like a blade finding the space between ribs.

This wasn't the ache of a lover's impending departure. This was the cold dread of a strategist realizing she had fundamentally misread the board. That what she'd thought was connection might have been conquest. That what had felt like mutual need might have been something far more one-sided.

He stirred. Not the drowsy, reflexive stretch of a man waking, but a conscious shift of weight. A decision made, deliberate and final.

She kept her own breathing even, maintaining the

flawless imitation of sleep that came to her as naturally as actual rest never did. Another reflex from that life she couldn't remember. Hiding in plain sight.

"Miera," he said in a perfunctory manner. He didn't look at her.

She didn't know what to make of it. His voice held none of the warmth from the night before. None of the raw vulnerability she'd heard when he'd whispered her name in the darkness, when barriers had fallen and something genuine had blossomed between them.

She turned her head on the pillow slowly, feigning sleepiness to buy herself a moment. Just enough time to school her face. Just enough time to rebuild her walls.

"Jareth." The name felt foreign in her mouth now, weighted with new meaning she couldn't quite parse.

He rolled to face her, but kept from touching her. A hand's width of space between them, negligible in measurement, infinite in implication. His eyes, those pale Vertharian grey eyes that had devoured her in the darkness, that had looked at her with something approaching desperation, now focused somewhere over her shoulder.

On the heavy tapestries depicting Vertharian conquest. On the morning light bleeding through curtains. On the cold hearth with its bed of white ash. On anything but her face. The evasion was a small, sharp pain, confirmation of a truth she hadn't wanted to accept.

"I have duties," he said. The words emerged smooth and polished, each syllable a brick being placed in the wall between them. "Correspondence awaits. Council meetings. My father will expect—" He stopped himself, jaw tightening fractionally. "The day's obligations cannot be postponed."

A dismissal. Wrapped in the language of necessity, but a dismissal, nonetheless.

She remained silent, her own stillness now a form of armor. If she spoke, if she allowed the hurt to show in her voice, it would give him power. It would reveal that this, whatever this was, had meant something to her. That she'd been fool enough to believe it had meant something to him as well.

Better to let him think her unaffected. Unconcerned. As practiced at these morning-after performances as he clearly was.

He leaned in, and for one traitorous half-beat of her heart, hope flared. Perhaps she'd misread this. Perhaps the distance was only in her mind, a product of her own insecurity rather than his withdrawal.

The kiss he pressed to her hair extinguished that hope like water on flame. Brief. Cool. Perfunctory.

It held no heat, no memory of the desperate hunger from hours before. It was the chaste, passionless gesture of a monarch bestowing favor upon a subject. A final seal on their returned distance. A goodbye that tasted like betrayal.

She absorbed the blow without flinching, were there years of training in her past, from a life she couldn't remember, teaching her how to hide wounds both physical and emotional? It was the strangest feeling, like some older version of herself stepped forward in that moment, showing her how to hold steady while her heart recoiled.

He rose from the bed, the mattress shifting with his weight, cold air rushing in to fill the space his body had occupied. She watched him move in the grey dawn light, each motion economical and controlled. The warrior prince reassembling himself, piece by piece, into the armor of propriety and duty.

Beside her linen nightgown, discarded on the floor, his clothing from the night before lay in a heap. The crimson and black wool of his formal coat. The fine linen of his shirt. Garments that marked him as royalty, as power, as something far above the woman in this bed.

She saw the rush in every movement. He pulled on his trousers, then his shirt, fingers moving so quickly that he missed a couple of buttons. He stopped, corrected them, and reached for his coat as if he couldn't leave fast enough.

She took in the details as he reassembled his public self. The dark wool of his high-collared coat, severe and militaristic. The glint of silver thread in the cuffs, catching the pale light. The perfect fit across his shoulders that spoke of wealth and tailoring and a life lived in palaces rather than hovels.

He was a portrait of Vertharian power now. Structured. Unyielding. Unreachable.

The man who had held her, who had traced the lines of her face with trembling fingers, who had breathed her name like a prayer, that man had vanished. This prince had taken his place, and she recognized him as a stranger.

When he was fully dressed, every button fastened, every line perfect, he finally looked at her. Not at her face, she noticed. At some point just past her shoulder, as if even meeting her eyes would cost him something he couldn't afford to spend.

His expression was a constructed mask of polite regret. The kind of look a man might wear after a minor political misstep. Apologetic without actually apologizing. Distant without being overtly cruel.

"Rest," he said.

Not an invitation. An order. A command to the woman in his bed to remain quiescent, to not complicate his departure with messy emotions or uncomfortable questions.

Then he turned and walked from the room, his boots barely making a sound on the stone floor. The soft click of the door's latch was unnaturally loud in the sudden, crushing emptiness.

The sound of a key turning in a lock, though the door had no lock. The sound of a cage closing, though the cage was invisible.

Miera lay back against the pillows, her gaze fixed on the dark canopy above the bed. The silk hangings seemed to press down on her, the weight of fabric matching the weight in her chest.

The warmth of his body was already fading from the sheets, becoming memory rather than sensation. The indentation on the mattress where he'd lain was all that remained, a hollow space that mirrored the new void opening inside her.

Her body remembered his closeness with an intimacy that now felt like betrayal. The weight of him pressing her into the mattress. The solid, steady beat of his heart against hers. The way his hands had mapped her body as if memorizing territory he intended to claim.

But her heart felt hollowed out, as if she'd misplaced something vital in the darkness and the cold morning light had revealed its theft.

She told herself this was natural. Perhaps this was simply how intimacy worked between people like them, people playing roles in a political drama she didn't fully understand. Unsteady. Complicated. A thing of fleeting warmth and lingering questions.

But the rationalization felt like a flimsy shield, offering no protection against the sharp edges of what she was feeling.

A disquieting thought surfaced, unwelcome and insistent as water seeping through cracks. Why did his silence feel so...wrong? Was his tenderness in the dark true, or a tactic to coax her to let her guard down? Was his cold withdrawal in daylight calculated to keep her off-balance? Close enough to be controlled, but never close enough to be dangerous. Near enough to use, but too distant to trust.

She saw it then, clear as the pale dawn light: a game board. She'd been moved like a pawn into a position of seeming strength, had believed herself advancing, only to discover she was more exposed than ever. More vulnerable than she'd been before surrendering to his touch.

The thought should have angered her. Should have sparked rage, indignation, the desire for retribution. Instead, it just made her tired. And sad. And achingly, desperately alone.

The familiar, cool weight of the veilstone against her throat should have steadied her. That anchor in every storm, that source of manufactured peace that had carried her through confusion and fear. She clutched the soft oval of the stone, thumb tracing the polished silver setting with its falcon-talon prongs. She closed her eyes, willing the gentle, magical calm to descend. Needing its peace. Desperate for the steady, muted rhythm that would quiet the storm of questions and hurt rising inside her.

She needed it to quiet this new, raw ache. To blur the sharp edges of rejection. To help her forget the way his kiss had felt on her skin and the way his departure had felt like abandonment.

She waited for the wave of tranquility to wash over her, to mute the hurt, to soften the confusion into something manageable. She waited for the familiar fog to descend, that gentle numbness that made everything bearable. The stone remained cool and inert against her skin.

Its pulse, always so steady, so reliable, felt distant now. Tinny. Weak. As if the magic itself was a failing heartbeat, struggling against something too strong to overcome.

The hollow ache in her chest didn't recede. The questions didn't soften. The hurt didn't blur into comfortable vagueness.

If anything, everything grew sharper. More insistent. More real.

For the first time since Jareth had clasped the silver chain around her neck, presenting it as a gift of healing and protection, the magic failed her.

The veilstone's peace was no match for the strength of this emotion. This grief. This sense of being used and discarded, of offering something precious and having it treated as worthless.

The failure terrified her more than his departure.

The pendant had been her shield. Her solace. Her one piece of solid ground in a world that shifted like sand beneath her feet. When memories threatened, the stone had quieted them. When fear rose, the stone had soothed it. When confusion overwhelmed, the stone had provided clarity, or at least the illusion of it.

Now, for the first time, she understood with sickening clarity: the magic hadn't been a comfort. It had been a cage. And she'd been rattling its bars without even knowing it.

The realization struck her with the force of physical impact. How many thoughts had been erased before they could fully form? How many questions had died on her lips because the veilstone smoothed them away? How many truths had tried to surface, only to be pushed back down into darkness?

Her mind reeled backward, examining weeks of memories through this new, terrible lens. The dreams of salt air and foreign sigils, had those been trying to tell her something? The visceral reaction to Corthen being slandered in that history book, why had it felt so personal? The face in the mirror, staring back with cold knowledge, whose face had that been?

The veilstone had answered each question the same way: by deleting the question itself. But this pain was too strong. Too real. Too rooted in the present rather than the buried past.

The magic couldn't erase what she'd just experienced. Couldn't smooth away the memory of his hands on her skin or the ice in his eyes when he'd left. Couldn't make her forget the taste of his kiss or the sound of the door closing behind him.

Her objective shifted, born of desperation. She had to quiet this turmoil herself. Had to find a way to navigate this new, unfiltered reality where her own feelings were a treacherous landscape and her only guide had just revealed himself as the architect of the maze.

She had to convince herself that this was normal. That this was simply how these things worked. That the difficult start of something real was always painful, and pain didn't mean it was a mistake. She had to believe that, or the alternative was too terrible to face.

She drew the heavy coverlet up to her chin, a futile barrier against the cold that had settled not just in the room, but deep within her bones. The velvet felt heavy against her skin, more burden than comfort.

The fire was dead. The room was grey. And she was alone. In the corridor beyond her locked door, Jareth's footsteps faded down the stone hall. Each step was precise, measured, carrying him back to his world of duty and secrets and the brutal pragmatism of Vertharian rule.

She tracked the sound until it was swallowed by the vast, echoing silence of the fortress. The silence that followed was different from the one she'd grown accustomed to. Not empty. Not peaceful. It filled the room like water filling a drowning woman's lungs. And in that quiet, questions began to surface again, one after another, relentless as waves breaking on the shore.

Who am I? Why did he really bring me here? What is this pendant actually doing to me? Why does Corthen matter to me?

The veilstone pulsed weakly at her throat, trying to push the questions back down. But for the first time since she'd woken in this fortress with no memory and no name, her own mind was stronger than the magic meant to control it.

The questions remained. The ache remained. And somewhere in the dark spaces of her fractured memory, a truth waited, patient and terrible and inevitable. A truth about who she'd been before the veilstone had locked her away. A truth about kingdoms and treaties and the price of peace bought with deception. A truth that, when it finally surfaced, would shatter everything she thought she knew. But that was still to come.

For now, she lay alone in the cold grey dawn, wrapped in velvet that couldn't warm her, clutching a pendant that couldn't save her, grieving for a connection that had been built on lies from the very beginning.

And for the first time since waking in Durevin Hold, she wondered if perhaps the greatest mercy would have been if she'd never woken at all.

CHAPTER

SIX

Guilt was a poison, and it had worked its way through Jareth all night, spreading through his veins like venom with no antidote. The pale wash of dawn brought no relief. If anything, morning light made everything worse, illuminating what darkness had allowed him to ignore. It chased back the shadows where his conscience had feasted upon the memory of her trust, exposing the full magnitude of what he'd done.

Not just the veilstone. Not just the manipulation and lies that had brought her here. But last night. Using her body to silence his guilt, taking comfort in her warmth while knowing every touch was built on deception. Whispering her false name against her skin while hiding her true one. Making love to a woman he'd imprisoned in her own mind.

The door to her chamber closed behind him with a soft, final click that echoed down the stone corridor like a key turning in a lock. A lid closing on something precious and far too fragile. Something he'd broken with his own hands.

Her quiet disappointment had been visible despite her attempts to conceal it. He'd seen it in the slight tremor of her smile when he'd kissed her hair with all the warmth of a man dismissing a servant. Had seen it in the way her hands had stilled on the coverlet, gripping velvet as if it were the only solid thing in a tilting world.

She'd hidden it well. But he'd spent weeks learning to read her, learning which expressions the veilstone allowed and which it suppressed. He knew disappointment when he saw it. The knowledge sat in his chest like broken glass.

He stood in the cold corridor, forcing his breathing to steady, his expression to smooth into the mask he wore for the world. Composing himself. Reassembling the pieces of the prince from the wreckage of the man.

The two guards posted at her door straightened as he emerged, their expressions blank. Professional. They'd seen him enter last night. They'd seen him leave this morning. They knew exactly what that meant.

They were his men, their loyalty sworn and tested. But loyalty was currency that rumor could debase into worthlessness. One whisper in the wrong ear, one servant's observation reaching his father's network of informants, and everything he'd built would collapse.

"You saw nothing. You heard nothing." His voice came out low and clipped, stripped of warmth or humanity. The voice of a prince and commander, not the man who'd just fled a woman's bed like a coward. "The lady was unwell during the night. I was ensuring her safety. That is all."

"Your Highness." They murmured in perfect unison, gazes fixed on the stone wall opposite, giving him the privacy of their professional blindness.

The order was absolute. The matter sealed. Another lie added to the fortress he'd built from deception.

He turned and strode down the empty hall, his boots echoing against stone. Each step carried him away from her chamber, away from the warmth and softness he'd destroyed with his cold departure. Away from the wreckage of whatever they'd had, or whatever she'd believed they had.

He needed to reestablish control. Not just over the court's perception, but over the chaos churning inside him like a storm battering at fortress walls. The intimacy he'd sought as balm for his guilt now felt like a brand burned into his skin, marking him. A secret that made him vulnerable. A weakness his father would exploit without hesitation or mercy.

The corridors of Durevin Hold stretched before him, lit by morning sun slanting through arrow-slit windows. Torches from the night still smoldered in their brackets, adding smoke to air already heavy with the scent of baking bread rising from the kitchens far below. The fortress was waking.

Soon the halls would fill with courtiers and servants, all of them watching, cataloging, reporting. He was halfway to the central stairwell when a familiar voice stopped him.

"Cousin."

Jareth's entire body went rigid before training

reasserted itself. He forced his shoulders to relax, his posture to shift into practiced ease, even as tension coiled tighter in his gut. He turned to see Lord Rilen emerging from an adjoining corridor.

Rilen. His cousin by blood, though several times removed. A few years younger, with the same dark hair but steadier eyes that hadn't yet learned to hide everything they felt. A soldier by trade and temperament, straightforward in a court built on duplicity.

The composition of Jareth's inner circle had shifted considerably since Miera's arrival. Captain Vale, the man who had most vocally demanded she be put to the question, had been reassigned to the northern garrison—officially a promotion to command the Frostwatch outpost, privately a removal of a threat to her safety. Commander Kerr had returned to the capital on the king's orders, recalled to brief Halric on border defenses in person. In their absence, Jareth had drawn Rilen closer, elevating his cousin from peripheral advisor to essential confidant. Blood loyalty, he had learned, was harder to corrupt than oath-bound duty.

Perhaps the only man in Durevin Hold that Jareth trusted without reservation. A rare moral anchor in the treacherous currents of his father's court.

Which made this encounter dangerous. Because Rilen would see. Would know something was wrong. And Jareth couldn't afford to drag him into this disaster.

"Rilen," he said.

His cousin's concerned gaze swept over him, cataloging details Jareth couldn't quite conceal despite years of practice. The tension across his shoulders. The faint shadows beneath his eyes from a sleepless night spent tangled in sheets that smelled like her. The haunted quality he couldn't quite smooth from his expression.

"You're about early," Rilen observed. His voice was low, meant only for Jareth's ears beneath the distant clatter rising from the kitchens below. Not an accusation. An opening. An offered hand in the dark.

"Matters of state don't wait for the sun." The words came out polished and hollow, the response he'd give any courtier who presumed to question his movements.

Rilen's jaw tightened fractionally, the only sign Jareth's deflection had landed like a blow. But he recovered with the grace of long practice, falling into step beside Jareth as they walked. His presence was meant as comfort, as solidarity.

Jareth couldn't afford to accept it.

"Of course." Rilen matched his stride, boots hitting stone in synchronized rhythm. They walked in silence for several paces before his cousin spoke again. "Though some matters seem to carry more weight than others."

His tone sounded purposefully neutral, but Jareth heard the concern beneath. "The king's mood has been foul since the Avenali delegation arrived. He grows impatient for results." A pause, weighted with meaning. "Regarding your guest."

The warning was pragmatic, the kind of intelligence Rilen had always provided. Alert him to shifting political winds before he was caught in the gale. But the concern beneath it was genuine, not for politics, but for Jareth himself.

"The king's impatience is a constant," Jareth said, deflecting with practiced ease. "I have the matter in hand."

Evasiveness as cruelty. Necessary cruelty. Because to share this secret, to tell Rilen the truth about Miera, about the veilstone, about his father's order to kill her, would be to place his cousin's head on the same chopping block as his own.

Better to wound him with distance than destroy him with truth. He saw hurt flicker in Rilen's eyes, quickly suppressed. His cousin was perceptive enough to know something was deeply wrong. Loyal enough not to press the point. He understood the rules of this game, even if he didn't know which game they were playing.

"As you say." The words came out even and composed, the natural deference of a subordinate acknowledging his superior's decision.

The moment passed. The curtain drawn between them again. But the encounter left Jareth feeling even more isolated, walls of his own making closing in from all sides. He was hiding truth not just from his enemies now, but from his only friend.

When they reached the Great Hall, the vast vaulted chamber was already filling with morning court. Early risers claiming the best seats, servants carrying platters of food from the kitchens, the low hum of conversation building like gathering storm clouds.

The air hung rich with scent: roasted meats, fresh

bread still steaming, spiced porridge, and the sweet tang of preserved fruit from the southern provinces.

Long tables glittered with pewter dishes and pyramids of golden fruit, the carefully constructed image of prosperity. His father's stage. His father's theatre of power. And there, at one of the lower tables, sat Miera. Jareth's breath caught despite himself.

She was a solitary figure of grace among the boisterous, armored soldiers who'd claimed the surrounding benches. She wore a gown of deep blue wool, mourning colors in Corthen, though she wouldn't know that. Her dark hair had been arranged simply, pulled back to reveal the elegant line of her throat. And the veilstone pendant, silver falcon talons gripping crystal, catching morning light.

She looked up as he entered, her expression composed and calm. Perfectly serene. But he felt the weight of her gaze like a physical touch across the cavernous room, across the impossible distance between them.

The memory rose unbidden: her warmth in his arms, the softness of her skin, the way she'd sighed his name in the darkness. The trust in her eyes when she'd looked at him as if he were something more than the monster his father had raised.

He crushed the memory before it could take root. He had to create distance. A chasm. A gulf so wide and unbridgeable that his father would see her as nothing more than a passing interest, safely dismissed.

Deliberately, Jareth bypassed her table without a glance. His long stride carried him toward the high table, toward the carved ironwood seats reserved for royalty and their inner circle. He didn't look at her. Didn't acknowledge her presence with even the briefest nod of recognition. The public severing was unmistakable.

He heard the ripple of reaction, conversations pausing, heads turning, courtiers noting this new development with the keen attention of predators scenting blood in water.

He slid onto the bench beside Rilen, the scrape of wood against polished marble unnaturally loud in the suddenly attentive hall.

"Rilen, a word about the border patrols in the west." He pitched his voice loud enough to carry, performative. Theatre for the watching eyes. "I reviewed the reports last night. I'm not satisfied with their reconnaissance patterns."

His cousin caught the cue instantly, his expression shifting to serious consideration. Playing his part perfectly. "The terrain is difficult, Your Highness. And with winter setting in, the Whisper Road becomes treacherous. We've lost two scouts already to early storms."

Professional. Political. The business of running a kingdom.

Jareth felt Miera's gaze leave him. The connection cut. The performance complete. He'd succeeded. The court would see exactly what he wanted them to see: a prince attending to duty, the mysterious woman already forgotten.

The feeling wasn't triumph. It was hollow, aching emptiness, like a cavity carved in his chest.

He was using his cousin as a social shield, a buffer against the vulnerability she represented. But the court would see nothing suspicious. Just a prince and his most trusted lord attending to the business of the realm. The secret was safe. For now.

Throughout the meal, Jareth forced himself into the role. The Crown Prince. Cold. Focused. Discussing provisions and troop movements with clinical precision that left no room for emotion. He debated grain tariffs with visiting merchants. Reviewed supply chain logistics with the fortress quartermaster. Made decisions about patrol routes and watch rotations.

All of it necessary. All of it hollow.

Rilen matched his composure, providing quiet, observant loyalty, a small point of stability in Jareth's fracturing world. He didn't judge. Didn't press for explanations. Just supported, his silence a tacit acknowledgment of pain he didn't understand but respected.

But the strain of concealment pressed against Jareth's throat like a blade's edge. Every polite nod cost him. Every forced bite of food tasted like ash. Every feigned moment of interest in grain production or border security was an exercise in suppression.

He was becoming the man he despised. The cold, calculating strategist his father had always wanted. The prince who could use people without conscience, who could separate desire from duty.

The irony sat bitter on his tongue, more potent than the spiced wine in his goblet. He would make the distance real, not just performance. He would bury himself in duty, let the armor of his office grow over the wound of his guilt. It was the only way to protect her, from himself, from his father, from the consequences of his weakness.

As the court began to disperse, lords and ladies drifting toward their morning obligations, servants clearing dishes, Jareth rose. He gave Rilen a final, formal nod. His plan for the day was set. He would retreat into duty, into maps and reports, into the cold logic of military strategy.

He would not allow himself to seek her out again. His conviction firmed, a layer of ice forming around his heart as he took two steps toward the arched exit.

A royal page intercepted him. A boy no older than twelve, wearing a stark white tunic bearing the king's personal sigil, not the falcon, but the coiled dragon reserved for the throne itself.

The boy executed a clipped, perfect bow. "Your Highness." His voice rang clear and unwavering across the hall, loud enough that nearby courtiers turned to look. "The King requires your presence in the solar. Immediately."

The words fell like stones into still water, ripples spreading outward. Every eye in the hall turned to watch. His father's summons. Public. Immediate. Impossible to refuse or delay.

Jareth felt the weight of speculation settle over him like a heavy cloak. They all knew what this meant. The king didn't summon his son publicly unless he intended to make a point. Unless there was a lesson to be taught.

He kept his expression perfectly neutral, betraying nothing of the ice forming in his gut. "Of course," he said, his voice carrying the appropriate deference. "Tell His Majesty I attend him at once."

The page bowed again and hurried off, his small form quickly swallowed by the morning crowd. Jareth straightened his coat, adjusted the silver falcon ring on his finger, and walked toward his father's solar with measured, unhurried steps.

Every eye followed him. Every ear strained to catch whispers about why the king might summon the prince so publicly, so urgently. Only Jareth knew the truth.

This wasn't about border patrols or grain tariffs or the Avenali delegation. This was about last night. About the order he'd failed to carry out. About the woman he should have killed but instead had taken to his bed. This was his father calling him to account. And there would be consequences.

SEVEN

The tense meeting with Jareth's father had resolved nothing, Jareth had told himself in the days that followed. Their stances had only hardened, the brittle peace between them stretched thinner with each passing hour. But that was his burden to bear, not hers.

Miera wouldn't know about those confrontations. Wouldn't know that her existence had become the fault line threatening to split the royal family apart.

The days that followed the breakfast hall rejection settled into a new rhythm, one Miera constructed for herself from discipline and necessity, from the sheer determination not to disappear into the grey stone walls of Durevin Hold.

Several days had passed since Jareth had taken his seat beside Lord Rilen, his polite distance a chasm she couldn't cross. The initial shock had dulled to a persistent, low ache, like a wound that refused to close properly. To quiet it, to feel useful rather than decorative, to be something more than a ghost drifting through cold corridors, she built herself a routine.

A structure. A purpose. Even if that purpose was simply to survive each day with dignity intact. Her mornings began with long walks in the fortress gardens.

The space was nothing like what she imagined gardens should be, no riot of color, no wild profusion of blooms, no gentle chaos of nature allowed to express itself. This was a monument to Verthar's obsession with control. Stone paths cut through precisely clipped yew hedges that rose like dark green walls, their shadows falling sharp and geometric in the pale winter light. Every branch had been trimmed to exact specifications. Every stone placed with mathematical precision.

There was little softness here, little mercy. Only the stark, dramatic beauty of the Emberrose. The roses were everywhere, their deep crimson blooms defiant splashes of color against relentless grey stone. They shouldn't survive in this climate, the air was too cold, the growing season too short. But they endured anyway, hardy and stubborn, bred over generations to thrive in harsh conditions.

The fortress gardener, an elderly man with scarred hands and kind eyes, had told her the Emberrose was Verthar's symbol of unconquerable love. Love that survived despite brutal conditions. Love that refused to yield to winter's siege.

The irony wasn't lost on her. She walked these paths for hours each morning, her shoes scraping softly against gravel, her breath misting in cold air. The scent of damp earth and the faint, peppery fragrance of the roses grounded her, pulled her out of the endless circling of her thoughts. The act of movement, of placing one foot in front of the other, of feeling her muscles work, of occupying space in the world, was its own kind of defiance.

She existed. She mattered. Even if only to herself.

Sometimes she encountered other early risers. Ladies of the court taking their morning constitutionals, bundled in fur-lined cloaks and jeweled gloves. They would offer polite nods, and neutral greetings that acknowledged her presence without committing to anything more substantial.

They never invited her to walk with them. Never paused for conversation beyond the minimum courtesy demanded. She learned not to expect otherwise.

After her walks, she sought refuge in the aviary.

The structure rose in a sheltered corner of the inner bailey, a tall dome of iron and glass that caught morning light and held it like a jewel. Inside, the air smelled of musty seed, dry feathers, and a surprising warmth that contrasted sharply with the fortress's perpetual chill. The great black ravens of Verthar's messenger corps watched from their perches with intelligent, unblinking eyes.

She'd discovered this place by accident, wandering the fortress grounds in search of somewhere, anywhere, that felt less like a cage. The aviary was a cage too, technically, but the birds seemed content. Fed. Cared for. Given purpose. She envied them that.

The attendants were two older men, Garrick and Thom, brothers who'd tended the ravens for thirty years between them. They had gentle hands despite their soldier's builds, quiet voices that calmed the birds, and an easy manner that suggested they'd spent more time with ravens than with people.

They'd been surprised by her interest at first. Ladies of the court didn't typically venture into the aviary, it was too practical, too unglamorous, smelling of bird waste and raw meat rather than perfume and wine.

But Miera's genuine curiosity had won them over. She learned the birds' names: Shadowflight, Nightwhisper, Ironbeak, Stormcaller. Learned their habits, their calls, the subtle differences in their plumage that marked age and temperament. She watched Garrick and Thom train the younger birds, teaching them to return to specific towers, to recognize certain signals.

The work was methodical. Peaceful. Honest in a way the court could never be.

"You've a gentle hand with them, my lady," Garrick had said one morning, watching her feed scraps to Night-whisper. "Most nobles treat them as tools. Forget they're living creatures with their own natures."

The compliment had warmed something in her chest that had been cold since that morning in Jareth's arms.

Here, in this glass-domed sanctuary smelling of feathers and seed, she wasn't the prince's discarded interest or the mysterious woman with no past. She was simply someone who cared about birds. Someone useful. Someone real.

She found herself spending longer and longer stretches in the aviary, helping with feeding schedules, cleaning perches, learning the intricate art of maintaining the message cylinders that attached to the ravens' legs.

Garrick and Thom seemed grateful for the company. Their unguarded conversation was a balm, the kind of steady, everyday talk she had almost forgotten. They spoke about weather patterns that affected flight times, the best grain mixtures, and stories of remarkable birds from years past.

No hidden meanings. No careful word choices designed to reveal nothing while implying everything. Just honest talk between people who shared an interest. It was the closest thing to friendship she'd found in Durevin Hold.

Afternoons were for reading. She retreated to either the library or her own chamber, settling into the high-backed chair by the hearth while firelight danced across pages and shadows lengthened outside her windows. The heavy crimson velvet drapes seemed to grow darker as day faded, until the room felt like a cocoon, safe and isolated in equal measure.

She hadn't opened *A History of Vertharian Court and Culture* again. That book sat on her shelf now, spine facing inward, its lies safely contained. The emotional devastation it had triggered, the grief she couldn't explain, the rage that had felt so personal, still unsettled her when she thought about it.

The veilstone had failed to suppress those feelings. That failure haunted her more than the feelings themselves.

Instead, she lost herself in poetry and tales of the old

Dynasty of Elvedain, stories far enough in the past to feel safe. Mythical kings and tragic queens, dragons that were probably just metaphor, battles fought with honor rather than deception.

Fantasy. Comfortable lies instead of uncomfortable truths. The words on the pages couldn't hurt her. The characters had been dead for centuries. Their tragedies were complete, contained, safely distant from her own.

This new routine worked, in its way. It restored a fragile sense of balance, gave her structure when everything else felt formless and uncertain. The ordered tasks were anchors in a sea of confusion, giving her purpose beyond simply waiting for Jareth's favor to return.

Beyond hoping he would look at her again the way he had in the firelight, before dawn had turned him cold.

That fragile peace, however, rarely survived beyond the sanctuary of the gardens, the aviary, or the library. Her attempt to blend into the fabric of the court was foiled by constant, quiet scrutiny.

When she moved through the public halls, which she had to do, had to be seen, had to maintain some presence lest she disappear entirely, conversations didn't stop. That would have been too obvious, too rude. Instead, they shifted in tone and substance. The easy flow of gossip and complaint tightened into formal pleasantries. Laughter died to polite smiles.

She would catch their glances in reflections: polished shields hanging as decoration on stone walls, panes of glass in doorways, the silver surface of serving platters carried by servants. Sidelong looks. Measuring. Assessing. Not curiosity. Calculation.

One afternoon, crossing the Great Hall, its polished black marble floor reflecting the falcon banners hanging from high rafters, she passed two lords in conversation. Their clothing marked them as wealthy: dark silk embroidered with silver thread, fur-lined cloaks, rings that caught the light.

They offered stiff, correct bows as she approached. Protocol demanded it. Their eyes, however, held something that made her skin prickle with unease. Not the polite emptiness of courtly etiquette. Not even disdain or contempt, which she might have understood.

Watchfulness. The keen, predatory intensity of men assessing a new piece on the game board. Weighing her value. Calculating her position. Determining whether she was threat or opportunity.

She inclined her head in acknowledgment and continued past, feeling their gazes track her across the hall like arrows trained on a target.

The encounter followed her back to her chambers, settling over her shoulders like a heavy cloak. She finally understood.

Jareth's public withdrawal of favor had changed everything. She was no longer the mysterious guest under the prince's personal protection. That shield had been removed, deliberately and publicly, and now she stood exposed.

A political variable. An unknown quantity with no

declared allies and no clear purpose. An unmoored asset, or a potential threat.

She sank into the high-backed chair by her hearth, hands cold despite the fire burning steadily. Her mind worked through the implications with a clarity that surprised her. Some part of her, some buried instinct, understood court politics with disturbing ease.

To befriend her now was to risk inviting the prince's displeasure. Or worse, the king's scrutiny. She'd heard enough whispered conversations, caught enough fragments of gossip, to know that King Halric was not a man who tolerated unknowns in his court.

But to ignore her might be equally dangerous. What if she held hidden power? What if she had secret claims or valuable knowledge? What if dismissing her proved to be a grave political miscalculation?

So they watched. Waited. Calculated. Kept their distance while keeping her under observation.

The unforgiving political reality of the Vertharian court was laid bare before her, and it was as cold and hard as the stone fortress itself.

She was alone. Truly, completely alone. No allies. No protection. No path forward she could see.

Just the gardens in the morning, the ravens at midday, and books in the afternoon. Small routines that kept her sane while the court circled like wolves watching wounded prey, waiting to see if she would survive or fall. Waiting to see what the prince would do next. Waiting to see if she mattered at all.

That night, lying in her bed with the coverlet pulled to

her chin and the fire burned down to embers, she willed the veilstone to quiet her fears. She was desperate for its peace to descend and quiet the growing certainty that she was in terrible danger. The magic pulsed weakly, pushing at the edges of her awareness. Trying to suppress the questions. Trying to smooth away the fear.

But it was weaker now than it had been. Failing more often. As if whatever spell powered it was degrading, or as if her own mind was growing stronger, learning to resist.

The questions remained: *Who am I really? Why did Jareth bring me here? What happens when the veilstone stops working entirely?*

And most terrifying of all: *When the court decides I'm more threat than opportunity, will anyone protect me?*

She had no answers. Only the cold certainty that time was running out, that some crisis was building, and that when it finally broke, she would face it alone.

The veilstone pulsed against her throat. But it couldn't protect her from the truth any longer. Something was coming. And she wasn't ready.

EIGHT

The fortress of Durevin Hold possessed a heart, a low, steady thrum of life that resonated through its stone bones like a pulse through ancient veins.

In the hours past midnight, when torches burned low and shadows claimed the corridors, Jareth could feel it beneath his boots. The rhythm was composed of layered sounds: guard patrols on the ramparts, their footfalls synchronized from years of practice. The distant clatter from the kitchens where night staff prepared for dawn. The soft sigh of wind over battlements, whistling through arrow slits and around towers.

Tonight, however, another pulse beat beneath the familiar rhythm. A discordant cadence of anxiety and suspicion. A tempo of whispers and speculation. He had set this rhythm in motion. And it was quickening beyond his control.

He stood alone in his private study, the only illumina-tion a pool of golden light from a single candle on his massive blackwood desk. The fire in the hearth had collapsed hours ago, leaving nothing but glowing embers that cast skeletal shadows across stone walls. Those shadows swayed and stretched like living things, distorted and unsettling.

The air hung thick with the dry scent of old vellum and the sharper perfume of ink, metallic and bitter, like blood turned to liquid.

He'd spent the entire day forcing disciplined efficiency upon himself. A rigid routine of administration and correspondence meant to armor his thoughts against the chaos beneath. He'd reviewed supply manifests. Approved patrol rotations. Responded to dispatches from border commanders. Buried himself in the minutiae of running a kingdom. It hadn't worked.

Her presence, even in her absence, unsettled his equilibrium. She was a constant, quiet distraction that frayed the edges of his focus. A problem for which he had no clean solution. No military strategy, no political maneuver that could extract him from the trap he'd built with his own hands.

His father's impatience pressed down on him like the weight of the fortress itself. The king demanded answers Jareth didn't possess, or rather, answers he possessed but couldn't give. Who was she? Why was she still alive? When would Jareth stop being weak and do what needed to be done?

The court's whispers were a thousand tiny cuts, each one a question about the mysterious guest the prince kept secluded. Each one speculation about what she meant to him. Each one wondering why she mattered enough to defy the king.

The fragile calm Miera had constructed, her walks in the gardens, her hours with the ravens, her quiet reading, was eroding under relentless scrutiny. His public distance, a stratagem intended to shield her, had only made her a more compelling target.

The court circled like wolves around wounded prey, waiting to see if she would survive or fall. Passive secrecy was failing. It was time for active deception.

He moved to his desk, the oiled leather of his high-backed chair groaning softly as he settled into it. Before him lay everything he needed: a stack of blank parchment, cream-colored and expensive. A freshly sharpened quill, its nib glinting in candlelight. A pot of Vertharian gall ink, black as pitch.

The tools of forgery. The instruments of construction. The lie he was about to build needed to be a fortress in itself, constructed on a foundation of plausible truth, buttressed by calculated obscurity, defended by the impossibility of verification. He would forge her a past.

He dipped the quill, and its scratch against parchment was the only sound in the oppressive stillness. The noise felt loud in the midnight quiet, like a blade being drawn from its sheath.

He chose his materials with care. A minor noble house from the northern Marches, a region known for harsh climate and fiercely independent lords who kept poor records and asked few questions of the crown.

The House of Caelen. The name sounded northern.

And he imagined they were the kind of family that survived through grit rather than anything else.

From his extensive study of Vertharian histories, specifically the *Roll of Extinguished Peerage*, a grim catalog of families whose lines had ended, he knew the Caelen family had been terminated two generations ago. A border skirmish with wildling clans from beyond the mountains. The entire household slaughtered in a single night of violence.

No direct heirs remained to contest any claims. No cousins who might remember distant relatives. The line was extinct.

More importantly, their records were notoriously incomplete. A fire had consumed their ancestral keep half a century past, taking with it birth records, marriage contracts, property deeds. Everything that might prove or disprove a connection had been reduced to ash.

It was the perfect blend of historical precedent and convenient ambiguity. A ghost family for the woman he'd made a ghost. With painstaking care, he began to draft the narrative.

Lady Miera of House Caelen, sole surviving daughter of Lord Torven Caelen, a reclusive northern lord who'd kept his household isolated in the Whispering Hills.

Sent to the capital for a suitable match following her father's death from winter fever. Accompanied by only a single aging servant who'd perished in the attack that had nearly claimed Miera's own life.

The story was tragic. Nearly impossible to verify without a royal inquest, an action his father wouldn't take without more cause than curiosity.

He sketched out a genealogy chart with meticulous care, his lines clean and sharp. Three generations of imagined ancestors. Lord Torven married to Lady Elaine of House Morwyn (also extinct). A brother who'd died young in a hunting accident. Grandparents with northern names that sounded appropriately harsh and practical.

Each fabricated relative was another layer of protection. Another detail that made the lie feel solid. He even designed a sigil for the house, something that would satisfy Vertharian heraldic tradition without being so distinctive that anyone might remember seeing it before.

A solitary winter hawk, wings folded in repose, set against a field of grey stone. In the language of Vertharian heraldry, it symbolized a line in waiting. Dormant power. Patience rewarded by survival. The irony was a private, bitter satisfaction.

The act of creation absorbed him completely. The precise, methodical work was balm to his frayed nerves. He was a master strategist, and this was merely another form of campaign planning. He was marshaling facts and falsehoods as he would marshal battalions, positioning them for maximum effect.

Birth date. Place of origin. Father's titles and holdings. A small dowry, not so large as to invite excessive interest, not so small as to suggest poverty. Details about education: tutored at home by a retired court scholar. Accomplished in needlework and music but not courtly intrigue, explaining her initial awkwardness at Durevin Hold.

Layer upon layer. Each detail supporting the others. Each fact referencing foundations that seemed solid but were built on nothing.

As he worked, candlelight flickering across the parchment, a colder thought took root. He wasn't just shaping a narrative. He was erasing a person. He was burying whoever she truly was beneath layers of invention, just as the veilstone buried her memories. The methodical precision, the calculated manipulation, the use of lies as tools of control, these were his father's methods.

He was using the very tactics he despised, rationalizing them as necessary shields for her protection. The ink on his fingers felt like a stain that wouldn't wash away.

Is this what it means to hold power? The question echoed in the silence of his study. *To use the tools of the corrupt to forge something good? Or am I simply proving I'm my father's son after all?*

He stared down at the documents spread before him. They looked authentic, every detail perfect, every line convincing. They would pass any casual inspection, would satisfy any courtier's curiosity. They were also a prison. Another cage he'd built for her, this one made of parchment instead of crystal.

When the documents were complete, when the lie was fully constructed and ready to be unleashed, he summoned his guards. Not the King's Guard, whose captain reported directly to his father. Not the fortress garrison, whose loyalty was to the crown first and foremost.

He sent for two men from his own household retinue. Sergeant Kael and Corporal Vorne. Their families had served his own for generations, not as subjects of the king, but as personal retainers of the prince's line. Men whose loyalty was to him, not to the throne. Men he could trust with treason.

They entered the study and stood at attention as they awaited their prince's orders. Jareth rose from his chair, the fabricated documents in his hands. He looked each man in the eye, letting the quiet stretch on and on. Weighing them. He needed more than their obedience tonight. He needed their complicity. Their silence, if it ever came to trial.

"This is for her safety," he said finally, his voice low and firm. He didn't specify who 'she' was. Every man in his service knew. The mysterious woman. The prince's obsession. The liability the king wanted eliminated. "Rumors endanger her. This will give her a name. A history. A shield against speculation."

He handed the folio to Kael, who took it with steady hands. "You'll deliver this to the sub-archivist in the records office. It's to be logged as a late discovery from the Northern Survey, documents that were misfiled decades ago and only just found during the reorganization." He held the sergeant's gaze. "No name is to be attached to the delivery. It must simply appear, as if it had been there all along."

He turned to Vorne. "You'll take the story itself, the details of her lineage, and ensure it reaches the right ears. The ladies in waiting first. They gossip with the stewards. Then the stable master, who drinks with the garrison. Let it spread like a natural discovery. A piece of exciting court gossip that everyone believes they heard independently."

He paused, his gaze hard. "Your loyalty in this is to me. To no one else. Not to the king. Not to the crown. To me."

The words hung in the air between them, a direct order to place personal loyalty above duty to the throne. Treason, spoken plainly.

"Your Highness." Kael's voice was a low rumble, steady as stone. He and Vorne gave a single, sharp nod.

It wasn't the automatic response of soldiers to a commander. It was an oath. A quiet moment of trust that belonged to him alone, purchased with years of service and mutual respect. A small, solitary point of honor at the center of this grand deception.

They took the papers and departed, their footfalls receding down the stone corridor. The sound faded to nothing, leaving him once more in the echoing silence of his study. It was done.

The lie was set. A shield of parchment and whispers, cast out into the court like a net to catch speculation before it became accusation.

By the following evening, the first tendrils of the new narrative had taken root.

He saw it in subtle shifts. A steward who'd previously avoided his gaze now met his eyes with a look of respectful understanding, *ah, the poor northern lady, how tragic.* Two court ladies he passed in a corridor, their voices hushed with sympathetic tones as they discussed Lady Miera's sad history. The speculative glances that had followed her like knives were replaced by something softer. Curiosity, yes, but no longer dangerous. Pity rather than suspicion.

He'd succeeded. He'd bought her time. The relief was temporary, as thin and fragile as the parchment on which his lies were written.

It did nothing to quiet the conflict churning within him. He was her protector, and he was her jailer. The two truths stood in opposition, and he was the fulcrum upon which they balanced, being slowly torn apart by the weight on either side.

As if summoned by the thought, a page arrived bearing a small scroll sealed with crimson wax. The weekly report from Archmage Lyren, tasked with monitoring the veilstone's effectiveness.

Jareth broke the seal with his signet ring, the wax cracking with a clean, sharp sound. He unrolled the parchment, eyes scanning the precise script.

Lyren had explained the stone's limitations with scholarly precision in his initial consultation. The enchantment could suppress memories tied to identity, names, places, training, but it struggled against memories tied to emotion. Terror, love, betrayal, all these emotions carved deeper grooves in the mind than knowledge did. Strong emotional triggers could crack the suppression, and once cracked, the damage spread.

The veilstone was not a wall but a dam, and every

breach weakened the whole structure. Jareth had dismissed the warning then, confident that Miera's life in Durevin Hold would be calm enough to prevent such triggers. He had not anticipated Silven Drael. He had not anticipated falling in love with her.

The language in Lyren's note was arcane, filled with technical terms that described magic in cold, clinical detail.

Harmonic attunement. Psychic dampening field. Memory engram suppression.

But the message was simple: The veilstone was working. Its calming influence remained undiminished. It continued to actively suppress intrusive memories, ensuring the subject remained placid and forgetful. No degradation in the enchantment's efficacy. No signs of resistance from the subject's consciousness. Complete success.

A final note, penned in Lyren's distinctive angular script, gave him pause.

The enchantment remains stable under normal conditions. However, I must reiterate my earlier warning: intense emotional states such as fear, rage, passion can create harmonic interference with the suppression field. The stone's efficacy may be temporarily compromised during such episodes. I recommend the subject be kept in a state of calm routine. Emotional volatility is the enemy of this magic.

He set the report aside and stared into the candlelight, his thoughts circling back to the night he had found her. The lavender silk. The Corthen accent. And beneath the mud and desperation, that faint, unmistakable scent clinging to her hair: Nightshade Moonflower, a bloom that grew nowhere but the royal gardens of Mirenweald. He had known from that first moment she was no common refugee. The question had never been if she was connected to the Corthen crown—only *how* deeply, and what it would cost him to protect her from the answer.

He saw himself as the strategist. The player moving pieces on a board for a necessary victory. The prince making hard choices to save a life.

But to her, if she ever learned the truth, he would be nothing more than the architect of her prison. The man who'd stolen her identity. The monster who'd locked her in her own mind and pretended it was love.

He lowered the scroll, parchment crackling in his tight grip. The lie he'd just released into the world was a shield, yes. Protection against the court's suspicion. A false identity to satisfy their curiosity.

But it wasn't only for her. Not entirely. A colder, more terrifying thought crystallized in the stillness of his study: He wasn't just hiding her from the court. He was hiding the court from her.

If she ever remembered who she really was, if the veil-stone ever failed, if the truth ever surfaced, she would see this court for what it was. Would see Verthar's history, its conquests, its crimes against her kingdom.

Would see him for what he was. And she would hate him for it. Rightfully. Completely. With the focused rage of someone who'd been caged and lied to and used.

He had absolutely no idea which was more dangerous: the court discovering her true identity, or her discovering it herself. Both paths led to destruction.

Both truths were weapons that could kill them both. He sat in his study until the candle burned down to a stub, until the embers in the hearth went cold and grey, until the first pale light of dawn crept through the window.

He had considered telling her a dozen times. Had composed the words in his head during sleepless nights.

You are Seraya of Corthen. Your kingdom believes you dead. My father ordered your execution. I have been lying to you since the moment we met.

But the confession was not a gift he could give her. it was a trap he would spring on them both. The moment she knew, she would act. She would try to contact Corthen, to reclaim her throne, to reach her people. And the moment she acted, his father would know.

The veilstone was not just protecting her from painful memories. It was protecting her from herself—from the princess who would walk into a blade before she understood whose hand held it. He needed time. Time to neutralize his father's threat. Time to find allies who could shield her when the truth emerged. Time to build a path to safety before the truth set her free to destroy herself.

Every day he delayed was another day she remained alive. That had to be enough. It had to be.

He needed time. Time to neutralize his father's threat. Time to find allies who could shield her when the truth emerged. Time to build a path to safety before the truth set her free to destroy herself. Every day he delayed was another day she remained alive. That had to be enough. It had to be

And he had no answers. Only the growing certainty that he'd set something in motion that he could no longer control. The lie was out there now. Growing. Taking root. And lies, once planted, developed appetites of their own.

CHAPTER
NINE

The lie Jareth had spun was a fragile mantle, but it offered more warmth than the cold shroud of anonymity had ever provided.

In the days that followed its telling, the court of Durevin Hold transformed around Miera. The shift was subtle, a change in the currents of a deep and dangerous river. The hard, speculative stares that had followed her like hunting dogs softened into something more benign. The whispers that had fallen silent when she approached now continued, their cadence changing from sharp suspicion to respectful curiosity tinged with sympathy.

She was no longer a nameless phantom haunting the fortress corridors, a mystery that needed solving. She was Lady Miera of House Caelen, a tragic figure from the wild northern Marches. A story just plausible enough for this court to sheath its knives.

The title gave her a single secure foothold on the sheer face of this stark, militaristic world. Emboldened by this newfound acceptance, fragile though it was, she began to test its boundaries. She ventured more confidently into the public spaces of the fortress, moving beyond the quiet solitude of the gardens and the honey-colored light of the library.

She learned to navigate the eddies of courtly life. Her posture straightened. Her steps became more assured. She learned which ladies could be approached with polite conversation and which preferred to keep their distance. She learned the rhythm of morning audiences, the hierarchy of seating in the Great Hall, the unspoken rules about who could speak to whom and when.

She began to feel less like a prisoner but knew they were still watching her. The deep calm the veilstone afforded her felt less like a necessity and more like a natural state of being, as if peace were simply who she was, rather than something imposed from outside. It was a peace built upon lies. A beautifully constructed game, and she was learning how to play her part.

That fragile peace shattered with the arrival of the Avenali trade delegation. Their entrance into the Great Hall for the formal reception was a splash of garish color thrown into Verthar's world of grey stone and crimson banners. Where the Vertharian court favored severe, structured lines, wool and leather in blacks and deep reds, practical and austere, the Avenali were a flowing river of jewel-toned silks.

Sapphire blue and emerald green. Cloth-of-gold that caught torchlight and threw it back in dazzling reflections. Rich purple silk embroidered with silver thread that depicted exotic birds and flowering vines. Every garment was a statement of wealth so excessive it bordered on offensive.

The very air changed with their arrival. The Great Hall usually smelled of woodsmoke and the sharp scent of beeswax from polished floors. Now it was suddenly thick with unfamiliar, heady perfumes, the cloying sweetness of imported spices, night-blooming flowers from southern gardens, amber and sandalwood and something that smelled like honey fermented into wine.

The invasion of the senses felt deliberate. Calculated. A colonization through sheer sensory excess.

The Avenali laughter was louder than Vertharian reserve allowed, their gestures more expansive and theatrical. They moved through the hall like actors taking a stage, their performance one of indulgent power. A demonstration that their strength came not from iron mines and disciplined armies, but from coffers so deep they could afford to be careless with wealth that would feed a Vertharian village for years.

It was a performance of power as surely as Verthar's military displays were performances of power. Just a different kind, wealth instead of steel, abundance instead of austerity.

The Vertharian court watched with predictable reactions. Miera saw envy in the eyes of the younger ladies as they appraised the visitors' gowns, their fingers unconsciously touching their own garments. She saw contempt in the tight jaws of the men, in the way they stood with military rigidity as if their posture alone could rebuke such ostentatious display. Disgust and fascination in equal measure.

Miera stood at a polite distance among the other ladies, positioned near one of the great pillars where she could observe without being thrust into the center of attention. She wore a gown of deep crimson wool, borrowed Vertharian colors, the uniform of her adopted court. Her hair had been arranged in the northern style, practical and elegant, befitting a minor noble from the Marches.

She was camouflaged. Safe in her false identity. She watched as Jareth and his father welcomed the visitors at the base of the dais. King Halric's expression was a mask of cold cordiality, his smile as thin and sharp as a shard of winter ice. Every gesture was precise, controlled, giving nothing away beyond the minimum courtesy demanded by diplomacy.

Jareth stood beside him, a study in flawless, princely composure. Every nod measured. Every word carefully chosen. The perfect heir performing his role.

She felt a distant pang of sympathy for him, forced to play gracious host to men whose ostentatious display was an unspoken challenge to everything Verthar represented. Every shimmering thread on their clothes was a taunt. Every perfumed gesture a mockery of Vertharian restraint.

The delegation's leader was announced, Lord Havren, a portly man dripping in gold chains who spoke with the booming confidence of someone accustomed to being heard. His Vertharian was flawless but heavily accented, each word rounded and musical where Vertharian speech was clipped and harsh.

Other members of the delegation were introduced. Trade ministers. Economic advisors. A scholar of agricultural practices. Each bowed with flourishing gestures that seemed designed to display the richness of their garments.

Then, he was introduced. "Silven Drael, diplomatic attaché to the Avenali merchant council."

He was not as richly attired as the others. His silks were a more muted shade of sapphire, the color of deep water rather than gaudy jewels. The gold embroidery on his cuffs was subtle, almost understated by Avenali standards. Where the others wore their wealth like armor, he wore his like a whisper.

Yet he moved with a fluid grace that made the others seem clumsy by comparison. He was tall and lean, with the bearing of a dancer or a swordsman, someone who understood his body as an instrument of precision. His face was sharp and intelligent, framed by dark hair that fell to his shoulders in a style that would have seemed too long and impractical by Vertharian standards but somehow suited him.

He was handsome, undeniably. But it was a dangerous kind of beauty, all sharp angles and knowing eyes. His smile was charming, and deeply, instinctively predatory.

As he made his way through the formal introductions, bowing to the king and then to Jareth, his eyes swept the assembled court. They didn't merely look. They assessed. Catalogued. Measured. He was mapping the room, identifying power structures, noting who stood where and with whom.

He was a hunter in a room full of posturing prey. When his gaze finally fell upon her, the low murmur of the hall seemed to fall away into sudden, rushing silence. Not a glance. A collision.

A jolt went through her, sharp and electric, a feeling of impossible, terrifying familiarity. Like recognition, but twisted. Wrong. As if she'd been running from something for a very long time, her own shadow perhaps, and had just turned a corner to find it standing directly in her path, barring the way forward.

I know you. The thought came unbidden, certain, devastating. But how? She knew no one. She was no one. A northern lady from an extinct house, alone in the world, unknown to everyone but the prince who'd saved her.

For a single, suspended heartbeat, Silven's polished smile faltered. His eyes widened fractionally, a minute fracture in his perfect mask of courtly grace. It was barely perceptible, gone in an instant, concealed with practiced perfection.

But she'd seen it. Startled recognition. An unguarded reaction he'd immediately suppressed. He knew her. Or believed he did.

The certainty of it was a cold, solid weight that settled deep in her gut, anchoring her to the polished black marble floor even as the world seemed to tilt beneath her feet.

The moment passed. Time resumed. The world rushed back in, the clinking of glasses, the distant strain of musicians in the gallery, the ceaseless hum of conversation washing over her like waves.

The delegation moved on, sweeping Silven Drael with them toward the high table carved from dark, gleaming wood. He went smoothly, seamlessly, never breaking stride or looking back.

No one else seemed to have noticed. No one had seen the silent, violent collision that had just occurred between two strangers across a crowded room.

But Miera couldn't breathe. The air in her lungs had turned to glass shards, each inhalation a fresh torment. Her heart hammered against her ribs like a prisoner beating against cell bars. The calm the veilstone had provided, that deep, steady peace she'd come to rely on, wavered like a candle flame in sudden wind.

The ache she thought had been banished returned with vengeance. That phantom pain that had haunted her after reading Verthar's biased history. The grief she couldn't explain. The rage that had felt so personal.

It came roaring back, amplified, undeniable. A ghost of memory screamed that something was terribly, terribly wrong. She needed to leave. Needed to be gone from this place, from his sight, from the weight of whatever knowledge lived behind those winter-sky eyes. Now.

With a murmured excuse to the lady beside her, a plausible fiction about a sudden headache brought on by the overwhelming perfumes, Miera slipped away from the assembled court. Her movements were graceful, unhurried despite the panic coiling in her gut. A flawless performance of a delicate lady retiring for the evening.

No one would see the terror beneath the composure. No one would know about the desperate urge to flee that clawed at her throat. She was a ghost again. But this time she fled not from anonymity, but from the chilling certainty of being seen. Known. Recognized by a stranger who shouldn't know her face.

As she passed through the great arched doors of the hall, she chanced a single look back. Across the vast, torchlit expanse of the Great Hall, through the crowd of silk-clad diplomats and armored Vertharian lords, Silven Drael was watching her.

He stood beside his host, a picture of polite engagement, nodding at something Lord Havren was saying. But his attention wasn't on the conversation. His eyes tracked her movement with focused, unwavering intensity.

His expression was once again one of disarming charm, perfectly calibrated for the political theater around him. But his eyes were sharp. Searching. Triumphant. He had found her.

Whatever he'd been looking for, he'd found it in her face. She didn't stop moving until the heavy oak door of her chamber was closed and bolted behind her, the iron bar sliding into place with a solid *THUNK* that still didn't feel secure enough.

The silence of the room after the noise of the hall was a physical blow. Her ears rang with it. The absence of perfume and crowd-noise felt almost painful after the sensory assault below. She leaned against the unyielding wood, her whole body trembling. Her heart hammered so violently she could feel her pulse in her throat, her wrists, her temples.

She reached instinctively for the peace the veilstone promised, craving it like a newborn babe wanted milk. Her fingers closing around the cool silver of the pendant. The veilstone had an energy all its own and it was supposed to be comforting. But it wasn't. A low, resonant hum vibrated from it, pulsing against her fingertips in a frantic rhythm that matched her own racing heartbeat. A sound she felt more than heard, thrumming through the bones of her hand, up her arm, resonating in her chest.

It was an alarm. A desperate, failing attempt to suppress something. The gentle peace it had always provided was absent. In its place was this frantic pulsing, this sense of magic straining against something too strong to contain. The veil was tearing.

She stumbled to the chair by the cold hearth and collapsed into it, her legs no longer reliable. Her whole body trembled with reaction, adrenaline and terror and something else. Something trying to surface through layers of magical suppression.

She was haunted. Not by a ghost, but by a flicker of impossible familiarity in a stranger's eyes. She tried to rationalize it. To dismantle the terror with logic, the way she'd learned to navigate the treacherous waters of court politics.

A trick of the light. Frayed nerves. The exotic perfumes had muddled her senses, made her imagine things that weren't there. It was impossible. She knew no one. She was no one. The name they'd given her was real, Lady

Miera of House Caelen, daughter of the north, alone in the world.

The rationalizations were as flimsy as smoke against a gale. That moment in the hall hadn't been coincidence. It had been recognition. Mutual, undeniable, terrifying recognition.

He knew her. And some part of her, some buried, locked-away part, knew him. The thought planted a seed of profound, devastating doubt in the barren ground of her memory.

She closed her eyes, fingers still clutching the frantically humming stone, trying to will the calm to return. Trying to push the fear back down into darkness where it belonged. But behind her closed eyelids, an image broke through the fog. Sharp. Unwelcome. Undeniable as a blade.

A windswept cliff under a sky bruised with twilight. A pale moon hung low on the horizon, its light washing the rocks in silver. The air tasted of salt and coming storms. The sound of waves crashing against rocks far below. The feeling of wind pulling at her hair, her clothes, threatening to send her tumbling over the edge into darkness. And a voice, someone calling a name that wasn't Miera.

The vision lasted only a heartbeat. A fragment of a second. Then it vanished, ripped away as the veilstone's pulse grew even more frantic, the magic fighting desperately to suppress the memory before it could fully form.

She gasped, eyes flying open, finding herself back in her chamber. Cold stone walls. Single window. One moon in a dark sky. But the vision left behind a residue. A certainty.

The chill that remained wasn't from the cold stone walls of Durevin Hold. It was the absolute, undeniable knowledge the vision left in its wake: It was real. That cliff. That moonlit shore. That other name. They were real.

Which meant everything else was a lie. The pendant pulsed frantically against her throat, magic straining to its limits. But for the first time since waking in this fortress, since opening her eyes to find herself nameless and lost, Miera felt something other than confusion. She felt rage.

Cold, clear, focused rage at whoever had done this to her. Whoever had locked her away from herself. Whoever had stolen her memories and given her false ones in their place. The veilstone couldn't suppress that.

It tried. The pulse grew more frantic still, the magic pushing at the edges of her awareness, trying to smooth away the anger, trying to restore the calm. But the rage was too strong. Too real. Too rooted in the present moment rather than buried past.

Someone had done this to her. And Silven's eyes had told her he knew who. She sat in the darkness of her chamber as night deepened outside her window. The single moon rose higher, pale and cold. Had she seen its reflection, or something else entirely? The memory was already blurring at the edges, but the certainty remained.

The veilstone pulsed against her throat, trying desperately to make her forget. But she wouldn't. Not this time. The first threads of her true self, so long held captive in a prison of gentle magic, were beginning to pull free. And once started, the unraveling couldn't be stopped.

CHAPTER

TEN

The formal drone of the royal herald echoed through the vaulted ceiling of the Great Hall, each syllable falling flat and lifeless in the vast space. The sound echoed the winter air that crept through the fortress walls, cold and dry, stripped of any warmth.

Jareth stood at his assigned place, a half step behind his father's massive ironwood throne. The very picture of a dutiful son. His expression was carefully composed, princely and unreadable, as hard as the throne itself. His posture remained rigid, every muscle locked in place.

Beneath the stillness, his nerves were drawn taut as bowstrings. He'd known this day would be a crucible from the moment word had reached him. The Avenali delegation's arrival hadn't been announced through official channels, no formal diplomatic correspondence, no advance notice allowing for proper preparation. They'd simply appeared at the gates yesterday with documents bearing the royal seal of Avenal and expectations of immediate accommodation.

The irregularity was calculated. Deliberate. A power play.

A coded message from his spymaster, Eldric, had arrived mere hours before the formal reception. The report had been lean on facts and heavy on warning. The delegation's lead attaché, Silven Drael, was a man whose reputation for perception was matched only by his ambition. He'd risen from minor merchant family to diplomatic prominence through a combination of intelligence, ruthlessness, and an uncanny ability to identify valuable information.

Eldric's counsel had been straightforward: *Observe. Do not engage.* Now, watching Silven Drael across the expanse of polished black marble, Jareth understood the caution with crystalline clarity.

The Avenali were a loud spectacle, a deliberate performance of wealth staged in the austere heart of Verthar. Gold-threaded silks that cost more than most nobles' annual incomes. Jewelry that caught torchlight and threw it back in dazzling displays. Perfumes so heavy they felt like physical presence, cloying and sweet, an olfactory assault on the clean, cold stone of the hold.

The message was clear: *We can afford to be excessive. What can you afford?*

His father sat rigid on the throne, enduring the display with the stony tolerance of a man who viewed such ostentation as weakness. Every Vertharian in the hall maintained similar composure, backs straight, expressions neutral, silently judging the visitors' lack of restraint. But Silven Drael was different.

He was a whisper in the midst of his delegation's clamor. Where the others performed their wealth like actors on a stage, Silven wore his more subtly, expensive but understated, a sapphire silk coat that suggested refinement rather than shouting it.

As he offered polite, meaningless pleasantries to the king, his gaze swept the room with methodical precision. Calm. Unreadable. The gaze of a hawk charting its hunting ground, cataloging every face, every position, every relationship. It missed nothing.

Jareth felt the pressure of that gaze when it passed over him, a brief, assessing glance that took in his position, his bearing, his carefully neutral expression. Measuring him. Finding him worth noting but not immediately threatening. Then it moved on.

The question that gnawed at him was not whether Silven knew who she was—the emissary's pointed provocations in the days since his arrival made that obvious. The question was *how*. Avenal's intelligence network was legendary, their agents embedded in every court on the continent. The Gilded Ring's merchant lords had eyes in places even Jareth's own spymaster could not reach.

Had they identified her before Jareth had? Had they, perhaps, known of her survival when the rest of the world believed her drowned in the Shardspine passes? The thought chilled him to the marrow. If Avenal knew, then her existence was not his secret to keep. It was a weapon others were already positioning to use—and he was merely the fool who had provided them a clear target.

Jareth kept his own expression perfectly neutral, hands clasped loosely behind his back. The picture of a prince attending to duty, present but not engaged. He'd learned this posture in childhood, how to be visible yet forgettable, how to occupy space without drawing attention.

But when Silven's eyes found Miera, standing quietly among the ladies of the court in a gown of borrowed crimson, they did not move on. They lingered.

It was a masterclass in subtlety. There was no overt stare, no vulgar change in his charming expression that would have drawn notice. Just a slight angling of his body toward her, so subtle most wouldn't register it consciously. A fractional pause in the easy rhythm of his breathing that only a trained observer would catch.

To anyone else, it would have been invisible. To Jareth, who'd spent a lifetime reading the hidden languages of power, studying the micro-expressions that revealed truth beneath diplomatic lies, it was a declaration. Silven wasn't merely observing. He was targeting.

The suspicion Eldric's report had planted bloomed into chilling certainty. This was not coincidence. The Avenali delegation arriving now, unannounced, with this particular attaché known for his intelligence gathering, this was an audit.

Someone had sent them to investigate. To verify information. To confirm suspicions. The question was: what did they know? And who had told them?

The formal introductions concluded with all the tedious ceremony such occasions required. The herald announced each member of the delegation, their titles and positions. The Avenali bowed with flourishing gestures. The Vertharian court responded with stiff, minimal acknowledgments. Political theatre at its finest.

As the court began to dissolve into smaller clusters, conversations forming and reforming like water finding its level, Jareth remained at his post. His father engaged the lead Avenali merchant in conversation, their low rumble of feigned cordiality drifting up to where Jareth stood.

His own attention remained fixed on Silven, who now charmed a stern-faced duchess with effortless grace. His laughter was natural, his interest seemingly genuine. He asked questions that displayed flattering knowledge of Vertharian history. He complimented the fortress's architecture with insights that proved he'd actually studied it. Perfect diplomatic performance.

And yet Jareth could feel the man's awareness, a palpable, invisible line drawn across the room, connected directly to Miera. Like a spider sensing vibrations on its web, Silven remained constantly attuned to her position, her movements, her reactions.

Jareth saw her too, though he didn't let his gaze linger. Her face was pale, her composure fragile as spun glass. She stood among the other court ladies with perfect posture, her hands folded with studied grace, but he knew her well enough now to read the tension in her shoulders, the slight stiffness in her smile.

She was terrified. The sight of her unease, a mirror of

his own, twisted something sharp and ugly in his gut. Guilt. Fear. Rage at his own helplessness.

He needed to get her away from here. Needed to extract her from Silven's scrutiny before the man could approach her, before he could speak words that might shatter the veilstone's grip entirely.

But any overt move to protect her would be an admission of her importance. A confirmation of the very thing he sought to conceal. Moving to shield her would draw every eye in the court, would signal to his father that she mattered more than a minor northern noble should.

Trapped, he could only stand and watch, a silent guardian helpless to prevent the hawk from circling its prey.

The audience finally ended. King Halric rose, the signal for formal dismissal. The Avenali delegation was escorted to their prepared suites in the eastern wing by a contingent of guards whose instructions would be to watch as much as to serve.

As the hall began to empty, Jareth turned to leave, his mind already racing. He needed to speak with Eldric, needed more information about Silven's background and connections. Needed to understand what game was being played and who had set the pieces on the board.

"A word, cousin." Rilen's voice was low and urgent, cutting through the polite murmur of the departing court.

Jareth stopped in the shadow of a heavy tapestry depicting a long-dead Vertharian king slaying a dragon. The woven beast's eye, a single black thread against crimson, seemed to watch them with cold knowledge.

Jareth glanced around. No one was close enough to overhear. He gave a fractional nod.

Rilen moved closer, his face carved with concern beneath his careful composure. "His Majesty is not pleased," he said, voice barely above a whisper. "The Avenali arrive unannounced with an attaché known for his guile, and their questions are too precise, too informed. They know more than they should."

Avenal had remained neutral in the Verthar-Corthen conflict for three generations, watching from across the Sundering Sea as two kingdoms bled each other white. Officially, they sought only trade agreements and safe passage for their merchant fleets. But Jareth had read the intelligence reports his spymaster compiled. Avenal's neutrality was a position of strength, not weakness. They were waiting to see which kingdom would emerge weakened enough to exploit. A restored Corthen heir would destabilize Verthar's claim to the conquered territories.

A war of succession would bleed both realms further. And Avenal, with its merchant fleets and mercenary companies, would be positioned to pick up the pieces. Silven was not here to negotiate trade routes. He was here to light a fire and watch the world burn—then sell water to whoever survived.

Jareth's jaw tightened. "What questions?"

"About trade routes through the northern passes. About noble houses in the Marches." Rilen's gaze held Jareth's. "About recent arrivals to court."

The information landed like a physical blow. They were already asking about her. Already probing.

"The King's patience with secrets is wearing thin," Rilen continued. "He wants to know why you've found nothing about the woman. Why your investigations have produced no results. He's beginning to suspect you're protecting her rather than investigating her."

The pressure, now given voice by his cousin, felt like the weight of the entire fortress pressing down on his shoulders.

"I am handling it," Jareth said, the words clipped and cold. It was the same answer he'd given his father, and it sounded just as hollow now. Just as much a lie.

"Are you?" Rilen's question was gentle but unflinching. "That man, Drael, I watched him. He looked at her as if he were a jeweler assessing a familiar stone. As if he recognized her, Jareth. If he does recognize her, if he tells the King before you do..."

Rilen let the sentence hang in the cold air between them, unfinished. The unspoken consequences were more powerful than any explicit threat. Disgrace for deceiving the king. Imprisonment for treason. War if she proved to be who Jareth feared she was. And for Miera herself, something far worse than any of that.

Execution. Or being handed over to enemies who would use her as a political weapon.

"The King's trust is conditional," Rilen pressed, loyalty warring with fear in his expression. "He will not tolerate being made a fool in his own court. Not by the Avenali, and not by his own son."

Jareth's first instinct had been to shield her. Every

decision, every lie, every forged document had been built around that single imperative: protect her at all costs.

But Rilen's warning illuminated a darker truth. He was no longer just protecting a woman. He was managing a state secret that could bring down his house. That could tear the kingdom apart. The realization settled over him like ice water.

"The Royal Guard are his eyes and ears," Jareth said, his voice dropping even lower. He was thinking aloud now, mind shifting from defense to offense, from protecting to controlling. "I can't use them. They answer to him first, to me second."

Rilen's expression hardened with understanding. He knew what Jareth was asking. It was a line they'd never crossed. "My men are loyal to me, Jareth. But spying on an official guest of the crown..." He paused, weighing words. "That is treason."

"Protecting the crown from its own ignorance is not treason. It's duty."

The words came out cold, pragmatic. They tasted like his father's logic, like the brutal calculus of power that Jareth had spent his life resisting. He was becoming the man he despised. Using the tools he hated. And he couldn't stop himself because the alternative was worse.

"I need to know what Silven is planning," Jareth continued, urgency sharpening his voice. "I need to know who he contacts, what he says, what he reports back to Avenal. I need this information before my father's paranoia gives him reason to act preemptively."

A long silence stretched between them, thick with

the weight of shared risk. Heavy with the knowledge that what Jareth was asking could get them both executed.

Rilen's men weren't official soldiers. They were a private force, a mix of household guards and paid loyalists, an inheritance from his father's vast estates. To use them this way was to step outside the law. To create a shadow conspiracy within the walls of the citadel itself.

To commit treason in the name of protecting someone who might be an enemy of the state.

Finally, Rilen gave a single, almost imperceptible nod. "What do you need?"

The relief that washed through Jareth was so profound it almost buckled his knees. He hadn't realized how truly alone he'd been until this moment, until someone chose to stand with him despite the cost.

"Surveillance. On Drael and his entire retinue. I want to know everything. Where they go, who they speak to, what messages they send. I want eyes on them every hour of every day."

"It will be done," Rilen said quietly. Then he melted back into the flow of the departing court, disappearing among the crimson and black of Vertharian nobles, leaving Jareth alone in the shadow of the dead king.

Hours later, the fortress had settled into its evening rhythm. Most of the court had retired. Guards changed shifts with muted efficiency. Servants cleared the last remnants of the feast, their footsteps echoing in empty corridors.

Jareth sat in his study, the door barred from inside.

The only sounds were the crackle of fire in the hearth and the frantic scratch of his quill on parchment.

He was no longer a prince. He was a spymaster, drafting a battle plan in ink and wax.

The instructions were detailed, precise. He listed the routes of communication to monitor, the eastern wing where the Avenali were housed, the messenger stations they might use, the public houses in the city below where information was traded like currency.

Attendants to watch. Not just Silven, but every member of the delegation. The guards assigned to them needed to be his people, not his father's.

A list of potential contacts in the city to shadow. Merchants with Avenali connections. Foreign traders who might serve as intermediaries. Informants who sold intelligence to the highest bidder.

He poured all his strategic acumen, all his fear, onto the page. Years of military training distilled into surveillance protocols. Every contingency planned for. Every vulnerability identified and exploited.

He wore his formal princely attire still, the crimson coat with its silver fastenings, the high collar that marked his rank. But a slim, serviceable dagger was concealed beneath the coat, pressed against his ribs where he could reach it in a heartbeat.

It had always been there, a standard precaution for anyone of noble blood in a court where political rivalries could turn violent. But tonight, the cold weight of it felt more necessary than ever. A small, sharp comfort against the chaos.

When he finished writing, he folded the parchment carefully. Three precise folds, the way military dispatches were sealed. The way orders were given that couldn't be spoken aloud.

He lit a stick of deep red sealing wax from the candle flame. The scent of melting beeswax filled the air, rich and slightly sweet. He watched the wax drip onto the seam of the paper, pooling like blood.

A pool of crimson spreading across white parchment.

Then he took the heavy silver signet ring from his finger. The black falcon of his house was carved into its face, the symbol of his authority, his lineage, his right to command.

He pressed it into the hot wax. The seal was made. The order was given. The act of treason was complete.

He stared at the mark for a long moment. The symbol of his loyalty, the emblem of his house, now seared onto a document of profound disloyalty. He'd turned his kingdom's tools of statecraft against itself. He'd ordered his own private army to spy on official guests of the crown.

If his father discovered this, there would be no mercy. No allowance made for filial bonds. The king would see it as betrayal of the most fundamental kind, a prince building power structures independent of the throne, conducting shadow operations without royal sanction.

Execution would be the kindest outcome. But he'd done it to protect her. Every treasonous word on that parchment, every illegal order, every line crossed, all of it was for her.

The realization didn't comfort him. It terrified him.

Because protecting her had become more important than his duty. More important than his honor. More important than his life.

When had that happened? When had she become more vital than everything he'd been raised to value? He didn't know. Couldn't pinpoint the moment. It had been gradual, insidious, a slow poison that had worked its way into his blood until he couldn't imagine cutting it out without bleeding to death.

He was trapped. A man caught in a cage of his own making, standing between his father's brutal suspicion, Silven's piercing perception, and the terrifying, unknowable truth of the woman he was trying to save.

A woman who might hate him if she ever discovered what he'd done to her. A woman who might destroy him even if she never learned the truth. He had no idea which of them would destroy him first, his father, Silven, or Miera herself. All he knew was that destruction was inevitable now.

The only question was what form it would take, and how many people it would consume along the way.

CHAPTER

ELEVEN

The Great Hall of Durevin Hold was a spectacle of power, a vaulted cavern of stone and shadow transformed into theater by the glow of a thousand candles. Their light glittered on gold filigree worked into the edges of serving platters. On polished pewter dishes that reflected flames like mirrors. On the black falcons woven into crimson banners hanging between carved pillars, their wings spread in eternal descent.

The air hung thick and heavy with competing scents. Roasted boar, its skin crackling and glazed with honey. Spiced wine steaming in silver carafes, aromatic with cinnamon and cloves. The clean, waxy smell of beeswax from hundreds of candles burning in their sconces. Underneath it all, the perfumes of the Avenali delegation, heady, exotic, overwhelming.

Beneath the distant, elegant strains of strings and flutes played from the musician's gallery, a low murmur of hundreds of conversations created a constant, humming undercurrent. The sound rose and fell like ocean waves, punctuated by the sharp clink of silver on stone, the ring of crystal touching crystal, occasional bursts of laughter.

It was a performance of royal splendor, carefully orchestrated down to the last detail. And Miera was a part of the cast, playing a role she didn't fully understand.

She sat midway down the high table on the raised dais. Her position among the Vertharian court ladies was deliberate, she suspected. Not important enough to sit near the king, but elevated enough to be visible. A decorative figure. A curiosity on display.

Her spine was perfectly straight, years of training she couldn't remember keeping her posture flawless. Her hands rested with studied grace in the lap of a borrowed gown of dark velvet that felt too heavy, too formal, like armor disguised as clothing.

To any casual observer, she was the picture of placid nobility. A northern lady at ease in opulent surroundings, comfortable in her place at court. It was a lie. Her serenity was a mask, thin as paper. Her composure was a fortress wall built from pure will, and behind it, she was a city under siege.

Her goal, formed in the panicked solitude of her chamber the night before, after hours of clutching the frantically humming veilstone and trying to make sense of impossible visions, was simple: Disappear. Not in body, but in presence. She would be so perfectly composed, so flawlessly serene, so unremarkable that she would become part of the scenery. Invisible to the one pair of eyes she could feel on her skin like a physical touch.

Silven Drael. The Avenali diplomat sat three tables away, positioned at an angle that gave him a clear view of most of the hall. He never looked at her directly. To all appearances, he was the epitome of a charming courtier, fully engaged in lively conversation with a grizzled Vertharian general to his left.

His smiles were easy, genuine-seeming. His gestures fluid and expressive. He laughed at a shared joke, his head tilted back in a picture of unguarded warmth, the candle-light catching in his dark hair.

It was a devastatingly effective performance. But Miera's reawakened instincts, sharper and colder than any fear she'd known before, cutting through the veilstone's suppression like a blade through silk, screamed that it was all an act.

His surveillance was a masterpiece of subtlety.

He spoke animatedly to the general, gesturing with his wine goblet to emphasize a point. He kept her perfectly positioned within his peripheral vision. Not directly in his line of sight, that would be too obvious. But positioned so that any movement she made would register immediately.

She tested it once, shifting slightly in her seat to reach for her wine goblet. His conversation didn't pause. His smile didn't falter. But she saw the minute adjustment of his posture, the way his awareness tracked her movement without his eyes ever leaving the general's face. It was intentional. Absolutely intentional.

When a servant stepped forward to refill his wine, bending between Silven and his conversational partner, Silven's gaze didn't follow the motion. It remained fixed ahead, focused on the general, while his hand held out his goblet with the automatic precision of someone who didn't need to look.

His awareness of her was unwavering. An invisible pressure against her skin, like a hand pressed against her throat. He observed her as a constant, a fixed point in his strategic map of the room.

She was not a person to him. She was a target. The knowledge settled in her stomach like a cold stone, heavy and immovable.

She forced herself to breathe slowly, evenly. To mimic the calm rhythm of the lady beside her, whose chest rose and fell with the measured ease of someone who had nothing to fear. Etiquette was her shield. The rigid structure of the feast, the prescribed actions, the formal choreography of courses and toasts, was her only defense.

She picked up her goblet, keeping her fingers steady through sheer force of will. She took a sip of wine, barely tasting it. The liquid was warm, spiced, sliding down her throat like liquid heat, but she registered none of it.

She focused on minutiae. On small, prescribed actions. The proper way to hold the goblet. The correct angle to tilt it. The appropriate moment to set it down. Each movement was a brick in the wall of her composure, built carefully to hide the panic churning beneath.

The veilstone hummed against her skin. It was a low, almost subsonic vibration, a separate pulse that didn't match her heartbeat. The magic tried to enforce calm her mind now actively rejected. What had once felt like a gentle tide pulling her toward peace now felt like a hand pressing down on her thoughts, trying to smother them before they could fully form.

Its magic strained against something sharper, older. An instinct that knew the shape of predators. That understood the deadly geometry of a room where power was the only real currency. That could read threat in the angle of a body, danger in the timing of a glance.

A toast was called. A minor lord, one of the King's advisors, she thought, though she couldn't remember his name, rose and proposed the health of the Avenali delegation. Standard diplomatic courtesy.

Miera rose with the others, her movements fluid and practiced. Muscle memory from a life she didn't remember carried her through the motions.

She watched as the Vertharian courtiers lifted their pewter goblets in the traditional manner, holding them by the delicate stems, raising them to chest height. The gesture was restrained, controlled. Very Vertharian in its precision. Then her eyes found the Avenali.

As one, they performed a different ritual. They cupped the bowls of their goblets, made of dark, smoked glass that caught candlelight and turned it amber, with both hands. Their fingers laced together in a gesture that looked almost like prayer. They gave a slight, almost imperceptible bow of the head as they drank.

It was beautiful. Reverent. A gesture of practiced grace that spoke of centuries of tradition.

When her gaze fell on Silven, he performed the movement with liquid precision that was almost hypnotic.

Every finger placed deliberately. The bow perfectly angled. The timing exact.

It was another piece of information. Another confirmation. Everything he did was deliberate. Every gesture freighted with meaning. Every movement a word in a language she was only beginning to remember how to read.

She sat, her own goblet untouched despite having risen for the toast. The breach of etiquette would be noted, but she couldn't bring herself to drink. Her throat had closed up, her body refusing to cooperate with the performance.

The isolation was profound. She was adrift in a sea of faces, surrounded by courtiers and nobles, by ladies in velvet and men in military dress, by servants moving between tables and musicians playing in the gallery. Surrounded by humanity. And yet still alone.

Her silent, one-sided war was invisible to everyone around her. The allies and enemies surrounding her had no idea she was fighting for her sanity, her identity, her very sense of self.

"The spiced pears are simply divine tonight, are they not, my dear?"

The voice startled her from her paranoid vigil. Thin and reedy, but kind. An elderly lady seated to her right was smiling at her, her face a roadmap of fine wrinkles that spoke of decades of laughter and sorrow. Her eyes were gentle, entirely oblivious to the tension crackling through Miera like lightning.

A brooch of unadorned Vertharian silver was pinned to

her shoulder, a family piece rather than a political statement. She wore no rings except a wedding band. Her gown was elegant but understated.

Miera was forced to turn, to break the invisible line of tension connecting her to Silven. She summoned a smile, feeling the unfamiliar pull of muscles in her face. It felt genuine, if brief. A moment of actual human connection in this theater of masks.

"They are wonderful," she agreed softly, her voice sounding strange to her own ears. Too quiet. Too fragile.

The mundane pleasantry was like a brief gasp of air in a suffocating room. For a heartbeat, she was just a woman discussing dessert. Just someone making polite conversation at a formal dinner.

But the moment highlighted her utter solitude. The chasm between her internal reality, the terror, the fragmented memories, the certainty of being hunted, and the polite fiction of the feast.

For one brief, beautiful moment, she was just a woman talking about pears. Then the elderly lady turned back to her plate, attention captured by a servant offering more wine, and the weight of Silven's awareness settled back onto Miera's shoulders. Heavier than before, as if it had been building pressure during that brief reprieve.

The courses progressed with formal precision. Servants cleared away the main dishes, platters that had held roasted boar, braised vegetables, fresh bread that steamed when broken open. They brought forth the final course: glistening fruits arranged in elaborate pyramids, intricate pastries dusted with sugar that sparkled like frost, delicate confections that looked too beautiful to eat.

The music shifted to a livelier tempo. A signal the feast was winding down. She had almost made it. Had survived the evening. Her performance had held. She hadn't cracked, hadn't drawn attention, hadn't given anything away.

She must escape, and retreat to her chamber before he could corner her. Before he could speak to her and shatter the last remnants of her control with words that might undo everything the veilstone tried to suppress.

King Halric pushed his chair back. The sound of wood scraping across the floor cut through the ambient noise. A signal. He rose, his movement stiff and formal, and the entire hall followed suit. Hundreds of people standing in near-unison, a wave of motion rippling outward from the high table. The formal dinner was over.

Courtiers began to move, to form new clusters of conversation. The rigid structure of the feast dissolved into the fluid social dynamics of the court at leisure. It was her chance. She needed to confirm his location before she moved. Needed to know where he was so she could slip away in the opposite direction. She dared a single, fleeting glance across the hall toward where he'd been sitting.

At that exact moment, he turned. For the first time all evening, Silven's gaze locked directly onto hers. No pretense now. No charm. No mask of polite diplomatic interest.

His eyes were filled with triumphant certainty. Absolute knowledge. The look of a hunter who'd finally cornered his prey after a long chase. *He knew.*

A small, knowing smile touched his lips. Not cruel, which would have been easier to face. Just satisfied. Certain. The smile of someone who'd solved a puzzle and was pleased with his own cleverness.

Her heart stopped for a frozen moment, her blood stilling in her veins. And then, as she watched in dawning horror, he began to walk. Not toward the great doors where the other Avenali were gathering. Not toward his delegation or toward the king. But with casual, predatory grace, the unhurried confidence of someone who knew his quarry couldn't escape, he started along the high table. Directly toward her.

Every head turned to follow his path. The movement was subtle but unmistakable, courtiers tracking the foreign diplomat's progress with the avid interest of people who sensed drama unfolding. The ambient noise of the hall didn't stop, but it seemed to recede in Miera's perception. Her vision narrowed to a tunnel, focused entirely on his approach. His measured steps. The way he moved through the crowd like water flowing around stones, effortless and inevitable.

She couldn't move. Couldn't breathe. Couldn't think. The veilstone pulsed frantically at her throat, magic straining to suppress the panic flooding through her. But it was too late. Too strong. Too real. He was coming. And she had nowhere to run.

TWELVE

From his seat at the high table, Jareth watched the feast with the detached focus of a general observing enemy lines through a spyglass. The Great Hall was a sea of calculated motions, a symphony of polite warfare where true battles were fought in spaces between words, in the subtle turn of a head, in the deliberate choice of which wine to pour. Banners bearing the black falcon of Verthar hung still as death between carved pillars, their shadows falling across courtiers like judgments.

His gaze was a weapon. He swept the hall methodically, cataloging allegiances, dissecting threats, measuring the distance between potential allies and confirmed enemies. But his attention always returned to two fixed points on his mental map.

Miera, a study in fragile composure, her dark velvet gown making her look like a shadow among the crimson-clad Vertharian ladies. And Silven Drael, the Avenali emissary who was a serpent coiled in silk, venom disguised as charm.

For the duration of the interminable meal, Jareth had maintained a passive defense. A strategy born of grim necessity and his father's watchful presence. He'd observed Silven's masterclass in non-verbal intimidation, a relentless pressure applied with such elegance it was entirely deniable. The perfect crime.

Every instinct screamed at him to cross the hall, to place himself physically between them, to shield her from that calculating gaze. But he couldn't.

Any overt act of protection would be a confession of her importance. A signal flare for his father's ever-watchful suspicion. The king sat three seats away, his pale eyes missing nothing, his stillness that of a predator waiting for prey to reveal itself.

So Jareth had remained frozen in place, a prince trapped in his own court. His knuckles had gone white where they gripped the carved ironwood arms of his chair, a silent signal of the fury he kept caged behind diplomatic composure.

The feast was ending. King Halric rose, the scrape of his chair a definitive sound that cut through ambient noise. The formal proceedings were over.

Jareth felt a breath of relief expand in his chest. She'd weathered the storm. His passive strategy, however agonizing, had worked. She was safe for now. He could extract her from the hall, escort her back to the quiet solitude of her chambers, away from the hawk's piercing gaze. Then his blood ran cold.

Across the dais, Silven Drael turned. The movement was fluid, unhurried, but it cut through the room with the force of a drawn blade. For the first time all evening, his gaze locked directly onto Miera's, no pretense now, no polite artifice masking his intent.

It was a look of pure, triumphant certainty. A small, knowing smile touched his lips. Sharp as a shard of glass. Predatory and satisfied.

Jareth's muscles coiled. Every nerve fired with the urgent need to move, to intercede, to do *something*. He was half out of his seat when Silven began to walk. Not toward his delegation, gathered near the great doors. Not toward the king, who was engaged in quiet conversation with his advisors. But with casual, predatory grace, Silven started along the high table. Directly toward Miera.

Every head in the immediate vicinity turned to follow his path. The movement rippled outward like stones dropped in still water, courtiers tracking the foreign diplomat's progress with the avid interest of people who sensed drama unfolding. The ambient noise of the hall didn't stop, but it receded in Jareth's perception, fading to a distant drone. All that was real was the Avenali emissary's deliberate, unhurried approach.

Jareth's mind raced, charting possibilities, seeking a countermove that wouldn't reveal too much or provoke his father's scrutiny. There was none.

Silven had chosen his moment with surgical precision. In the chaotic interlude between the feast's formal end and the court's dispersal, when movement was expected, when approaching other guests was normal, he'd created the perfect cover.

It was public, yet intimate. An ambush staged in plain sight. Brilliant and devastating.

Silven stopped beside Miera's chair, his presence casting a shadow across the table that seemed to swallow the candlelight. He held two crystal goblets of unmistakably Avenali make, their impossibly thin stems designed to ring with a faint musical note upon the slightest touch. The wine within was deep crimson, almost black in the flickering light.

He offered one to Miera with a smile that radiated charm, his posture the picture of polite diplomacy.

"Lady Miera." His voice was a low, smooth melody that cut effortlessly through the noise, pitched just loud enough for those nearest to hear. Jareth included. "I could not let the evening end without you tasting a true Avenali delicacy. A gift from my own family's estate."

Jareth's jaw clenched so hard his teeth ached. Every word was a trap being set, each syllable weighted with layers of meaning.

Miera looked up, her face pale in the candlelight. Her expression was a mixture of apprehension and polite confusion, the look of someone trying to navigate social obligations while fighting rising panic.

She was trapped. To refuse would be a public insult to a powerful foreign emissary. To accept was to walk into whatever snare he'd prepared.

She took the goblet. Her fingers trembled almost imperceptibly as they brushed his. A detail most would miss. Jareth saw it. Silven saw it. And the slight widening of Silven's smile confirmed he'd noted her fear.

He raised his own glass in a subtle toast. "It is said to pair wonderfully with the Cortheni-style roasted pheasant we were served tonight." He paused, letting the words hang in the air between them. "A bold choice for the Vertharian kitchens, incorporating such foreign techniques. You must tell me if you agree with the pairing."

Jareth's heart hammered against his ribs like a prisoner beating against cell bars.

No. No, no, no. It was a test. Silven wasn't asking her opinion. He was presenting her with a deliberate cultural trigger, a piece of bait poisoned with homeland nostalgia, waiting for her instincts to betray her. Betting that her deeply ingrained training, years of education about food, wine, culture, would override the veilstone's fragile hold. Betting she would correct him. Because the dish hadn't been prepared in Cortheni style at all.

Miera, caught off guard by his proximity and the weight of courtly attention suddenly focused on her, lifted the goblet to her lips. She took a small, hesitant sip, her brow furrowing in concentration.

For a horrifying second, Jareth thought she might see the trap. Might recognize the deliberate wrongness of his statement and deflect with vague pleasantries. But the bait was too specific. The trigger too deeply embedded in a life she didn't consciously remember.

"The vintage is bold," she said, her voice distant, almost dreamy. Reflexive. Her eyes had a faraway look, as if she were reading from a script written in her bones. "But it lacks the finish of the Sunstone varietals from the southern Cortheni vineyards. Their soil gives the grape a cleaner note, less tannin."

The words fell into sudden stillness. Not true silence, the hall was still full of conversation, music still played from the gallery. But a pocket of quiet opened around them, a vacuum where time seemed to stop.

Miera froze. Her eyes widened with dawning, abject horror as her own words echoed back to her. Words she shouldn't know. Knowledge she shouldn't possess.

She stared at Silven, her face draining of all color until she looked like a ghost. The goblet clinked hard against the table as she set it down, the sound like a bone breaking in the sudden quiet.

A sharp, reflexive gasp escaped her lips. The veilstone at her throat pulsed frantically, visible even from where Jareth sat, a desperate attempt to suppress what had just surfaced. To push the knowledge back down into darkness.

Too late. Silven's smile widened into something that approached genuine pleasure. Slow, satisfied, the expression of absolute victory. He'd done it. He'd cracked the lock on her lost memory and shown her a glimpse of the treasure inside.

More importantly, he'd proven his suspicion to himself, and to her. And he'd done it all while demonstrating his power to break her careful composure at will, in full view of the court. It was a catastrophe.

Jareth moved without conscious thought. His chair screeched back against polished marble, the sound grating and violent in the attentive silence. Every eye at the high table swiveled toward them, toward him standing abruptly, toward Miera's stricken face, toward Silven's satisfied smile. He'd been so elegantly, so completely outmaneuvered.

This public failure would be noted. Reported to his father as a moment of lost control, a crack in his composure. Weakness the king would exploit. But none of that mattered in the face of Miera's terror.

He forced his voice to steadiness, though it came out tight with barely suppressed fury. "Her Ladyship has become quite the scholar." The words tasted like ash on his tongue. He moved to stand behind Miera's chair, placing a hand on its carved back, a gesture of protection that felt hollow. "She's spent the better part of the last month devouring every book in the library of Durevin Hold. It seems our histories on winemaking have left quite an impression."

The excuse was laughably thin. A scrap of paper held up to shield them from a bonfire.

No book could impart the instinctive, sensory knowledge she'd just displayed. The mention of Sunstone varietals specifically, an obscure detail known only to Cortheni nobility and wine merchants, wasn't in any Vertharian text. He knew for a fact the single chronicle on Cortheni agriculture contained only passing references to their vineyards, nothing about specific grape varieties or soil composition.

That was the arcane knowledge of a native. A connoisseur. Someone who'd been raised in those southern vineyards, who'd learned to distinguish vintages from childhood. Not a line in a history text. Not something learned from books.

Silven's gaze shifted to Jareth, winter-pale eyes glittering with amusement. He gave a slight, dismissive nod, the polite acceptance of an explanation they both knew was a lie. He knew. Jareth knew he knew. And in that shared, unspoken acknowledgment, the power dynamic of the entire evening shifted.

Silven Drael now held a leash. And the collar was around Jareth's neck.

"How very studious," Silven murmured, his voice laced with silken mockery. He gave a final, charming bow to Miera, who looked as if she might shatter into pieces. "I am delighted the library has provided such a comprehensive education. A kingdom's greatest asset, after all, is its knowledge."

The words were innocent enough on the surface. Underneath, they were a threat. *I know what you're hiding. I know who she is. And I will use this knowledge however I see fit.*

With that final, veiled warning hanging in the air like smoke, Silven turned and melted back into the crowd. His retreat was smooth, unhurried, the movement of someone who'd accomplished exactly what he'd set out to do.

He left Jareth standing in the ruins of his carefully constructed strategy.

The court's attention lingered, dozens of eyes watching, measuring, speculating about what they'd just witnessed. The mysterious northern lady displaying impossible knowledge. The prince intervening with an implausible explanation. The Avenali diplomat's knowing smile.

Whispers would spread before the hour was out. By morning, everyone would be talking about it.

Jareth was exposed. Miera was terrified, her cognitive dissonance a palpable wave radiating from her rigid posture. The entire test had been performed in full view of the court, turning them into the center of hushed speculation.

His passive, observational stance had been shattered. He was no longer a player controlling the game. He was a piece, and Silven had just moved him into check. The need for caution, for secrecy, had been incinerated in a blast of cold rage that threatened to overwhelm all calculation.

He knew his next move: seize back control. Rip the leash from Silven's hand before he could tighten it. Protect Miera from the consequences of what she'd just revealed, to herself, to Silven, to anyone paying attention.

The last echo of his weak excuse still hung in the air, sounding more pathetic with each passing second. Jareth's gaze left Silven's retreating back, no longer tracking the diplomat with the careful attention of a strategist, but with the focused rage of someone marking a target.

He mastered the burning urge to draw the dagger concealed beneath his coat. Channeled that violence into controlled action. He moved to Miera's side, placing his hand firmly on the back of her chair. His silent, unyielding pressure was a clear command.

Stand. Now. We're leaving.

She looked up at him with eyes that held too many questions, too much confusion, too much dawning awareness of truths the veilstone couldn't suppress anymore. But she rose.

He offered his arm, the gesture formal, appropriate, giving the watching court no ammunition. She took it, her hand trembling as it rested on his sleeve. Together, they walked from the Great Hall. Every step measured. Every movement controlled.

Behind them, the whispers began in earnest. And somewhere in the departing crowd, Silven Drael watched them leave with the satisfied smile of a hunter who'd just drawn first blood.

THIRTEEN

Horror coiled in Miera's stomach, cold, absolute, visceral. A tide of ice rising to her throat, stealing her breath. Her own voice, moments before so reflexive and certain, now felt like a foreign, treacherous instrument that had betrayed her.

She stared at Silven Drael. His satisfied smile was a masterpiece of cruelty, a slow and deliberate twisting of the knife he'd just slid between her ribs.

Her face had drained of all color, she could feel it, the blood fleeing to her core, leaving her skin cold and clammy. The goblet in her hand trembled. She set it down on the table with a sharp clink that sounded, in the ringing quiet, like a bone breaking.

A thin, sharp gasp escaped her lips before she could suppress it.

Panic seized her, pure and primal, bypassing thought entirely. The walls of the hall with their falcon banners and wavering torchlight seemed to press inward, the vast space contracting to a coffin. The low murmur of the court and distant strains of music became a roaring in her ears, a rushing sound like blood pounding.

She had to escape. The thought was a singular, desperate command that drowned out everything else. *Can't breathe here. Can't think.*

She turned to Jareth, her eyes wide with a plea she couldn't voice. She saw his face, pale and tight with a fury so cold it was almost serene, and watched him rise. His chair scraped back with that violent sound. His flimsy excuse about her studies was a meaningless drone in the background, a pathetic shield against a killing blow that had already found its mark.

But she seized upon it anyway. Because what else was there?

"I do not feel well." The words came out fractured, barely a whisper. It was a lie that was also the truest thing she'd ever said. A wave of dizziness swept over her, real and nauseating, the room tilting on its axis.

Jareth's hand closed on her arm instantly. His grip was firm, almost painful. Grounding. "Forgive us," he said to the table at large, his voice a low command that brooked no argument. He was already pulling her to her feet, moving her away from the dais, away from Silven's triumphant gaze.

She allowed him to lead her, her focus narrowed to the act of placing one foot before the other. Her borrowed Vertharian court gown, dark velvet that had felt elegant hours before, was now a heavy, suffocating shroud. Jareth's hand on her arm was a brand, burning through fabric. His touch wasn't gentle reassurance. It was a declaration of urgent ownership.

Mine. My problem. My disaster to contain.

They moved through the dispersing crowd of courtiers, a silent, grim procession cutting through silk and jewels and curious stares. Miera kept her head down, eyes locked on the floor, unable to bear the weight of the other eyes she felt upon her.

Speculation. Assessment. The beginning of whispers that would spread like wildfire.

As they passed through the great arched doorway, the sounds of the feast cut off abruptly. They were left in the comparative quiet of a stone corridor, torch-lit and empty.

Miera dared a single, fleeting glance over her shoulder. Through the press of bodies still visible in the hall, she saw him. Silven Drael stood watching them go, a glass of crimson wine held loosely in his hand. His expression was one of cool, unassailable victory, the look of a hunter who'd brought down his prey.

He gave a slight, almost imperceptible nod. As if to himself. Or perhaps as if saluting a worthy opponent who'd finally been defeated. The gesture was a final, damning confirmation. He had won.

She stumbled, and Jareth's grip tightened immediately, steadying her. She expected him to turn left, down the long, familiar passage toward the guest wing, toward her chambers. The thought of that quiet room with its low fire and solitude was a desperate prayer. A place to hide. A place to piece together the shattered fragments of her composure in private.

He turned right. The abrupt, unexpected change in direction sent a fresh jolt of alarm through her. He led her down a narrower, darker corridor she didn't recognize. His pace was quick, unforgiving. His boots echoed against stone in a sharp, angry rhythm that matched the tension radiating from his body.

The silence between them was taut, vibrating with his barely contained rage. He wasn't taking her to safety. He was taking her somewhere else entirely.

The corridor ended at a heavy, iron-strapped door. He pushed it open onto raw, cold night. A sharp whistle of wind whipped at them, tearing at her hair and the delicate fabric of her gown. It smelled of damp stone and the threat of rain, a clean, wild scent that stood in stark contrast to the cloying richness of perfume and wine they'd left behind.

They were on an outer rampart, a wind-scoured stone walkway high on the fortress walls. He didn't stop but pulled her along the battlement to a recessed alcove, a deeper pocket of shadow set between two massive stone merlons.

It was a private place. Hidden. Shielded from view of the main guard walk, whose distant, unsteady lights seemed a world away. A sliver of moon hung in a starless, ink-black sky, casting rough-hewn stone in stark silver relief. This wasn't a place of comfort. It was a place of secrets. An observation post for a battle.

Jareth finally released her arm. He turned to face the empty dark of the valley below, his back to her. He braced his hands on the cold, damp stone of the parapet, shoulders rigid with tension that looked painful. The wind tore at his dark formal attire, whipping fine wool.

"He knows." The words were almost stolen by the wind. Not a statement meant for her. A curse. A raw admission of defeat spoken to the night itself.

The confirmation of her deepest fear, spoken aloud by the man who was supposed to protect her, forced the air from her lungs like a physical blow.

The last vestiges of the veilstone's magical peace, already strained past breaking point, shattered completely. There was no hum now. No gentle pulse. No quiet tide of calm to soothe her racing thoughts. There was only the blood rushing in her ears like the ocean and the icy grip of terror.

"What?" Her voice trembled, thin against the wind's howl. "What does he know?"

Jareth turned from the wall. The look on his face frightened her more than Silven's knowing smile had. The mask of princely control was gone, replaced by something raw and desperate. His eyes, in the faint moonlight, burned with a hunted light she'd never seen before.

"He's playing a game with us." The words came out harsh, clipped. "With *you*." He took a step toward her, his presence overwhelming in the small enclosed space. "Did he speak to you before tonight? In the library? In the gardens?"

She shook her head mutely, unable to form words.

"Listen to me." It was a command, his voice growing harsher, clipped with an urgency that bordered on cruelty. "You will not go anywhere alone. You will not speak to him. If you see him, you walk away. If he approaches you, you will find a guard, you will find a servant, you will find *me*. Do you understand? Stay away from him."

The order wasn't a comfort. It was a threat. The desperate command of a man who no longer controlled the board, who'd been cornered and was now lashing out. He was her protector, the one who'd offered her a shield against the world's cruelty. But standing here in the cold and the dark, his face a mask of rage barely held in check, he felt like part of the danger.

A second threat circling her. The realization was a new kind of terror, worse, somehow, than Silven's calculated menace. Because at least with Silven, she knew where the threat came from. But Jareth...he was supposed to be safe.

"What's happening?" The question tore from her throat, desperate. "What does he know about me that I don't know about myself?"

His jaw worked, muscles clenching and unclenching. For a moment she thought he might tell her. Might finally explain the mystery of her own existence, the gaps in her memory, the knowledge that surfaced unbidden from depths she couldn't access.

"It doesn't matter." The words came out flat, final. A door slammed in her face. "What matters is keeping you away from him."

"It matters to me!" The words exploded from her, surprising them both. Rage flooded through her, hot and clean and real, burning through the fear. "I have a right to know who I am! What I said in there, I knew things. Things I shouldn't know. Things I don't remember learning. And that man—" She gestured wildly back toward the fortress "—that man *recognized* something in me. Recognized *me*. While you stand there telling me it doesn't matter!"

Her voice had risen to nearly a shout, wind tearing the words away almost before they formed.

"You don't understand—" Jareth started.

"No, I don't! Because you won't tell me!" Tears burned in her eyes, tears of frustration, of rage, of helpless confusion. "I trusted you. I thought you were helping me. But you're just... you're keeping secrets. And those secrets are mine. They're *about me*. I have a right—"

"You have a right to be *alive*." His voice cut through hers like a blade, sharp and absolute. "And that's what I'm trying to ensure. Your curiosity, your need to know, those are luxuries. Right now, survival is all that matters."

They stared at each other across the small space. The wind howled between them, carrying with it the scent of rain and stone and distant smoke.

She was trapped on a dark, windswept rampart, miles from a home she couldn't remember. Caught between a man who knew her past and a man who was terrified of it. Between a hunter who'd marked her as prey and a protector whose protection felt increasingly like imprisonment.

Her sense of safety, so carefully constructed over the past weeks, had been a lie. Jareth's protection had been a beautiful prison, and its bars were now dissolving, leaving her exposed to dangers she couldn't name.

The world had been a fog, soft, indistinct, a landscape

where she was safe but blind. The veilstone had kept her there, wrapped in its peace.

Now the fog had been ripped away. She was standing on a cliff edge in a storm, with the ground crumbling beneath her feet.

Her purpose, for so long, had been simple. *Survive. Wait. Remember who she was.* But that was no longer enough.

The deadly contest Jareth spoke of was real, and she was the prize. With her protector's control shattered, with his stability revealed as a fragile performance barely holding together, she couldn't afford to be passive anymore.

The questions burned in her mind with new urgency:

Who am I?

What is Jareth hiding?

Why did Silven recognize me?

What are these southern vineyards I shouldn't know about?

What does the veilstone really do?

Looking at the prince, at the raw fear and fury warring in his eyes, at the desperate control fraying at its edges, she understood with chilling clarity. Waiting to be saved was no longer an option. She had to uncover the truth of this deadly game herself. Had to discover who she'd been before the veilstone stole her memories. Had to understand what made her valuable enough for Jareth to lie, for Silven to hunt.

Because the only way to survive was to understand what she was surviving. And no one was going to tell her willingly. She would have to find out herself.

CHAPTER

FOURTEEN

He left her in the gilded prison of her chambers, the scent of her terror and the sharp night air still clinging to him like a second skin. The order he gave the guards stationed at her door was clipped, absolute. Spoken with the full, cold authority of his station, a voice that tolerated no questions, no hesitation, no deviation. No one was to enter. No one was to leave.

He'd contained the prize. But the hunter still moved freely through the halls. And that was unacceptable.

The image of Miera's face on the rampart was branded into his mind. Pale and fractured in the moonlight, her eyes wide with questions he couldn't answer and rage he couldn't contain. He'd done that to her.

His careful lies, his partial truths, his suffocating web of protection, all of it had led to this moment. He'd constructed a fortress of deception to keep her safe, and Silven Drael had walked through the main gate holding a torch.

Worse, he'd locked her in that fortress while the fire spread. Told her to trust him, to wait, to accept his protection without question. And she'd finally stopped accepting.

"I have a right to know who I am!" Her words echoed in his skull, each syllable an accusation. She was right. She deserved answers. Deserved truth.

Jareth didn't return to the Great Hall, where the last of the courtiers were likely dispersing, carrying their speculation and whispers into every corner of the fortress. He moved through the lesser-known passageways of Durevin Hold, his steps making no sound on the stone. His body was a study in coiled violence barely restrained.

He was no longer the prince. He was a predator on his own territory. He stalked the corridors, his mind a razor-sharp map of the fortress. Every shortcut, every hidden passage, every private route the courtiers didn't know. Silven wouldn't return to his quarters immediately. He'd be savoring this moment, letting the venom of his public triumph seep into the court's gossip like slow-acting poison.

Jareth followed the faint, muffled echo of music drifting from the Great Hall. The distant scent of beeswax and smoke. Letting instinct guide his hunt through dimly lit passages where torchlight flickered against stone.

He found him in the eastern gallery, its walls hung with immense tapestries depicting the grim victories of Vertharian kings. Conquests rendered in thread and dye, cities burning, armies fleeing, kings kneeling in submission.

A single torch in a wrought iron sconce bled weak, unsteady light, casting long shadows that writhed across the floor like tormented spirits. The air was cool and still, heavy with the oppressive silence of a place few ever walked. The stones had been quarried from the Ironridge Bluffs and were known to hold winter's chill deep into summer.

Even now, in the fading warmth of autumn, the cold seeped from the walls like a living thing.

Silven stood examining a tapestry that showed a Vertharian dragon immolating a field of Cortheni knights at the Battle of the Mourning Trail. His posture was relaxed, almost contemplative. One hand rested lightly against the woven fabric, tracing the flames devouring the fallen soldiers.

He was alone. The glint of torchlight on polished floor reflected his solitary, elegant figure. He'd made himself an easy target, a deliberate act of supreme confidence more insulting than any phalanx of guards could ever be.

I don't fear you. I don't need protection from you.

Jareth's hand went to the hilt of the Vertharian stiletto concealed at his belt. The worn leather of its sheath was a familiar, grim comfort. It had been a gift from his weapons master, a thin, rigid blade designed for finding gaps in an enemy's armor. For slipping between ribs to puncture lungs. For ending threats quietly, efficiently.

The urge to draw it, to feel its perfect deadly weight in his palm, was a primal scream in his blood. To cross the distance in three swift steps. To put the blade to Silven's throat and demand silence, demand surrender, demand satisfaction for the violation committed in the Great Hall.

He mastered the impulse with an effort that left him trembling. Forced his hand to fall to his side. His fingers curled into a fist so tight his knuckles ached, nails biting into his palm hard enough to draw blood. This confrontation required a different kind of weapon.

He approached without sound, a shadow detaching itself from other shadows. He stopped a dozen feet away, letting the silence stretch. Allowing his presence to become a pressure in the air before it was a shape in the gloom.

Silven didn't turn. "A lovely piece, is it not?" His voice was calm and crisp, echoing lightly in the stone passage. No surprise at Jareth's appearance. As if he'd been expecting company. "Such a clear depiction of the natural order. The strong consuming the weak. Might rendering judgment upon those who lack the will to defend themselves."

He finally pivoted, the movement fluid and unhurried. The predatory smile he'd worn in the Great Hall was gone, replaced by a look of polite, academic interest. The diplomat once more, discussing art and history with a fellow scholar.

"Can I help you, Your Highness?"

The calculated innocence was a spark to dry tinder. Jareth closed the distance between them in three long strides, stopping so close he could see the fine silver threading on the Avenali's coat. Could smell the lingering sweetness of Avenali wine on his breath, Goldwine, a vintage famous for its ability to mask the taste of poison.

"The game is over." His voice was a low, dangerous growl, stripped of all courtly artifice. The voice of a commander on a battlefield, not a prince in his father's keep. "You will not speak to her again. You will not look at her again. You will not think her name. She is no longer your concern."

Silven didn't flinch. Didn't retreat even a fraction of an inch. Genuine, infuriating amusement lit his pale eyes, and the ghost of his predatory smile returned. He met Jareth's barely contained violence with unshakable calm, the stillness of someone who'd faced down far worse threats and survived. It was like shouting at a mountain.

"I confess, I am not familiar with the game to which you refer," Silven replied, his tone one of light curiosity. The very picture of innocence.

Then his voice dropped, losing its silken edge and taking on the cold, hard weight of steel.

"But a prince's secrets are his kingdom's vulnerabilities."

The words weren't a threat. They were a statement of fact, a core tenet from the brutal calculus of nations. A line from every textbook on statecraft ever written, delivered with the chilling precision of an executioner reading a death warrant.

Silven took a small, deliberate step closer, invading Jareth's space, closing the distance the prince had meant to weaponize. His gaze held Jareth's with an insolent lack of fear.

Jareth's entire body screamed for him to react. To strike. To drive the man to his knees and feel the satisfying snap of bone beneath his fists. He remained frozen, transfixed by the sheer, elegant audacity of the move.

"You should guard yours more closely, Your Highness." Silven's voice dropped to a confidential whisper, more menacing than any shout could ever be. His eyes moved down Jareth's body in a subtle, dismissive assessment, then back up to his face. "Especially when they have such beautiful, familiar eyes."

Familiar. The word detonated like a bomb in Jareth's chest. Not interesting eyes or unusual eyes. *Familiar ones.*

Silven knew. Not just that Miera was Cortheni that much had been obvious from her instinctive knowledge. But he recognized her specifically. Knew who she was. Had seen her face before, in another context, another life.

The cold fire of Jareth's rage was doused by a wave of icy, impotent horror. The stiletto at his hip felt a thousand miles away, a useless toy. He'd come here to reassert his authority, to put the fear of a prince into a meddling diplomat. To reclaim control through threat of violence if necessary.

"What do you want?" The question tore from Jareth's throat, raw, desperate. No longer a command. A plea.

Silven's smile returned, no longer amused but filled with quiet, professional satisfaction. The look of an artisan admiring his finished work.

"Want? I want what every civilized nation wants, Your Highness. Peace. Prosperity. Fair treatment of those who've been wronged." He paused, letting the words settle. "And I want to ensure that Princess Seraya of Corthen receives the justice she deserves."

Princess Seraya. Her true name, spoken aloud. The secret Jareth had killed to protect.

"Think carefully about your next actions," Silven continued, his voice soft as silk over steel. "The Avenali Empire has long maintained neutral diplomatic relations with both Verthar and Corthen. It would be... unfortunate... if information about a certain missing princess were to reach the wrong ears. Information about who holds her. Who has kept her imprisoned. Who has used forbidden magic to suppress her very identity."

The threat was explicit now. No more veiled language, no more diplomatic dancing. *Do as I say, or I expose everything.*

"What do you want?" Jareth asked again, each word like pulling teeth.

"For now?" Silven's smile widened fractionally. "I want you to do nothing. Make no moves. Take no action. Let events unfold naturally." He paused. "I'll be watching to ensure you comply."

He gave a slight, formal bow, an impeccable gesture of respect that served as the final, crushing insult. The bow of an equal. Or perhaps of someone who'd just won a decisive victory and could afford to be gracious.

"If you will excuse me, Your Highness. It has been a long evening."

He turned and walked away down the dark corridor, his footsteps echoing on stone with unhurried confidence. He didn't look back. Didn't need to.

Jareth stood motionless, heart hammering a frantic rhythm against his ribs, listening to the sound of Silven's footsteps fade into oppressive silence. The single torch on the wall cast his solitary shadow, long and distorted, against the tapestry of the victorious dragon consuming its prey.

His hand went to his signet ring, thumb pressing hard against the cold gold crest of his house. A desperate, futile search for an anchor in a world that had just been torn from its moorings.

The rage was still there, but it was a caged, powerless thing now. Seething in the pit of his stomach with nowhere to go, no outlet, no release.

He was a prince of Verthar. Son of a king. Commander of armies. And he'd never in his life felt so powerless.

His secret was no longer his. It was a weapon, and it was pointed directly at the heart of the one person he'd risked everything to protect.

Princess Seraya.

The name felt foreign in his mind. Wrong. She was Miera, the woman he'd saved, the woman he'd held, the woman who'd looked at him with trust that had burned like acid in his gut. But she wasn't Miera. Had never been Miera.

She was Princess Seraya of Corthen. Enemy of his kingdom. Daughter of the nation his father had spent decades trying to dominate. A political weapon of incalculable value. And he'd fallen in love with her anyway.

The realization struck him with devastating force. Not new, he'd known it for weeks, had felt it every time he looked at her, every time he heard her voice. But facing it here, in this cold gallery with his authority in ruins and her true name hanging in the air like smoke, made it undeniable.

He loved her. And he'd imprisoned her.

And now Silven Drael held both truths in his hands like weapons, ready to deploy them however he saw fit.

How could he possibly defend her now? How could he shield her from an enemy who held the very truth as hostage? How could he protect her from the consequences of his own crimes against her?

The dragon on the tapestry seemed to mock him with its woven flames, consuming Cortheni knights who'd never had a chance against such overwhelming power. He'd thought himself the dragon: strong, protective, dominant.

But standing alone in this cold gallery, he finally understood. He was one of the knights. And the flames were already burning.

CHAPTER

FIFTEEN

The silence of her chamber was no longer a comfort. It was a vacuum, amplifying the sharp echo of Jareth's words, the memory of raw fury in his eyes. The command had been a shield thrown far too late, the desperate, angry act of a man who had lost control. Stay away from him. The anxiety that had been a low hum since the feast now sang a high, sharp note of alarm in her mind. Jareth's protection, which had once felt like a fortress, now felt like a cage.

Sleep had offered no respite, only a battlefield of fractured images and formless dread. She rose with the thin morning light and paced the confines of her room, the plush Vertharian rug a path worn by her own spiraling thoughts. She needed to escape. Not the fortress itself, but the suffocating confines of her own mind. She needed a space where the world was ordered and calm, where the sheer weight of accumulated knowledge could press down upon her fear and restore some semblance of peace.

There was only one place in Durevin Hold that had ever offered such a promise. The library.

The decision was a grasp for a familiar anchor in a storm. The library had been her first sanctuary here, a place of silent companionship and discovery. The memory of its profound quiet beckoned her, a promise of solace. She dressed in a court gown of deep blue, the color of a twilight sky, and approached her chamber door. Two new guards stood posted outside, their faces unfamiliar and grim. Jareth's lockdown. They blocked her way, their expressions impassive stone.

"Lady Miera," one said, his voice flat. "The Prince's orders are that you are to remain in your chambers."

She met his gaze, projecting a calm she did not feel. "His orders were that I was to be protected, was it not? I am simply going to the library. Surely you do not believe I am in danger from a book?" She offered a small, disarming smile. "I will be within the main wing.

You are welcome to follow at a distance if it eases your mind, but confining me will only draw the attention the Prince wishes to avoid."

The guards exchanged an uncertain glance. Her argument had found the seam in their orders, the conflict between keeping her isolated and keeping her situation discreet. After a moment, the first guard gave a stiff, reluctant nod. "As you say, my lady. We will be close."

The walk to the library was a journey through a fortress holding its breath. The tension from the night before lingered in the air, a subtle static that clung to the stone walls. Courtiers spoke in hushed tones, their glances quick and furtive. Miera kept her head high, her expression one of serene neutrality, a mask she was learning to wear with practiced skill. No one could be permitted to know the terror that churned within her.

The great, carved doors of the library stood open, a silent invitation. She stepped across the threshold, and a familiar, beloved scent washed over her. It was the dry perfume of old paper, the rich aroma of leather bindings, and the faint trace of beeswax from a thousand burned candles. It was the scent of history, of order, of quiet contemplation. A long sigh of relief escaped her lips.

The library of Durevin Hold was a cavern of knowledge. Towering blackwood shelves soared into the vaulted darkness overhead, creating deep canyons of shadow between them. Sunlight, thin and pale, slanted through high, arched windows, illuminating solitary motes of dust that danced like forgotten sprites in the still, honey-colored air. The silence was profound, a living presence that muffled the outside world. It was a place built for thought, for refuge. It was precisely what she needed.

She moved deeper into the labyrinth of shelves, her fingers trailing along the spines of handsome, leather-bound tomes. She was not looking for a specific book, only for the comforting weight of one in her hands, the tactile reality of its ordered pages. She turned into a narrow aisle, a secluded alcove far from the main reading tables, and froze.

He was there. Silven sat in a high-backed leather chair, a single volume resting open in his lap. He had been hidden from the entrance by the towering shelves, his placement a matter of strategic design. He was not reading. He was waiting. The sight of him in her sanctuary was a violation, a sacrilege. Her every instinct screamed at her to turn, to flee. But he looked up, and his expression was not one of triumph, but of gentle, disarming concern.

"Lady Miera," he said. His voice was a low, melodic murmur that seemed to be absorbed by the silence rather than breaking it. He rose to his feet in a single, fluid motion. "Forgive me. I seem to have chosen the same refuge as you."

She could not move, trapped by the rigid politeness of the court. Jareth's warning thundered in her ears. If you see him, you walk away. But how could she? He blocked the narrow aisle. To retreat would be a panicked, graceless scramble, a clear admission of fear. A concession of ground.

"I hope I did not startle you," he continued, taking a step to the side to clear her path. It was a gesture of courtesy that only heightened her sense of being cornered. He was giving her the illusion of choice.

"You did not," she lied, her voice tight.

His smile was warm, laced with what appeared to be genuine regret. "I am glad. I must confess, I have been hoping for an opportunity to apologize. My suggestion of wine last night was clumsy. I fear I caused you some distress, and for that, I am truly sorry."

The apology was a masterful stroke. It was smooth, sincere, and disarming. It positioned him not as an aggressor, but as a gentleman mortified by a social blunder. How could she hold his apology against him? How could she flee from a man offering such polite contrition? She could not. He had boxed her in with courtesy.

"There is no need for an apology, my lord," she said, the formal words feeling like ash in her mouth.

"But there is," he insisted softly. "It is a particular failing of my people, I think. We in Avenal are lovers of stories, of patterns. We see them everywhere, and sometimes, we press too hard to find them where none exist." He gestured to the chair he had vacated. "Please. Do not let me drive you from this lovely quiet."

She remained standing, her body rigid. He did not press the point, simply returning to his own seat with relaxed posture. He had created a pocket of placid, social decorum in the middle of her ambush. After a moment of taut silence, he sighed, a sound of thoughtful melancholy.

"Your situation," he began, his gaze distant, as if speaking to himself, "reminds me of a rather tragic Avenali parable. A cautionary tale we tell our children about the dangers of good intentions."

She said nothing. She did not wish to hear his story. But she was a guest in this court, a lady of supposed gentility. She could not simply turn her back on an emissary. The silence stretched, expectant.

He took her silence as assent. His voice dropped, becoming hypnotic, a storyteller's cadence that coiled around her. "It is the story of a great lord, a man of power and fierce loyalties. One winter, he found a woman wandering near his lands, a stranger with no memory of her name or her past. She was beautiful, and she was lost, and he took her into his protection. He gave her a new name, a new life. He swore to keep her safe from a world he knew to be cruel."

The air grew heavy. The veilstone at her throat, a cool, familiar weight, seemed to offer no comfort. Its gentle, calming pulse felt distant, a weak and useless rhythm against the sudden, violent pounding of her pulse.

"The lord came to love this woman deeply," Silven continued, his eyes fixed on some point in the middle distance. "And because he loved her, he feared for her. Her past, he suspected, was dangerous. He believed that the truth of her identity would put her in harm's way. To protect her, he concealed it from her. He used his vast resources to weave a tapestry of lies, a beautiful, comforting world where she was safe, and ignorant, and his."

Miera's breath caught in her throat. This was not a story. It was a mirror, distorted and cruel, held up to her own life. Every word was a poison-tipped dart, aimed at the soft, vulnerable core of her trust in Jareth.

"He even commissioned a charm from his mages," Silven added, his voice barely a whisper. "A beautiful piece of jewelry, enchanted to quiet her mind, to soothe her nightmares, to keep the jagged edges of her true memories from breaking through the peace he had built for her."

Miera's hand flew to her throat, her fingers closing over the veilstone. The story was no longer a mirror. It was a key, unlocking a door in her mind to a room filled with a specific, terrible doubt. The magic of the stone was designed to soothe emotion, to blunt the sharp edges of panic and grief. But this was not an emotional assault. It was an intellectual one. Silven's parable was a narrative, a piece of logic. It was a question. The veilstone had no defense against a question. Its calm was the peace of an empty field, useless against a poison slipped into the well.

"For a time, they were happy," Silven said, a note of profound sadness in his voice. "She loved him for his kindness. He loved her for the gentle, trusting woman he had created. But truth, as it so often does, has its own allegiances. A rival lord, seeking to destabilize the great lord's power, discovered the woman's true identity. He saw the deception not as an act of love, but as a weakness to be exploited."

His gaze lifted, meeting hers. There was no malice in his eyes. There was only a deep, unnerving pity, the pity of a scholar observing a tragedy unfold according to immutable laws.

"The rival revealed the truth to the woman. He showed her who she had been, a princess of a neighboring land, a woman of power and importance. And he showed her the lies her lover had told. The shock of the betrayal, the knowledge that her entire reality had been a carefully constructed lie built by the man she trusted, broke her. She did not rail. She did not scream. She simply ceased to be. She took her own life, unable to live as the ghost she had become, or the stranger she had once been."

Miera made a small, choked sound.

"And the great lord?" Silven finished, his voice a somber finality. "He was ruined. He lost the woman he loved, his honor was shattered, and his political power collapsed under the weight of his own well-intentioned deceit. He was destroyed. Destroyed by the very protection he had built."

The last words hung in the profound silence of the library, an epitaph.

He had done it. He had taken her fragile trust in Jareth and poisoned it at the root. He had not accused Jareth of anything. He had not threatened her. He had simply told a story. A deniable, elegant, and devastating act of psychological warfare.

As he watched her flee, Silven allowed himself a moment of private reflection. The Gilded Ring had sent him here with instructions: destabilize, observe, report. But they did not understand, as he did, the true opportunity before them. Avenal had no love for Verthar's expansion. They had even less love for the chaos that would follow Verthar's collapse and disrupt the trade routes that were Avenal's lifeblood. What Avenal wanted—what the Gilded Ring had always wanted—was balance. A strong Corthen checking a strong Verthar. Both nations focused on each other rather than expanding toward Avenali interests.

The princess's supposed death had disrupted that balance, tipping power too far toward Halric's ambitions. Her survival might restore it. He was not here to destroy her. He was here to free her—and in freeing her, to set two kingdoms at each other's throats once more. It was not cruelty. It was commerce.

The need to escape was a physical force, a violent revulsion. The library was no longer a sanctuary. It was a tomb, and the air was thick with the dust of the story he had just told.

She turned, stumbling back the way she had come. She did not make an excuse. She did not say a word. She simply fled.

Silven did not try to stop her. He remained seated, the open book still in his lap, a portrait of calm, scholarly repose. He had accomplished his goal. The seed was planted.

As Miera burst from the library's suffocating silence back into the tense corridors of the fortress, the last line of the terrible parable echoed in her mind, a relentless, chilling refrain. Destroyed by the very protection he had built.

The question that bloomed in the ruins of her peace was cold and sharp as a shard of ice. Was Jareth's secrecy the same kind of protection? Was he the great lord from the story, his love a cage, his kindness a lie?

And was she the woman in the story, being led so gently, so lovingly, to her own destruction?

CHAPTER
SIXTEEN

The impotent rage had burned itself out like a fire consuming its own fuel, leaving behind only cold, heavy dread, a stone settled deep in Jareth's gut that grew heavier with each passing hour. Time had moved strangely since his utter dismantlement in the eastern gallery, the afternoon crawling by with the sluggish quality of a nightmare where running gets you nowhere. He'd retreated to his study, but the familiar scent of ink and parchment offered no comfort, the strategic maps on his walls no clarity.

They were just lines on a page now, a child's drawing of a world he no longer controlled. Silven's victory had been absolute, a masterpiece of quiet political evisceration that left Jareth bleeding from wounds no one else could see.

He stood by the tall, arched window, his hand resting on the cold glass as he stared out at the fortress grounds below. The afternoon light was failing, casting long oppressive shadows that bled across the stone floor like ink spilled on a ledger, staining everything they touched. Durevin Hold was quiet, but it was the quiet of a hunter's blind, not the quiet of peace, the stillness before violence rather than after. He'd been so focused on the external threat, on Silven as a piece on the board to be countered and contained, that he'd neglected the more immediate front. Miera.

He'd left her on the rampart last night, shattered and afraid, her questions ringing in his ears. He'd posted guards at her door like a jailer rather than a protector. He'd confronted her tormentor and accomplished nothing except confirming the enemy's power. He'd performed all the requisite actions of someone trying to keep her safe, and every single one had compounded the disaster, adding fuel to a fire that was already consuming everything he'd built.

Terror, a more potent and insidious emotion than his earlier rage, coiled through him now like a serpent wrapping around his chest. Silven was a master of the mind's battlefield, a strategist who understood that the most effective weapons were words and doubts planted like seeds in fertile soil. He wouldn't have stopped with the public unmasking at the feast. That had been opening moves, establishing control of the board. He would have found her since then. He would have spoken to her in private.

He needed to see her. Needed to assess the damage, to

repair what he could before the cracks spread too far. He needed to deliver his reassurances before Silven's poison could take root completely, to shore up the crumbling walls of her trust with the familiar cadence of his protection. It was the only weapon he had left in his arsenal, the only tool he knew how to use.

He found her in her chambers, and the sight of her stopped him cold in the doorway. She was not reading by the fire as she so often did, finding comfort in books when the world became too much. She was not pacing by the window, working through her thoughts with movement. She sat in a high-backed chair near the hearth, but her posture was rigid as carved stone, her hands laced together in her lap as if to still a tremor she couldn't quite suppress.

The fire burned low, providing barely any warmth, and the room was filled with the fading light of afternoon and the faint, clean scent of dried lavender from sachets meant to soothe. On the wall behind her, a grand tapestry depicted the grim founding of Durevin Hold, its black-armored figures a stark and unyielding backdrop to her fragile stillness.

She stared at nothing, her face pale and drawn like someone who'd seen something terrible and couldn't look away from the memory, her eyes holding a haunted, distant look that made his heart clench painfully in his chest. She looked like a finely crafted statue with a fracture running deep inside, one that hadn't yet reached the surface but would inevitably shatter everything when it did.

She didn't seem to notice him at first, lost in whatever dark thoughts consumed her. He stood in the doorway watching her, a silent observer, and the distance between them felt like a chasm that had opened overnight. This was not the withdrawn but trusting woman of yesterday, the one who'd looked to him for protection even when confused and afraid. This was someone else. Someone guarding a new and terrible wound with walls he didn't know how to breach.

"Miera," he said softly, carefully, as if speaking to someone standing at the edge of a precipice.

Her head snapped toward him with startling speed. Her eyes were wide and startled, as if he'd woken her from a nightmare she'd been trapped in while awake. For the briefest of moments, a heartbeat, perhaps less, he saw raw, undiluted fear in them. It was the look a cornered animal gives a predator, the instinctive recognition of mortal danger, and it was directed at him.

The expression vanished as quickly as it had appeared, replaced by careful, blank neutrality that was somehow worse than the fear. But he'd seen it. He'd seen how she looked at him now, and the knowledge cut deeper than any blade.

"Your Highness," she said, her voice a quiet, formal whisper that held none of the warmth or familiarity they'd shared.

She made to rise, a gesture of courtly deference she'd never once used with him in private, treating him like the distant authority figure he'd tried so hard not to be with her.

"Don't," he said quickly, perhaps too quickly, moving into the room and closing the door behind him with a soft click. The sound of the latch catching felt unnervingly final, like a cell door closing. "Stay seated. Please."

He approached her slowly, as one might approach a frightened horse or a wounded animal that might bolt at any sudden movement. He stopped a few feet from her chair, his own body feeling stiff and foreign, every gesture requiring conscious thought when it should have been natural.

He searched for the right words, the soothing tone that had always worked before, the reassurances that had carried them through every previous crisis. It felt like trying to remember lines from a play he'd once known by heart but had somehow forgotten in the moment of performance.

"I came to see how you were," he began, forcing his voice to smoothness he didn't feel, projecting a calm that was entirely false. "Last night was difficult. I was harsh with you. My anger, it wasn't for you. It was for him, for what he'd done. I should have made that clearer."

She said nothing in response. She simply watched him with those dark, unreadable eyes that had once looked at him with trust and now held only wariness. The silence stretched between them, heavy and suffocating, pressing down on him like physical weight. It was a silence that demanded to be filled with words, explanations, reassurances. And he, like a fool walking into a trap he could see but couldn't avoid, obliged.

"Has there been any word?" she asked suddenly, her

voice barely audible, each word seeming to cost her effort. "From my family? Does anyone know I'm here? Is anyone looking for me?"

It was the question he'd been dreading, the same question she'd asked before but different now in its weight and implication. This was not the plea of a lost woman genuinely seeking connection to her past. This was a test, a trap laid with the precision of someone who already suspected the answer. He knew it in his bones, felt it in the careful way she watched for his response. And still he walked right into it, unable to deviate from the script he'd written for himself.

"No," he said, and the lie slipped from his tongue with the practiced ease of long repetition. "Nothing yet. I've had inquiries sent to every major house in every kingdom we have diplomatic relations with. No one has reported a missing daughter, a lost cousin, any woman matching your description. But don't despair, please don't."

He took a step closer, then another, kneeling down beside her chair so their eyes were level in what he hoped was a gesture of intimacy and care. His gaze fell for a moment on the silver pendant at her throat, the veilstone he'd commissioned from the court mages, and he could almost feel its cool, suppressive magic working to keep her calm. A magic as false as the words he was about to speak, as hollow as the protection he claimed to offer.

"It means nothing. The lack of response only means we haven't found them yet, that our search hasn't reached the right people. I will keep you safe here until we do. You have my word on that. I swear it on my family's honor. No one will harm you while you are under my protection."

As he spoke the words, the familiar, comforting script he'd delivered dozens of times before, a strange thing happened that had never occurred in any of their previous conversations. For the first time, he truly heard what he was saying. He heard the hollow, rehearsed quality of the sentences, the smooth, polished surface that concealed the lie beneath. The words tasted of rust and falsehood in his own mouth, bitter as poison he was asking her to swallow. This was not comfort he was offering. This was a performance, a recitation of lines meant to manipulate rather than heal. And it was failing spectacularly.

He saw it in her eyes with devastating clarity. As he spoke of protection, as he delivered his carefully crafted reassurances, he didn't see relief dawn on her face. He didn't see the tension leave her shoulders or trust return to her expression. Instead, he saw something else, a subtle wince, an almost inaudible flinching away as if his words caused physical pain. He saw the doubt crystallize into certainty, no longer a vague fear but a raw, gaping wound that his words only made worse. Her trust wasn't just fractured anymore. It was gone. His reassurances, the very foundation of their fragile relationship, weren't healing her. They were salt in her wound, acid on raw flesh, poison masquerading as medicine.

He watched as a wall rose between them, invisible but as solid as the stone of the fortress itself. It was a wall built of his good intentions, mortared with his own well-intentioned lies and the growing weight of all he'd concealed from her. He'd claimed to be her shield against the world's cruelty, but she now saw him, he could see it in her eyes, as the bars of her cage.

As the architect of her imprisonment rather than her salvation. The corrosive genius of Silven's work was laid bare before him in this moment. The Avenali hadn't needed to prove Jareth was a liar or present evidence of his deception. He'd simply given her the lens through which to see the truth for herself, and now she was looking at Jareth through that lens and seeing something monstrous.

His voice faltered mid-sentence, the last words of his practiced speech dying in his throat like birds falling from the sky. He saw the pain in her eyes, the deep and terrifying distress his words were causing rather than alleviating, the way each reassurance landed like a blow instead of a comfort.

And in that moment, his overwhelming need to control the situation, to maintain the deception that had become his entire world, was completely overridden by a singular, desperate need that cut through everything else. He had to stop hurting her. Whatever it cost him, whatever it meant for his carefully constructed plans, he couldn't continue inflicting this pain.

He fell silent, the words simply stopping as if his voice had been cut off at the source. The silence that descended was worse than any that had come before. It was a tomb, the final resting place of the trust he'd so carelessly cultivated and so thoroughly destroyed. He stayed there, kneeling beside her chair like a supplicant before an altar, the great prince of Verthar rendered mute and powerless by the consequences of his own tender-hearted cruelty.

He watched, helpless and frozen, as a single tear escaped the corner of her eye and traced a slow, silent path down her pale cheek. She didn't sob. She didn't make a sound. She simply broke, quietly, in front of him, and there was nothing he could do to stop it because he was the cause.

His carefully constructed world, his control, his plans, his vision of how this would all work out, all of it was dust scattered by wind he couldn't contain. It no longer mattered what Silven planned for his kingdom or what political machinations were unfolding in the shadows. The more immediate and devastating damage was already done, complete and irreversible. He'd lost her. Not to another man, not to politics or war or any external force. He'd lost her to his own deception, to the prison he'd built with his own hands while calling it protection.

He rose to his feet slowly, each movement feeling heavy and wrong, a cold hollow ache spreading through his chest like frost creeping across glass. His plan had failed. Soothing her was impossible now, his very presence caused her pain. Protecting her had become indistinguishable from harming her. His only path forward now was diagnosis, understanding the exact nature and extent of the damage. He had to know. He had to understand the precise shape of the poison Silven had poured into her ear, the specific words and implications that had armed her with this terrible, silent certainty that he was her enemy rather than her ally.

He turned toward the door, his heart a leaden weight in his chest, each beat a reminder of the life that continued despite feeling like death. He had to get out of this room, away from the evidence of his failure written so clearly in her tear-stained face and haunted eyes. As he reached the door, his hand closing around the cold iron latch, he paused.

The metal felt like the bolt on a prison cell, cold and unyielding, a reminder of all the ways he'd caged her while claiming to free her. He looked back at her one final time, a solitary, broken figure silhouetted against the dying fire, surrounded by shadows that seemed to reach for her like grasping hands.

How could he ask her what was wrong? How could he probe the wound without proving he was the one who'd inflicted it? Any question he asked now would be a confession of guilt, an admission that there was something to hide. He was trapped in a prison of his own making, walls built from lies and good intentions, and there was no way out that didn't involve more destruction.

He opened the door and left without another word, leaving her alone in the gathering darkness. The guards straightened as he emerged, their faces carefully neutral, pretending they hadn't heard anything from within. He walked past them without acknowledgment, his feet carrying him through corridors he barely saw, his mind turning over the disaster again and again like a scholar examining a text in a dead language he couldn't quite translate.

Silven had won. Not just the battle but potentially the

war. He'd destroyed Jareth's relationship with Miera, poisoned the well of trust so thoroughly that no amount of truth or explanation could purify it now. And he'd done it all without needing to tell a single verifiable lie, simply by helping her see what all had been there along.

The evening shadows lengthened as Jareth walked, and somewhere in the fortress, Silven Drael was likely smiling, satisfied with a day's work well done.

CHAPTER

SEVENTEEN

The day had left her hollowed out. A porcelain vessel scoured of everything but dread. Jareth's visit had been the final scouring, his words stripping away what little trust remained. The practiced reassurances echoed in the stillness. The smooth cadence of his lies. He had knelt before her, eyes full of earnest care, and with every gentle promise of protection, he had driven Silven's parable deeper into her heart.

Sleep had become a place she feared. Since Jareth had given her the veilstone, sleep had been a descent into thick, dreamless fog. A muffled quiet she'd mistaken for peace. Now that peace felt like a void. An unnatural emptiness. A silence where there should have been the restless murmur of a life lived.

Tonight, she would not have it. The thought was a quiet rebellion, a single seed of defiance taking root in barren soil. She needed rest. True rest, not the blanketing oblivion the stone offered.

The fire in the hearth had burned down to sullen, glowing embers. They cast weak orange light that barely pushed back the encroaching shadows. Moonlight cut through the silk-gauze curtains like a silver blade, striping the rich coverlet on her four-poster bed. The room was a study in contrasts. Cold light and dying warmth. It felt like a reflection of her own internal landscape.

She prepared for bed with slow, deliberate grace. Her movements were fragile armor against the turmoil inside. She brushed her long, dark hair until it fell like an ink curtain down her back. When she was finally ready, clad in a nightgown of soft linen, she stood before the narrow ebonized writing desk that served as her vanity.

The veilstone lay where she'd placed it. Its polished silver setting gleamed dully in the dim light. Even now, it seemed to whisper of peace. An end to anxiety. Its presence was a lure, a promise of quiet. Her hand trembled as she reached for it, fingers hovering over its cool surface. The habit was so ingrained, the seeking of its comfort so reflexive, that to deny it felt like a betrayal of her own survival.

With a final, resolute breath, she drew her hand back.

She would not wear it. She would face the night on her own terms, whatever it might bring.

She left the pendant on the desk, its clear crystal catching a sliver of moonlight. For a moment, she thought she saw a faint, rhythmic pulse of light from within the stone. A soft, slow beat like a distant heart. She dismissed it as a trick of the light and turned away.

Slipping between the cool sheets, she lay on her back,

staring into darkness. The silence in the chamber was different now. Heavier. More profound. Without the veil-stone's constant, low-level hum of magical suppression, the room felt vast and empty. She could hear the faint whisper of wind against the balcony doors. The distant, muffled sound of a guard's boot heel in the corridor. The soft sigh of dying embers. And beneath it all, the unsteady drumming of her own heart.

Sleep did not come easily. It was a skittish animal, refusing to be coaxed from shadows. Her mind, untethered from the stone's calming influence, raced. It replayed Silven's voice, the hypnotic cadence of his terrible story. It replayed Jareth's face, the earnest pain in his eyes as his lies fell flat.

Who was he? Her protector? Or her jailer?

She turned onto her side, pulling the coverlet up to her chin, seeking warmth that would not come. Eventually, exhaustion won its long war with anxiety. Her thoughts blurred. Her limbs grew heavy. She felt herself sliding into the dark, welcoming abyss of sleep.

There was no gentle descent. No foggy oblivion. She was plunged into a maelstrom of sensory chaos. The dream was not a dream. It was a memory.

Rain. The taste of it on her lips, sharp and cold. The smell of it on wet stone. She stands on a high, crumbling parapet. The sky is the color of a bruise. Below her, a man in a dark cloak looks up. His face is a pale oval in the gloom. His voice, carried on the wind, calls a name.

Not Miera.

A name of sharp syllables and regal weight. *Seraya.*

The sound of it struck her like a physical blow. It was her name. She knew it with a certainty that defied all logic, a truth that resonated in her very bones.

The scene shattered. Replaced by firelight and the glint of steel. A corridor. She is running. Men are shouting in a guttural tongue she doesn't recognize. The air is thick with smoke. A blade flashes past her face, close enough to feel the wind of its passage. She doesn't scream. Her body moves with terrifying, innate competence. She ducks. Twists. Her hand reaches for something at her waist that isn't there.

Another shattering. A room of maps and shadows. Her own hand, slender and pale, traces a route through a mountain pass. Her fingernails are clean. Her fingers unadorned. But they move with an authority that is absolute. She is giving an order. Her voice is low and calm, speaking in the lilting, formal cadence of Corthen. The words are clear. Precise. A string of tactical commands.

Then, the sigil.

It burns behind her eyes, an afterimage of impossible clarity. Carved into a slab of dark, rain-slicked obsidian. A monument or a tombstone. A silver hawk, its wings outstretched in predatory majesty. In its talons, it clutches a spear. The wooden shaft snapped in two. The image is alien, yet it fills her with profound, aching loss. A forgotten allegiance to a fallen house. A duty left undone.

She jolts awake with a choked, desperate gasp. Her body lurches upright in the bed. Her heart hammers against her ribs. A frantic prisoner beating against bone bars. The sheets are tangled around her legs, damp with cold sweat. The chamber is dark. Still. Silent.

But the dream images are burned onto the back of her eyelids, vivid and raw.

Seraya.

The name echoes in the hollow space of her mind. Terror seizes her. Pure and undiluted. A cold, gripping fist around her throat, choking the air from her lungs. This is not the vague unease of before. This is the sharp, specific horror of a truth too terrible to bear.

Her hands shake violently. Primal, instinctual panic overrides all thought. She needs it to stop. Needs the peace, the quiet, the blessed numbness. Her eyes dart to the desk, to the small, dark shape of the pendant resting in moonlight.

Comfort. Safety. An end to this terror.

She scrambles from the bed, stumbling over tangled sheets. Her bare feet are cold against the stone floor. She reaches for the veilstone with desperate, shaking hands. Her fingers close around the cool, smooth stone like a drowning woman grasping driftwood. It is the only medicine she knows for this sickness of the mind.

She fumbles with the clasp. Her ragged breaths fill the silence. Finally, she secures it around her neck.

The effect is instantaneous.

And it is the most terrifying thing she has ever experienced.

A wave of calm washed over her. So potent. So immediate. It felt like a physical blow. The frantic hammering of her heart slows to a dull, steady rhythm. The violent trembling in her hands ceases. The sharp, vivid dream images that had been seared into her mind blur. Fade. Then dissolve into formless, grey mist.

The name, *Seraya*, which had been a bell tolling in her soul, becomes a meaningless, distant whisper. And then nothing.

The terror does not vanish. It is simply muted. Encased in a thick, clear layer of magical apathy. She can still feel it. A cold, hard knot deep inside. But she can no longer properly access it. The sharp edges are gone.

She stands motionless in the center of the room. Her hand is still at her throat, clutching the pendant. She is breathing evenly now. The panic is gone.

And in its place, a new, colder, and far more profound horror dawns. The man she trusted, the man she allowed into her bed, the man whose kindness she clung to as her only anchor in a sea of confusion. He did this to her. He built this beautiful, elegant prison around her mind and called it kindness.

The realization does not come with a storm of rage or a flood of tears. It comes with chilling, absolute stillness. The woman from Silven's story is her. The great lord is Jareth. The enchanted charm is the lie she wears around her neck.

Dawn is beginning to break. Faint, grey light seeps into the chamber, turning shadows from black to soft, hazy blue. The world outside is waking up. And so is she.

Slowly, deliberately, she unclasps the necklace. She does not throw it. Does not smash it. She walks back to the desk and places it on the polished ironwood surface. It lies there, glinting in the growing light. A beautiful, perfect lock for a prison she hadn't known she was in.

She looks at the pendant. Then at her own reflection in the dark, polished wood of the desk. A stranger stares back. A pale, haunted woman with fear in her eyes. But beneath the fear, something new is hardening. A core of adamant forming deep within.

She is not Miera. Miera is a fiction, a ghost created to keep the true woman buried. She is someone else. Someone with a past. With skills. With loyalties represented by a silver hawk. She is Seraya.

Her new purpose, hard as a diamond, settled into place. She will have to continue being Miera. The docile, empty girl he so carefully created. She will have to smile and thank him for his kindness. Pretend to be soothed by the very magic meant to keep her chained.

And all the while, in the secret, silent corners of her mind, she will fight. She will fight to find the woman he tried so desperately to erase.

CHAPTER

EIGHTEEN

Something had shifted in the fortress during the night. He felt it like a change in air pressure before a storm. He told himself it was the weather or fatigue. He believed neither excuse.

His study was dim with weak winter light. The fire burned low, doing little to warm the book-lined chamber. He sat at his blackwood desk and tried to focus on the kingdom's business.

Before him lay stacks of parchment. The first was a dispatch about unrest along the Cortheni border. Coordinated raids on logging camps. Too organized for common bandits. He read the captain's report but the words wouldn't stick. He set it aside without answering.

The next was a ledger from the western mines. A delayed shipment of iron ore. Flimsy excuses about rockfalls and broken wagon wheels. It reeked of corruption, but investigating would mean war with a powerful family. He dipped his quill to draft a summons, but his hand stilled. His gaze drifted to the window where frost covered the glass. He found himself listening for something. A footstep. A voice.

His thoughts kept circling back to Miera. He reached for the third document. A note from Silven, delivered an hour ago. No formal heading. Just a few elegant lines.

A fascinating history, this fortress holds. One finds the most unexpected things in its archives.

Not a question. A threat. Jareth crumpled the note in his fist, the sharp crinkle satisfying in the silence. He needed to focus. Verthar was teetering. Border disputes. Resource shortages. A viper from Avenal prowling his court. And all he could think about was her.

An attendant entered to stoke the fire. As he turned to leave, Jareth spoke. "Has Lady Miera taken her breakfast?"

The attendant paused. "No, Your Highness. Her maid reported that she rose before dawn but has not left her chambers. She declined a morning meal."

He dismissed the servant and stared at the crumpled note. His first thought was the veilstone. The court mages had been clear. Its power wasn't infinite. A strong enough shock could weaken its hold.

What had happened in her room last night? Had Silven's poison broken through her defenses? Had the memory of the feast cracked the surface of her forgetting? He imagined the pendant's light dimming, its magic failing. Terror shot through him.

He pushed back from his desk and walked to the window. He pressed his forehead against the cold glass. The courtyard below was white and silver. He'd built a fortress of lies to keep her safe. Now he stood in its tower, feeling the walls tremble.

It would be easier if he didn't care. If she were only a political piece, his course would be clear. Isolate her. Control her. Use her. But she wasn't.

He'd seen the woman behind the amnesia. Felt the warmth of her trust. The sincerity of her smile. His judgment was compromised. His father's accusations of sentiment were now plain truth.

Strength Before Mercy. That was Verthar's creed, drilled into him since birth. Yet here he was, paralyzed by feelings he couldn't afford.

His first impulse was to go to her. To see if the pendant still glowed. He quashed the urge immediately. It would be foolish. Panicked. It would show too much concern and feed the very suspicions he was trying to starve.

He couldn't let Silven or his father see how much she mattered. He pressed his thumb against his signet ring, turning it. The falcon sigil dug into his skin. A weak anchor in uncertain waters.

He couldn't go himself. But he could send someone else. Someone whose presence wouldn't raise alarms. Someone he trusted. Rilen.

The plan formed. He would frame it as protocol. A wellness check to ensure the servants were attending properly to their guest. But he'd give his cousin a second, private instruction.

Look at the pendant. Tell me if it still shines.

It was roundabout. Covert. A way to gather information without revealing his concern. It gave him a course of action, a temporary illusion of control. He turned from the window, his face hardening. He would find Rilen. Give the order. Get his answer. Then he'd know what to do next.

But as he walked toward the door, a final thought slipped past his defenses. Cold and sharp. The unease wasn't really about the veilstone. The pendant was just a tool. Its failure was a symptom, not the disease.

The real terror, the thing he couldn't voice even to himself, wasn't about the magic. It was about what he would do when she remembered.

And he knew she would. The lie had a finite life. The truth was inevitable. And for all his planning, for all his power, he was completely unprepared.

CHAPTER

NINETEEN

When Miera woke, she felt like a shell of her former self. For the first time, she was a willing participant in Jareth's lie. Yes, it was because she needed to work out her escape, but it still felt horrid to pretend she didn't have her memories back. The veilstone lay cold on the writing desk, its magic inert and distant. Terror from the night's memories had receded, leaving not peace but sharp purpose.

She wanted to shout from the battlements of Durevin Hold that she was a princess of Corthen! She was Seraya. Lady Miera was a mask, and today she would learn to wear it not as a victim but as a spy seeking information to crush her enemies and return to her country.

She needed to know if the flashes of memory haunting her were random mental or emotional debris or the real fragments of her stolen life. The military map. The silver hawk. They felt too specific to be fantasy. But feelings were never to be confused with fact. She needed a trigger.

An external stimulus that could provoke another memory and confirm its truth.

She rose from the bed, her bare feet cold on the stone floor. The morning light was grey and weak through the curtains. She walked to the washing basin and splashed cold water on her face. The shock of it helped sharpen her focus.

She chose a gown of deep teal wool. The color was Vertharian in its sobriety. A safe choice. The fabric felt coarse against her skin. A uniform for the role she was about to play.

Once dressed, she sat at the writing desk and began to braid her hair. Her fingers moved with practiced economy. She watched herself in the polished surface of a heavy silver water pitcher. The face looking back was pale. Eyes wide and shadowed. But a stillness inhabited them now. A focus that hadn't existed before. The trembling was gone, replaced by cold intent.

The most dangerous part came last. She picked up the veilstone. Its weight felt heavier in her palm. A palpable burden. Clasping it around her neck was an act of self-violation. The familiar false calm seeped into her, muting the sharp edges of her clarity. Softening the steel of her purpose into pliable apprehension.

To all observers, she must remain Miera. The lost, gentle creature Jareth was protecting. Her ignorance was now her greatest weapon.

She left her chamber. Two guards stood outside. They straightened as she emerged. She nodded to them, the gesture demure and unthreatening. They relaxed slightly. Good. She was performing well.

The walk to the library took her through corridors she'd traveled a dozen times before. Now she noticed details. The spacing of the torch sconces. The patterns in the stone floor where centuries of feet had worn the surface smooth. The placement of the guards at each intersection. Her mind cataloged it all without conscious effort.

She passed a servant carrying linens. The woman curtsied. Miera smiled gently and continued. Just a lady taking a morning walk. Nothing suspicious. Nothing to report.

The palace library had once been a sanctuary. Now it was a proving ground.

She entered the still, dim room. The scent of old parchment, leather, and beeswax hit her. A familiar comfort that she now registered with analytical detachment. Motes of dust danced in pale shafts of winter light slanting from tall arched windows. They illuminated the gilded spines of books on dark polished shelves.

A small group of courtiers had gathered near the central hearth. Their voices were a polite, low murmur. They were discussing diplomatic correspondence, their postures stiff and formal in the Vertharian style.

Lady Elara. The king's hawk-faced cousin. And two junior lords whose names she'd committed to memory. Lord Borin and Lord Orin.

This was the stimulus she sought.

She approached slowly, adjusting her shawl. Making it

look casual. She joined them and offered a quiet greeting. Her expression was a careful blend of shy curiosity.

"Lady Miera." Lord Borin gave a slight, stiff bow. "We were just speaking of the recent frictions along the Cortheni border."

She inclined her head. Folded her hands demurely before her. Said nothing. Let the silence invite them to continue. It was a technique she didn't know she'd learned.

"Corthen grows bold." Lady Elara's voice was sharp as splintered bone. "They test our Ironwing patrols. Raid our timber camps. Arrogance has always been their primary export."

The words were meant as political opinion. But for Seraya, they were a key turning a lock deep within her mind.

Corthen. The name resonated in her soul, a plucked string in the architecture of her soul. She held her breath. Waited.

Lord Orin gave a dismissive wave. "They are a nation of poets and perfumers. Their recent past is a history of diplomatic defeats and poorly conceived strategies. They have no stomach for real war."

The phrase "recent past" struck her with physical force.

The library dissolved.

The image exploded behind her eyes. Not a dream. A memory of absolute clarity.

She was not in a library but in a poorly lit campaign tent. A massive map spread across an oak table. Its surface showed the jagged peaks of the Shardspine Mountains. The air smelled of canvas, lamp oil, and wet wool.

Troop markers. Small blocks of carved wood painted in different colors. Positioned along a trade route.

Her own voice, low and confident, was speaking.

"Orin's assessment is flawed. Their forces here are a feint. The real threat is the flanking maneuver through the Smuggler's Pass. They will cut off the Crownway supply line within three days if we do not move to reinforce it now."

She could see the Cortheni sigils on the markers. Knew the names of the commanders leading the battalions. She knew, with certainty as profound as breathing, that she was right.

The vision shattered.

The library rushed back into focus with a dizzying lurch. The faces of the courtiers swam before her eyes. An ache, sharp and blinding, pierced her temples. She swayed. Her hand flew to her forehead.

"Lady Miera? Are you unwell?"

Lady Elara's voice was laced with sharp concern.

Panic rose in her throat. Cold and acidic. She could not break here. Could not expose herself.

Her training, whatever it had been, took over. She summoned a look of fragile distress. Let her breath come in shallow, convincing flutters.

"Forgive me." Her voice was weak. "A sudden fatigue. The air is a little close in here."

It was the perfect excuse. A plausible weakness for the delicate, recovering woman they all believed her to be.

Lord Borin immediately looked flustered. Lady Elara's expression softened with condescending pity.

"Of course, my dear." The older woman's tone was solicitous. "You must rest. Shall I have a servant escort you?"

"No, thank you. I can manage." Seraya was already turning away. "You are too kind."

She walked from the room. Her steps were measured and even. A perfect portrayal of a woman fighting faintness. She did not run. Did not look back. Every instinct screamed at her to flee. To find a secure location. To record the intelligence she'd just accessed before it faded.

The corridor outside was blessedly empty. She moved quickly now, no longer pretending weakness. Her heart pounded against her ribs. She took the stairs to her floor. Passed a servant who barely glanced at her.

She reached her chamber. Closed the door. Leaned against it. The cool solid wood was a welcome anchor. She was breathing heavily. The facade of weakness dissolved into raw, shaking urgency.

The memory was already beginning to fray at the edges. Details losing their sharp focus. She stumbled to the narrow ebonized writing desk. Her hands fumbled to open the drawer. She pulled out a clean sheet of thick parchment and the pot of black ink.

She had to get it down. Now.

She dipped the pen. Her hand hovered over the page. She closed her eyes. Tried to recall the map. The troop positions. The name of the pass. As she brought the image to the forefront of her mind, she lowered the nib to the paper and began to write.

Her hand did not form the elegant, looping script of a courtly lady.

It moved on its own. A thing possessed of separate, procedural memory. The pen flew across the page. It formed a series of sharp, angular shapes. Precise and tight. A script of abbreviated symbols and geometric figures. A code that was alien to her conscious mind.

Lines connected symbols. Arrows indicated movement. She stared at the page. Her breath caught in her throat. The map was there. Perfectly rendered in a language she had no idea she knew.

Who was she? A cartographer? A strategist? A spy who dealt in coded intelligence?

The disquieting truth was that it felt natural. It felt correct.

Her hand was still trembling from the effort. She set the pen down. Her fingers were stained with ink. The paper lay on the desk. A tangible, incriminating piece of evidence.

Proof. Proof that her memories were real, strategic, and dangerous. Proof that she was not who she thought she was.

Cold dread washed over her.

Jareth. If he were to find this.

A new test presented itself. A final confirmation.

With a hand that felt strangely steady, she reached up and unclasped the veilstone. She held it in her palm for a moment. Then deliberately, coldly, she fastened it back around her neck.

She felt the familiar, hateful wave of placid calm wash through her. The sharp edges of her fear and excitement dulled. The ache in her temples subsided.

When the magical fog had fully settled over her mind, she looked back down at the parchment on her desk.

The effect was instantaneous and horrifying.

The neat, precise, meaningful coded script was gone. In its place was a chaotic scramble of meaningless, random markings. The lines and arrows had warped into nonsensical scribbles. The angular symbols had degraded into the frantic scratching of a madwoman.

It looked like nothing. It meant nothing.

She stared. Her heart turned to a block of ice in her chest.

It was true. The pendant did not just mute emotion or quiet nightmares. It actively obstructed her mind. It was a veil. A filter that warped reality. That rendered truth into gibberish. It was designed to keep her from understanding herself.

A mix of ice-cold fear and white-hot purpose flooded her. She had her proof.

Jareth's protection was a lie. His kindness was a cage. And she was standing in the middle of it.

Acting on pure, cold instinct, she took the paper. She did not burn it. An operative never destroyed intelligence.

She went to the writing desk. Using the fine tip of a letter opener, she carefully pried up a small section of the thin velvet lining inside the main drawer. The space beneath was shallow but enough. She folded the parchment twice and slid it into the hollow gap. Pressed the lining back into place.

Invisible. A secret hidden in plain sight.

She stood. Her movements were calm and deliberate. She walked to the small silver mirror on her vanity and looked at her reflection.

The same pale, placid face of Miera stared back. The eyes were calm. The expression serene.

But behind them, a different woman was now looking out. A woman who knew she was in a game for her life. A woman who had just discovered her opponent had been cheating from the beginning.

The calm the veilstone provided was her armor now. Her perceived ignorance was her sharpest weapon.

The game had begun. She would learn its rules. She had to, before Jareth realized his pawn had just remembered how to be a queen.

CHAPTER

TWENTY

The council audience began with a veneer of calm that fooled no one. The air in the chamber was heavy with unspoken threats. Thin winter light from the high windows caught the agitated dust in still air. Jareth stood at his father's right hand, his posture rigid. His gaze remained fixed on the Avenali envoy.

Silven civility was a weapon, polished to lethal sheen. His words were flawless. His tone impeccably courteous. Yet every question was a surgeon's scalpel, probing the tender edges of truth surrounding Miera's arrival.

"One hopes the recent disturbances have not overly taxed the fortress's resources." Silven's courtly smile was unreadable. He made a vague gesture toward the new stonework patching the window that had shattered days before. "Such events can often be traced back to unexpected arrivals. Unaccounted for variables."

The insinuation was a poisoned dart. Aimed not at Jareth but at the king himself.

Before his father could respond, Jareth answered. His voice was smooth and cold as the dark ironwood of the council table. "Fortress security is absolute. The disturbance was a deep-strata shift common to the Ironridge Bluffs. A settling of stone. Nothing more."

"Of course." Silven's eyes glinted with amusement that belied his words. He knew it was a lie. He knew that Jareth knew he knew. It was a move on the board. A piece slid forward to see how the opponent would react. "Still, it has led to a review of our own protocols. My attaché has been assisting your archivists with a tedious but necessary task. Cross-referencing our own guest logs with your northern patrol records from the past few months. We must ensure our diplomatic travel has been flawlessly documented."

Jareth felt profound coldness seep into his bones. The archives. Patrol records. Silven was not fishing for information. He was hunting, and he had found the scent.

Jareth offered a stiff, dismissive nod. A gesture of carefully performed indifference. "Your diligence is noted, emissary."

The delicate game of veiled threats continued for another hour. A masterpiece of diplomatic warfare fought with smiles and pleasantries. Jareth parried every thrust. Deflected every probe. But the damage was done. Silven had announced his stategy on the open floor of the council. It was a move of breathtaking arrogance. A challenge laid down in plain sight.

The audience dragged on. Discussions of trade tariffs. Border patrol schedules. Resource allocations. Each topic a mask for the real conversation happening beneath the surface. Jareth maintained his composure. Answered when required. Remained silent when prudent. His mind was already racing ahead to countermoves.

King Halric sat like a stone monument at the head of the table. His pale eyes moved between his son and the Avenali envoy. Calculating. Measuring. Missing nothing.

When the audience finally concluded, Jareth excused himself with a sharp, formal bow. His mind was already racing ahead. He found Rilen waiting in the corridor as planned. His cousin's face was a mask of grim concern.

They walked in silence. Their footsteps echoed in the stone passageway. Their path took them past high, narrow windows that showed a sky the color of slate. They did not speak until they reached the relative privacy of Jareth's study.

The walk gave Jareth time to think. To process what had just happened. Silven was moving faster than anticipated. More aggressively. The game was accelerating toward a conclusion Jareth could not predict.

They passed guards standing at their posts. Servants carrying firewood and linens. A scribe hurrying somewhere with documents clutched to his chest. All the mundane activity of a fortress going about its daily business. None of them knew the war being waged in their midst.

Rilen closed the heavy oak door behind them. The sound of the latch clicking into place was a final seal on their solitude.

"He knows." Rilen's voice was a low murmur. He

wasted no time on preamble. "His attendant has been in the archives for two days. I had him watched. He is pulling guest manifests and comparing them to the northern patrol logs from the ninth month. The heavy, wax-sealed vellum tomes of the northern command."

Rilen's gaze was direct. His soldier's mind cutting to the heart of the matter. "He is looking for a ghost, Jareth. A woman who arrived but was never officially recorded."

The confirmation was not a shock but cold, heavy certainty settling in his gut. Jareth turned away. Walked to the hearth where a low fire crackled. His strategy of hiding Miera in plain sight, of wrapping her in a cloak of quiet normalcy, had been a catastrophic failure.

He had not hidden her. He had turned her into an irresistible mystery. A puzzle that a mind like Silven's could not resist solving.

The game was more complex than he had anticipated. He had made a novice's error.

Before he could voice his next question, a sharp rap came at the door. Rilen turned, hand on his sword hilt. Jareth gave a minute shake of his head. "Enter."

A guardsman stepped inside, helmet under his arm. He presented a small, sealed note to Rilen. "From the gallery watch, Captain. As ordered."

The man bowed and retreated. His footsteps faded in the corridor outside.

Rilen broke the seal and passed the small slip of parchment to Jareth. The script was a soldier's scrawl. But the words were the ones Jareth desperately needed to hear. The words that would reshape the entire board.

Saw the lady Miera. Charm shines as brightly as ever. Her calm seems entirely undisturbed.

Jareth closed his eyes. A wave of relief, so profound it was almost painful, washed through him. The veilstone was holding. The core of his plan, the delicate magic that kept her memories chained and her mind placid, was secure.

That single vital piece of information clarified everything. The threat was external, not internal. Miera was safe from herself. All he had to do was keep Silven Drael from reaching her.

The relief was a dangerous luxury. A false comfort that allowed him to focus his entire strategic mind on his rival with chilling singularity.

"He has made her a mark." Jareth's voice was a low snarl of fury. He faced his cousin, his expression hardening into a mask of cold purpose. "My attempts to shield her have only painted a target on her back. Subtlety is no longer an option."

Rilen's brow furrowed in concern. "A direct confrontation is what he wants. It will draw the king's eye. You cannot risk that."

"I am not talking about a confrontation." Jareth's mind was already weaving the threads of a new, more aggressive strategy. The situation had shifted. The pieces rearranged by his own flawed assumptions. Now he saw the path forward. "I am talking about control. Absolute control."

The thought of Miera, so serene and unknowing, caught in the crossfire of this vicious political game was intolerable. It was a thought that went beyond politics, beyond duty. It was the raw, protective instinct of a man shielding something precious.

That instinct, the very thing his father would have scorned as weakness, now sharpened his mind to a razor's edge.

He would no longer hide her. He would hide the truth. He would build a new fortress around her. Not of stone but of misinformation and silence. He would control every word, every document, every rumor that flowed through Durevin Hold.

He moved to his desk. The firelight caught on the silver of his inkwell. "Post your best men on Silven and his attendant. Constant surveillance. I want to know when they sleep, when they eat, and who they speak to. Every whispered word. Every clandestine meeting."

He dipped his quill. "And I want the archives sealed. Effective immediately. Cite a mold infestation, a structural review of the foundation. I do not care which lie you choose. No one gets in or out."

Rilen nodded. His expression was serious. He understood the shift. This was no longer about deflection. This was about containment. This was a declaration of silent war.

"Consider it done." Rilen turned toward the door, then paused. "And the lady?"

"She stays where she is." Jareth's tone left no room for argument. "But I want additional guards. Discrete. She should not see them, but they should see anyone who approaches her chambers."

Rilen nodded again and left. The door closed behind him with a soft thud.

Jareth spent the rest of the night orchestrating his war from the deep shadows of his study. He sat in the dark. The only light came from the dying fire and a single candle. The scratch of his quill on thick Vertharian parchment was the only sound.

He drafted and sealed a dozen coded orders. His precise script moved swiftly across the page.

Instructions to his own network of informants within the city walls. Commands to border patrols to tighten their watch and report any Avenali movement. Missives to loyal vassals in the capital, subtly requesting information on Silven's own network of contacts.

He was methodically, systematically, closing every channel Silven could possibly exploit. He was building his fortress. One lie at a time.

Each letter was sealed with red wax. Each bore the impression of his signet ring with its imposing black falcon of Verthar. His authority. His responsibility.

He sent them with trusted messengers. Men who knew how to move through the fortress unseen. How to leave the city without drawing attention. How to deliver messages that would never appear in any official log.

The hours passed. The candle burned lower. The fire died to embers. Still Jareth worked.

As the first pale streaks of dawn painted the frosted windows grey, he took up a fresh sheet of parchment. This order was not for his spies. Not for the court. It was addressed to the garrison commander at a remote outpost in the northern Shardspine Mountains. The very outpost whose patrols would have been active during the ninth month.

The message was short. Devoid of explanation or apology. It was an order not to hide a record but to unmake it. A single, chilling command.

Destroy all patrol logs from the ninth month. Cite damage from water infiltration. Rewrite summaries from memory, omitting any reference to unidentified travelers. Confirm when complete.

He sealed the letter with black wax. Pressed his signet ring into the yielding surface with final, definitive motion.

He was no longer just hiding the truth. He was erasing it from history.

He held the sealed letter in his hand. Stared at it in the grey morning light. This was a line he could not uncross. Evidence destroyed could never be recovered. But if it kept her safe, if it kept Silven from his prize, it was worth the cost.

He placed it with the others to be sent.

Then he stood. Walked to the window. Looked out at the fortress awakening to another day. Smoke rose from chimneys. Guards changed shifts. Life continued, unaware of the war being waged in shadows.

He pressed his palm against the cold glass. Felt the chill seep into his skin.

He was becoming his father. Using the same methods. The same ruthless pragmatism. The same willingness to sacrifice anything for control.

But his father would sacrifice Miera without hesitation. Would use her as a pawn in whatever game served Verthar's interests.

Jareth would not. That was the difference. That had to be the difference.

He turned from the window. There was work to do.

CHAPTER
TWENTY-ONE

The veilstone was a leash, and she had learned how to slip the collar.

Over the next several days, Miera became a creature of meticulous, clandestine routine. Her existence, once a placid fog, now found its shape in the harsh geometry of risk and observation. She conducted her trials with cold precision, turning her gilded cage into a laboratory.

She had to understand the true nature of the magic that bound her. Was it a shield, as Jareth had claimed? Or was it a wall? She required data. To acquire it, she had to court the very danger she'd been taught to fear.

The first test was brief.

In the deep stillness of mid-afternoon, when the fortress was drowsy and guard rotations were at their most predictable, she retreated to her chamber. She unclasped the silver chain and set the pendant on the narrow ebonized writing desk. Its soft internal light pulsed once. A faint, questioning throb. Then went dark.

The change was not a tidal wave of memory but a sharpening of the world. The shift was subtle yet absolute. Like a lens clicking into perfect focus.

The muted colors of the heavy Vertharian tapestries on her walls resolved into rich, vibrant threads. Crimson and charcoal. The crimson, she noted without understanding why, was a specific shade derived from the kermes beetle. A dye whose production was a fiercely guarded monopoly of Verthar's southern provinces. A single tapestry was a declaration of wealth and power.

The intricate patterns of the carving on her four-poster bed, which had seemed merely ornate, now revealed themselves as the repeating falcon motif. The flaw she'd vaguely sensed in the design was suddenly obvious. The artist had given the bird the talons of an eagle. A small but glaring inaccuracy.

The knowledge arrived without context. A fact presented to a mind that had no reason to know it.

She walked to the window. Her gaze swept over the courtyard below. Where before she saw only guards, she now saw patterns. Two men at the main gate. Four on the ramparts. Their patrol routes intersecting every seventeen minutes. A blind spot existed near the western wall, just behind the buttress of the old armory.

It was a detail she had no use for. Yet her mind cataloged it with instinctive, unnerving competence.

An hour. She'd promised herself an hour. The clarity was intoxicating. A drink of cold, clean water after a lifetime of thirst. But it was a measured risk.

Before the guards on the rampart could complete their

fourth rotation, she retrieved the pendant. Fastening it was an act of violation. A willing return to the fog. The world softened again. The flaw in the carving became a mere quirk of design. The blind spot in the courtyard was just a shadow.

The calm returned. But it no longer felt like peace. It felt like a deficiency.

She lengthened the intervals.

Two hours, then three. The influx of sensory data was a deluge. She started to remember names she'd only over-heard once. The singsong cadence of a kitchen maid from the western provinces. The precise blend of spices used in the evening meal.

Her mind, once a still pond, was now a churning current of information. She was a sailor learning the tides.

At night, she dreamed. The dreams were no longer hazy nightmares but sharp, fragmented dispatches from an unknown front. She woke with words on her lips. Phrases in a lilting, elegant language she didn't recognize but understood perfectly.

The envoy lies. Check the manifests.

The words would dissolve into mist the moment she woke. Leaving only a residue of urgency. The risk of this new lucidity became terrifyingly real on the third day.

She was in the fortress gardens. A rare space of life amid the oppressive stone of Durevin Hold. The air was cold and clean, smelling of damp earth and the hardy, clove-scented petals of the Emberrose that bloomed even in weak winter sun.

She'd left the veilstone in her chamber. Hidden within

a folded silk chemise in her wardrobe. The three hours of freedom felt like a lifetime.

She walked the stone paths slowly. Observing. A servant tended the precisely clipped yew hedges. His shears made a soft, rhythmic snip-snip in the afternoon air. He was an older man with a kind, weathered face.

He looked up as she approached. Gave a respectful, hesitant nod. Unused to being addressed by the court's mysterious guest.

She noted the yew. How its dark needles promised a deep and final poison within its elegant form. Everything in this place, she thought, was a beautiful danger.

She meant to say, "The roses are beautiful this morning." The words were formed in her mind. Polite and Vertharian.

But what came from her mouth was something else entirely.

"*Nae'cala, ser. Anar caliath.*"

The phrase was liquid and smooth on her tongue. The accent perfect. It felt as natural as breathing.

The man froze. His shears held mid-snip. A deep furrow formed between his brows. A look of profound, uncomprehending confusion. He didn't look alarmed. Merely baffled. As if a songbird had suddenly spoken in the tongue of wolves.

Seraya froze, too. She stared at him. Her heart seized into a knot of cold iron in her chest. The language was Cortheni. She knew it. She knew it with a certainty that defied all logic.

The phrase meant, *A fine morning, master. The sun is*

warm. A courtly, meaningless pleasantry from her homeland. From the land of the enemy.

Panic threatened to shatter her composure. Cold and absolute. Her mind screamed. *He knows. He heard. He will report it. Jareth will know. They will all know.*

But her body, her training, reacted faster than her fear.

She summoned a look of faint, apologetic confusion. She touched her fingers to her lips. Her eyes wide with carefully crafted innocence. As if she were as surprised by the sound as he was.

"Forgive me." Her voice was a soft, flawless Vertharian murmur. "My thoughts are scattered today. I meant only to say how lovely the gardens are."

The servant blinked. The moment of strangeness passed. He was a simple man. A gardener, not a spy. The foreign words were just noise. A slip of the tongue from a woman known to be unwell.

His brow smoothed. He offered a small, awkward smile.

"Aye, my lady. They are." He mumbled, turning back to his hedge with palpable relief. He wanted the interaction to be over.

Seraya didn't wait. She inclined her head in a graceful nod. Continued down the stone path. Her posture serene. Her pace unhurried. She didn't look back.

To the servant, she was a strange but harmless lady of the court.

Inside, cold terror coiled in her stomach. The close call left her shaken. Her own mind was a traitor. Her own tongue was a liability. The skills returning to her were uncontrollable. Dangerous.

She could not trust herself. She walked until she found a secluded bench near the eastern wall. Out of sight from the main paths. She sat, hands folded in her lap. Breathing slowly. Steadying herself.

A maid passed by with linens. Glanced at her. Continued on. Just a lady resting in the gardens. Nothing unusual.

Seraya waited five more minutes. Then rose and made her way back inside. She passed through corridors. Climbed stairs. Her mind cataloging every detail. Guard positions. Servant routes. Windows. Doors.

She reached her chambers. Closed the door. Leaned against it. She needed a new method. A way to record her findings that couldn't betray her. Seraya waited until the fortress was deep in the silence of night. She lit a single candle. Its flame a small, brave point of light in the darkness. She took the veilstone from its hiding place but didn't put it on.

Instead, she sat at her writing desk. Before her lay a fresh sheet of stiff Vertharian parchment and the pot of ink. A black, viscous fluid meant for official decrees. She held the quill, its tip sharpened to a weapon's point. Feeling its foreign weight in her fingers.

She closed her eyes and let the memories come. The map from the library. The Cortheni phrase from the garden. The names of Jareth's commanders. Fragments of conversations, coded and significant.

She held them all in her mind. Then took up the pen.

She didn't consciously think about how to write. She simply let her hand move.

It didn't form the soft, looping script of Miera. It didn't even form the standard angular letters of Vertharian or Cortheni script. The quill moved with brisk, unnatural certainty. Forming a dense block of symbols.

Sharp, straight lines intersected with tight curves. Dots and hooks placed with geometric precision. It was a cipher. Complex and efficient. A language of pure information, stripped of all artistry. It was alien and frighteningly familiar.

She filled the page. Her hand aching from the speed and concentration. When she was finished, she stared at the parchment. It was a perfect record of her recovered intelligence. Incomprehensible to an untrained eye. It was safe. Or was it? One final test remained.

With a deep, steadying breath, she picked up the veilstone. Clasped it around her neck. The cool weight settled against her skin. The familiar, hateful tide of calm washed through her. Dulling the sharp edges of her mind.

When the magical fog had fully descended, she forced herself to look back at the page. She felt grim confirmation. The cipher was gone.

In its place was a chaotic mess of frantic, meaningless scratches. The precise, angular symbols had twisted into a child's senseless scribbling. The elegant efficiency of the code had warped into the visual noise of madness.

It was unreadable. It meant nothing. She had her answer. The pendant didn't just suppress memory. It actively interfered with the perception of truth. It was a blinder. A filter designed to render reality into nonsense.

Jareth hadn't given her a charm to quiet her thoughts. He'd given her a tool to break her mind. A cold, diamond-hard certainty settled in her soul.

She was two people now. There was Miera. The tranquil courtier. The gentle, grateful woman who smiled and walked the gardens. And there was the other one. The stranger who wrote in ciphers. Who analyzed guard patterns. Who spoke the language of the enemy.

The woman who was now methodically, patiently, uncovering a hidden and deeply dangerous past.

She folded the page of ciphered notes. Hid it with the first, concealed behind the velvet lining of a loose panel in her desk drawer. She would continue to gather her data. Would fill page after page with a truth that only she, in her brief hours of clarity, could read.

She blew out the candle. Stood in the darkness. Her hand at her throat. Her fingers resting on the cool, smooth surface of the stone. She looked toward the faint outline of the mirror, though she couldn't see her own reflection. The placid face of Miera was there, she knew but it was a mask.

But for the first time, she understood it was a mask she now wore by choice. The woman who wrote those ciphers was a stranger. An unknown quantity. And she had no idea if remembering who that woman was would be a liberation or a death sentence.

TWENTY-TWO

The summons arrived before dawn. It was not a request but a command. A sharp rap on his chamber door that cut through the predawn stillness.

The sound found Jareth sleepless. Staring into the dying embers of the hearth as the ghosts of a dozen failed strategies swirled in the smoke. A deep, damp chill seeped from the stone of the fortress. A cold that settled in his bones and felt indistinguishable from his father's displeasure.

He rose from the chair where he'd spent the night. His body stiff from hours of motionless vigil. He crossed to the washbasin. Splashed cold water on his face. The shock of it helped sharpen his focus.

He dressed in the dark. His movements economical and precise. He selected a coat of charcoal wool. Its high collar and severe lines a kind of armor. The only concession to his rank was the silver embroidery on the cuffs. It caught the faint light from the embers like slivers of ice.

He fastened the buttons. Buckled his belt. Adjusted his collar. Each action deliberate. Each a small piece of the mask he was constructing.

When he entered the council wing, the air was heavy with the scent of beeswax candles. The faint, metallic tang of oiled steel from the guards' armor. Torches burned low in their sconces. They cast long, distorted shadows that danced like accusations on the tapestries.

The corridor was long. His footsteps echoed. Guards stood at attention as he passed. Their faces impassive. He wondered if any of them reported his movements to his father. Probably.

His father was already seated at the head of the long table. A monolithic silhouette against the cold, grey light filtering through the high windows. The table itself was carved from a single petrified ironwood trunk. A spoil of some forgotten conquest.

King Halric's face was a mask of granite. The silver circlet on his brow a thin, cold band of authority. He did not look up as Jareth entered. A deliberate and calculated slight.

The other members of the war council stood rigidly by their chairs. Old men with faces like worn maps of harsh terrain. Their gazes were fixed on the polished wood before them. None of them met Jareth's eyes as he took his place at his father's right.

His posture was a perfect mirror of military discipline. He could feel Halric's gaze on him now. A physical weight. Cold and questioning.

"The Avenali delegation grows restless." The king's

voice was devoid of warmth. A low rumble that made the very air in the chamber feel brittle. "There are reports of friction. Your guards, Jareth, have been overzealous in their duties."

Jareth met his father's gaze without flinching. His own expression a carefully constructed veneer of calm competence. "The envoy's men have been testing the boundaries of their diplomatic access, Father. My guards have merely been reinforcing them. The situation is contained."

"Contained." Halric repeated the word, tasting it for scorn. He leaned forward. His hands flat on the table. The heavy royal signet on his finger catching the torchlight. "Containment implies control. This feels like weakness disguised as caution. The envoy requested a private audience. I denied it. I will not have it said that Verthar negotiates under the shadow of rumor and insinuation. You will handle this. You will project strength, not bureaucratic diligence."

The unspoken challenge hung in the oppressive silence. *Prove you are my son. Prove you are not weak.*

Jareth inclined his head. A single, sharp nod of acquiescence. "It will be done."

The dismissal was a wave of his father's hand. As the council members shuffled out, relief bleeding into their stiff formality, Jareth remained standing for a moment longer.

He had survived. He had parried the thrust without giving ground. But the encounter left a chill deeper than the morning air. His father's suspicion was no longer a passing mood. It was hardening into certainty. Setting like winter ice.

He turned and left the council chamber. The heavy doors closed behind him with a dull thud.

Rilen was waiting for him in the echoing corridor. His commander's uniform immaculate. His expression grim. As Jareth emerged, his cousin fell into step beside him. His voice was a low, urgent rasp that was lost in the vastness of the stone hall.

"The council was tense." Rilen observed, stating the obvious as if to test the waters.

"The king is impatient." Jareth's voice was clipped.

They walked on. Their boots striking a sharp, rhythmic tattoo on the flagstones. The corridor stretched before them. Lined with tapestries depicting Vertharian victories. Each one a reminder of the legacy he was meant to uphold.

They passed a pair of guards stationed at an intersection. The men straightened. Jareth nodded curtly. Kept walking.

Jareth's gaze drifted to a tapestry depicting the Vertharian victory during the Thornfall Betrayal. A brutal scene of fire and conquest woven in threads of crimson and black. He'd seen it a thousand times. Today it looked different. More prophetic than historical.

Rilen waited until they were clear of the council wing. Turning into a less-trafficked gallery where the thick wall hangings absorbed their words. Here they could speak freely.

"It is worse than impatience." Rilen's voice dropped

further. He stopped, forcing Jareth to turn and face him. "Silven has changed his tactics. He is no longer investigating. He is poisoning the well."

"Explain." The word was a blade.

"He is seeding rumors." Rilen's gaze was hard and direct. "Whispers, passed from his attendants to the court gossips. That the Avenali delegation knows more than it should about the 'unidentified woman' under your protection. That her origins are a secret Verthar is desperate to keep. He is not looking for proof anymore, Jareth. He is creating a political crisis and placing you at its center."

The danger was immense. A far more insidious threat than a spy in the archives. A rumor could not be intercepted. A whisper could not be contained.

Silven was bypassing Jareth's surveillance entirely. Aiming his attack directly at the one person Jareth could not control. His father.

If Halric heard these whispers from the court instead of from his son, Miera would cease to be a woman. She would become a pawn. A piece to be sacrificed in a game Jareth could no longer afford to play.

Jareth's first impulse was to scoff. To dismiss the threat with the very arrogance his father would expect. He opened his mouth to do so, but the words died in his throat.

He saw the earnest loyalty in Rilen's eyes. The unshakeable trust. He could not lie to the one man who had never lied to him. Not a complete lie, at any rate.

He gave a curt, dismissive wave. "Court gossip is a weapon for women and weak men. Let him whisper."

The lie was for Rilen's benefit. A pretense of confidence he did not feel.

Internally, a profound and chilling shift was taking place. The guilt that had gnawed at him for weeks, the moral weight of his deception, was being stripped away. The searing heat of this new, immediate threat burned it clean.

In its place grew something colder. Harder. A justification.

Every lie he had told, every secret he had kept, was no longer a failing. It was a necessity. His deceit was not weakness. It was a duty. He had to keep believing that. It was the only shield that stood between Miera and his father's cold, brutal pragmatism.

"I will handle Silven." His voice now held a new, steely resonance. He started walking again. His pace faster. More purposeful.

Rilen fell into step beside him. His relief was palpable. "What are your orders?"

"Double the watch on the Avenali wing. Confine them to their quarters after the evening meal. Cite a security review of all guest wing access. And I want Miera moved to the west tower. Her current rooms are too central. Too exposed."

He was thinking aloud. His mind a loom, weaving a new web of control. He needed her isolated. Completely. For her own safety. It was the only way.

They turned a corner. Passed through another corridor. This one lined with alcoves. Each held a suit of armor. Relics from Verthar's martial history.

As they passed a suit of polished black steel armor standing sentinel in an alcove, Jareth caught a glimpse of his own reflection. The armor had belonged to Halric's grandfather. A conqueror of renown.

The dim, distorted image in the curved surface of the breastplate stopped him cold.

For a disorienting second, it was not his own face that stared back at him. In the hard set of his jaw, the cold, calculating light in his eyes, the absolute lack of doubt, he saw his father. The face was younger, but the expression was Halric's.

The realization was a physical shock. A jolt that went through him like a blade.

In his desperate need to protect her, to control the situation, he had begun to adopt the very methods, the very look, of the tyrant he despised.

The quiet, reasonable lies he had told himself now sounded like his father's voice. Echoing in the hollow chambers of his own mind. *A ruler cannot afford sentiment. Neutralize the threat. Weakness is a form of treason.*

He had reaffirmed his mission. He would protect Miera, no matter the cost. But the cost, he now saw with terrifying clarity, might be his own soul.

He had reframed his deceptions as a noble sacrifice. A burden he must carry for her. He would be the villain to keep her safe.

The thought was both horrifying and strangely liberating. It was a path, and it was clear.

He tore his gaze away from the reflection. His own face now a stony mask.

"See to it." He commanded Rilen. His voice the clipped, authoritative tone of a prince who would be obeyed.

"And you?" Rilen asked quietly. "What will you do?"

"What I must." Jareth turned away from the armor. From his reflection. From the last remnant of the man he'd been. "I will speak to the master of the household. Ensure the move to the west tower happens today. Quietly."

Rilen hesitated. "She will ask questions."

"Let her." Jareth's tone was flat. Final. "Better she asks me than someone else."

He left his cousin to carry out his orders and strode on alone. The sound of his own footsteps echoed with a new, heavier finality. He walked through the great, silent halls of Durevin Hold. His mind already methodically plotting his next moves.

He would tighten his control over the court's information. He would reinforce Miera's isolation. He would become the monster his father always wanted him to be, if it meant keeping her from harm.

He passed servants. Guards. Courtiers. None of them saw what he was becoming. None of them knew the war being waged in shadows.

He reached the administrative wing. Found the master of the household in his cramped office. Gave his orders. The man's eyes widened slightly at the urgency but he nodded. "By nightfall, Your Highness."

"By afternoon." Jareth corrected. "And I want it done with minimal disruption. No one is to know except those directly involved in the move."

"Of course, Your Highness."

Jareth left. Returned to his study. Closed the door. Stood in the silence.

He was so focused on the threat posed by Silven. So convinced that his escalating protection was the only path to her safety. That he remained blind to the truth.

He did not know that the woman he was trying to cage was, at that very moment, in her own locked room, methodically rediscovering the skills to pick the lock.

His protection was not the sanctuary he imagined. It was the grindstone against which she unknowingly honed the blade of her own mind.

CHAPTER
TWENTY-THREE

The urge to validate the visions had become a physical weight, a restless current that moved just beneath her skin. For days, Miera had performed a state of suspended calm. Her public self was a mask of gentle curiosity while her true self stirred in stolen, silent hours. The splinters of memory that surfaced when the veilstone was removed were no longer sufficient. They were maddening glimpses of a life she could not hold. She required proof. She needed something tangible, an object that could not dissolve back into the fog when the pendant's magic settled over her once more.

Late that night, she sat by the low embers in her chamber in the west tower. The fortress was shrouded in the deep, velvet stillness that precedes a heavy snowfall. The firelight trembled across the stone, casting her shadow long and wavering against the heavy tapestries. She held the veilstone in her palm, its silver setting cold against her skin. Within the crystal, a faint, rhythmic pulse of light throbbed, a cadence that matched her own hesitant heart. It felt like a living thing, a tiny, captured star that seemed to watch her, to question her.

Her thoughts flew unbidden to her previous chamber, to the loose floorboard beneath the washstand where she had hidden her journal. The small book filled with her fragmented dreams and careful observations, the record of her resistance, such as it was. She had no way to retrieve it now without raising suspicion. The move to the west tower had been sudden, her belongings packed by servants she did not know, and she had not dared to ask them to wait while she pried up a floorboard.

That record of her slow awakening would remain behind, buried like a seed in hostile soil. Perhaps, if she survived this, she would find a way to recover it. Perhaps it no longer mattered. The woman who had written those confused, desperate entries was becoming someone else entirely.

With a breath that felt like a quiet betrayal, she removed it. She set the pendant on the narrow ebonized writing desk beside her and waited.

The shift was not a gentle sharpening but a deluge. A tidal wave of sensation flooded her. The scents of old parchment and cold sea wind filled her lungs. Voices spoke in the fluid, lilting cadence of Corthen. She was no longer in her chamber in Durevin Hold. She was somewhere else entirely.

She stood in a vast, circular room with a domed ceiling painted with the constellations of the southern sky. The polished stone floor beneath her feet was inlaid with a map of the known world. Her hands were spread flat on a military chart laid across a massive oak map-table, the vellum cool and smooth beneath her palms. She was pointing to a location, a pass through the Shardspine Mountains. Her own voice, low and confident, echoed in the chamber, issuing commands. It was a voice that expected obedience. It was the voice of a commander, a strategist, a princess.

"Their supply lines are overextended here," the voice said, the Cortheni words as familiar to her as breathing. A name surfaced with the words, a name she suddenly knew as her own. Seraya. "We will strike at the pass. A swift, surgical blow. They will not anticipate it."

Her gaze in the vision moved to the seal on a document beside the map. It was a heavy brass stamp with an ivory handle, its face carved into the shape of a precise, beautifully coiled hawk, its wings unfurled as if in flight. The Royal Seal of Corthen. The memory was so vivid, so complete, it felt more real than the quiet chamber around her.

The vision broke like a wave against rock, leaving her gasping on the floor, her cheek pressed against the cold stone of the hearth. Her heart hammered against her ribs, a frantic, terrified drum. The memory was not a fragment. It was a scene, whole and undeniable.

Shaking, she pulled herself to her feet and stumbled to the desk. She had to record it before it faded. Her hands trembled as she lit another candle, the flame unsteady in the still air. She took up her pen and began to write, her hand flying across the parchment in the dense, angular cipher that was her only trusted language. The hawk seal. The map room. Her own voice giving orders.

When she finished, she stared at the page, her breath coming in ragged bursts. It was there. Proof. But it was only her own word against the magic of the stone. She needed something more. She required external validation.

With a deep, steadying breath, she reached for the veilstone. The moment she clasped it around her neck, the familiar tide of calm washed through her, but this time it felt like drowning. The sharp clarity of the vision blurred at its edges. The Cortheni words in her mind became muffled, indistinct. The commanding presence she had just inhabited receded, leaving the quiet, uncertain Miera in its place. She looked at the ciphered notes. The precise symbols seemed to waver, their meaning suddenly distant, like a language she had once known but had long since forgotten.

The pendant was not just a suppressor. It was an eraser. The urgency became a cold knot in her stomach. She had to act now, while the residue of the vision was still strong enough to be her guide.

The next day, she put her plan into motion. The midday meal was the key. It was the one time of day when the fortress's rigid hierarchy relaxed, when senior staff were occupied and junior members were either in charge or eager to get to their own food. The public archives, usually overseen by a stern, unapproachable master archivist, would be at their most vulnerable.

She timed her arrival with precision. As she approached the grand, arched doorway of the archives, she noted the changes at once. Two guards now stood where before there had been none. Their posture was rigid, their gazes sweeping the corridor with a new, heightened vigilance. Jareth's orders. The realization sent a chill through her, but she let none of it show on her face. She wore the veilstone openly, its faint glow a signal of her harmlessness. She was Miera, the quiet, scholarly guest.

She did not approach the main desk. Instead, she lingered near the entrance, a book of Vertharian poetry, Sonnets of the Ironridge, held loosely in her hands. Her expression was one of polite, thoughtful curiosity. She waited for the shift change. The master archivist, a formidable man with a permanent scowl, emerged from the stacks, gave her a brief, dismissive glance, and headed toward the Great Hall. In his place, a much younger man took the desk. He was barely out of his teens, his face eager and his uniform still a size too large in the shoulders. She had seen him before, had exchanged a few pleasant words with him about a particularly dreary epic. His name was Elian.

She approached him with a soft, hesitant smile. "Pardon me, Master Elian," she began, using the honorific with a touch of gentle deference she knew would flatter him. "I know you must be busy, but I was hoping to find a different translation of this verse. The one I have is so very martial. I was hoping for something with a bit more heart."

Elian puffed up with importance, his chest swelling. "Of course, my lady. The martial poets of the Third Dynasty can be quite blunt."

She leaned in, her voice dropping to a conspiratorial whisper. "I was told the older trade ledgers sometimes have poems and notations in the margins. It is a silly notion, I know, but I have found such wonderful things in the past." She smiled again, a picture of innocent, scholarly charm. "I would not want to bother you. If you could just point me toward the older treaty records, perhaps from before the Redmere Accord? I am sure I can find my way."

It was a masterful piece of social engineering, a skill she did not know she possessed. She had given him a plausible reason, flattered his ego, and offered him an easy way to get back to his own thoughts of the midday meal. He hesitated for only a second, his eyes flicking toward the deep, shadowed rear stacks. The senior archivists rarely ventured there.

"The pre-Accord ledgers are in the east wing, my lady. Section Gamma," he said, gesturing vaguely. "They are quite heavy."

"Oh, I do not mind a bit of dust," she replied, her smile bright and grateful. "Thank you, Master Elian. You have been most kind."

He gave a brisk nod, his duty done, and turned his attention to a stack of scrolls on his desk. She had her opening.

The air in the rear stacks was cool and still, thick with the dry scent of old paper and crumbling leather. Dust motes danced in the thin shafts of light slanting from the high, narrow windows between towering shelves of dark ironwood. Her instincts, sharp and clear without the veilstone's interference from the night before, guided her. She moved with a quiet confidence, her fingers trailing along the spines of the massive, leather-bound tomes.

Her heart pounded, a steady rhythm against her ribs, but her hands were steady. She was no longer Miera, the lost guest. She was an operative in hostile territory.

She found it in the third row. A heavy ledger bound in dark, cracked leather, its gilt lettering faded to a dull brown. The Treaty of Redmere and Associated Accords. She lifted it from the shelf, its weight a solid, grounding presence, and carried it to a small, secluded reading table.

She opened it carefully, the old parchment rustling like dry leaves. Her gaze scanned the dense, formal script until she found what she was looking for. There, stamped into the dark red wax at the bottom of a page detailing a minor border concession, was a seal. The royal hawk of Corthen, wings spread in proud display. It was similar to the sigil from her nightmares—but not identical. That other mark, the hawk clutching a crescent moon, was something else. Something she had yet to identify.

It was exactly as she had seen it in her vision. The graceful curve of the wings, the sharp, predatory head, the intricate detail of the feathers. A wave of vertigo washed over her. It was real. The map room, her voice, the seal. It was all real. Her breath caught in her throat, a sharp, painful gasp.

But a seal was not enough. She needed a name. Another piece of the puzzle. She closed the treaty book, her mind racing. The vision had been of a military strike.

Trade manifests. The words from her dream echoed with an insistent clarity. Check the manifests.

She returned the treaty to its place and moved deeper into the stacks, toward a section marked Provincial Trade and Tariffs. Her heart was a steady drum now. The fear was gone, replaced by a chilling, absolute focus. She pulled down a ledger from two decades past, its pages filled with neat columns of numbers and names written in precise Vertharian script. She let her eyes drift over the entries, not reading, but searching, letting instinct guide her to the one detail that mattered.

And then she saw it. A manifest for a shipment of Cortheni silks to a Vertharian border garrison, dated a week before the treaty was signed. The manifest was co-signed by the quartermaster of the garrison and a Cortheni official. The Vertharian signature was a meaningless scrawl. But the Cortheni name, written in a clear, elegant hand, sent a chill through her.

Lord Vorlag.

The name struck her with the force of a physical impact. Lord Vorlag. The boastful, gregarious envoy from Tirnavale. The man Jareth had used to test her at that state dinner weeks ago. The man whose nervous lies and talk of the "late Princess Seraya" had confirmed Jareth's suspicions.

The pieces clicked into place with the sickening finality of a prison door locking shut. The vision. The hawk seal. The name. It was all connected. It was all true. Her past was not a phantom. It was a carefully buried corpse, and she had just found the bones.

Her trust in Jareth, the one anchor she had clung to in the sea of her amnesia, did not simply crack. It was unmade. Every kindness, every gentle touch, every reassuring word was a lie. He had not saved her. He had not protected her.

He had buried her.

She closed the ledger, her hands no longer shaking. A profound and terrible calm settled over her. She slid the book back onto its shelf with a smooth, silent motion. She walked out of the shadowed stacks and back into the main hall of the archive. Elian was gone, his post empty.

She stepped out into the bright, cold corridor, the guards at the door giving her a cursory, uninterested glance. She was still Miera. The picture of gentle, harmless serenity. Her face was a mask of placid calm. Her posture was relaxed, her movements graceful.

But beneath the mask, a new woman had been forged in the cold fire of betrayal. A strategist. A spymistress. A princess.

Her hand went instinctively to the veilstone at her throat. The faint, steady pulse of its magic against her skin was no longer a comfort. It was a cage. It was the symbol of her imprisonment. But it was also her greatest weapon. He thought she was still his pawn, his docile, grateful Miera. He had no idea the game had changed. He had no idea that a piece he believed to be captured was now a player.

And she was playing to win.

CHAPTER

TWENTY-FOUR

The day began with a veneer of calm that fooled no one. Jareth moved through his routine audiences with the flawless composure of a prince, each bow and each measured word a carefully placed stone in the wall of his authority. He used the mundane rhythm of the court as camouflage, a screen behind which he could observe Silven.

The envoy's civility was a masterpiece of political theatre. His words, chosen with the precision of a master assassin, wrapped their inquiries in the silken robes of diplomacy. They moved in deliberate, concentric circles, each one brushing the borders of Miera's arrival without ever speaking her name. The game was elegant, insidious, and maddening.

The morning's suffocating pageantry bled into an afternoon of strained silence. Jareth retreated to his study, the scent of old parchment and melting beeswax from the seals on his desk a familiar, grounding presence. He did not read the reports arrayed before him on the polished blackwood. His focus was elsewhere, tuned to the silent, invisible war being waged in the corridors of his own fortress.

Reports from Rilen's informants had already confirmed his deepest anxieties. Silven's designated messenger, a man with the forgettable face of a mid-level functionary, had been sending coded letters to a contact on the coast. The timing of the dispatches corresponded with unnerving accuracy to the key moments of Miera's confinement and her re-emergence in the court. The pattern left no room for coincidence.

The confirmation brought no relief, only the cold, sharp certainty of a blade pressed against the throat. He knew the king's own spies, men loyal only to Halric's paranoia, reported every deviation from the norm. Any overt action against Silven, any move that looked less like diplomacy and more like desperation, would bring his father's full, crushing power down upon him.

The irony was a bitter acid in his gut. The very act of protecting Miera had made her a focal point. His frantic efforts had become a signal fire for his enemies to follow.

Rilen's warning from days ago echoed in the quiet study. *Control the flow of information, but guard appearances above all.* Jareth had nodded then. He had offered the placid face of a prince who understood caution. He had not obeyed. Caution was a luxury he could no longer afford. Patience was a form of suicide.

The knock on his study door was soft, a prearranged signal. Rilen entered, closing the heavy oak door behind him. The sound of the latch clicking into place was a small, final note in the oppressive quiet.

He wore his commander's uniform, the polished Vertharian steel of his gorget glinting in the low firelight. He did not speak but placed a single, folded piece of parchment on the desk. The paper was thin, the wax seal broken.

"The courier was successful," Rilen said, his voice a low murmur. "Intercepted an hour ago. It was on its way to the coast."

Jareth picked up the dispatch. It felt lighter than it should, a fragile thing to carry the weight of a kingdom. His gaze fell upon the dense block of Avenali cipher, a script designed to look like decorative scrollwork to the uninitiated. "Has it been read?"

"Enough," Rilen replied grimly. The single word carried the weight of a dozen warnings. "Our man in Silven's circle provided the key to the first block. It was all he could risk."

Jareth's eyes scanned the translated lines his cousin had scribbled on a separate slip of paper, his blood turning to ice. The message was a declaration of victory. It spoke of progress in destabilizing Vertharian court politics. And then came the line that shattered his world. *The northern asset is confirmed. Lineage as suspected.*

Northern asset. Not 'the woman'. Not 'the amnesiac'. An asset. A piece on the board. A tool to be used. *Lineage as suspected.* Cortheni. Royal. Princess Seraya. Silven did not merely suspect. He knew. He had known all along.

Jareth read the line again, and then a third time, the

words burning themselves into his mind. His last fragile shield of hope, the belief that he was still a step ahead, that he was the keeper of the secret, disintegrated. He was not the puppet master. He was the fool.

"Jareth." Rilen's voice was low, laced with alarm. "Your own counter-espionage has not gone unnoticed. My sources say the king's men are watching your every move. An overt move now..."

Jareth was no longer listening. The carefully constructed walls of his patience, his pragmatism, his princely restraint, fractured and collapsed into nothing. All that remained was a cold, white-hot fury.

He looked at the dispatch in his hand, this flimsy piece of paper that held the power to destroy her, to destroy him, to plunge two kingdoms into war. It was proof. Evidence. A truth that could be wielded like a weapon.

An image formed in his mind, sharp and unwelcome. Miera, in the archives, her head bent over old ledgers, searching for truth in paper and ink. She sought to build a reality from fragments, to reconstruct a life from scattered pieces of the past. He, on the other hand, held a truth so potent it could burn the world down. And he found he had no desire to build. Only to destroy.

With a sudden, violent motion, he strode to the hearth and thrust the dispatch into the flames. The paper caught instantly, curling into a black, brittle scroll. The ink of the Avenali cipher flared, a brief, bright green, before it was consumed. The acrid smell of burning paper and chemical ink filled the small, silent room.

"What are you doing?" Rilen demanded, his voice tight with disbelief.

"Erasing it," Jareth said. His voice was a low, dangerous thing he did not recognize as his own. He watched the last corner of the message turn to grey ash and flake away into nothing. "This war will not be fought with evidence. It will be fought with control."

He turned from the fire, his face a mask of cold purpose. He saw his own choice reflected in Rilen's shocked expression. He was rejecting his cousin's caution, his honor, his pleas for restraint. He was choosing his father's path. The thought held no horror for him now, only a grim, liberating clarity. Tyranny was a tool, and he would wield it.

"Silven has made a fatal error," Jareth continued, his voice devoid of all warmth. "He believes he is a player in this game. He is not. He is a piece. And I am removing him from the board."

He stalked back to his desk. He took up a fresh sheet of heavy Vertharian parchment and dipped his quill into the inkpot reserved for royal decrees. The scrape of the nib on the paper was the only sound in the room. He wrote quickly, his hand steady, the script precise and unforgiving. He was not drafting a suggestion. He was issuing a decree.

When he was finished, he melted a stick of black wax over the flame of a candle. The drops fell like thick, dark blood onto the folded parchment. He pressed his signet ring into the cooling wax.

Then, he held the coded orders out to Rilen. His cousin

took the letter, his gaze fixed on Jareth's face, searching for the man he had known. He would not find him. That man was gone, burned away with the Avenali dispatch.

"Leave no trace," Jareth commanded. The words were quiet, but they held the absolute weight of a death sentence. "Intercept every message, every courier, every whispered word that leaves the Avenali wing. From this moment, the envoy is blind and deaf. We control what he knows."

Rilen looked from the letter to Jareth's unreadable expression. The finality of the command hung between them like a headsman's axe. This was a point of no return, a step into a darkness from which neither of them might emerge. The order was not for containment. It was for sabotage. Total, clandestine, and absolute.

Rilen gave a single, stiff nod. It was the gesture of a soldier, not a friend. He turned and left the study, the heavy door closing with a soft, definitive thud.

Jareth stood alone in the low firelight. The faint, mineral smell of the fortress stone mingled with the ghost-scent of burned ink. He had seized control. He had become the jailer. And in his desperate, misguided love, he had just built the final wall of a prison from which there would be no escape.

TWENTY-FIVE

The morning passed under a veil of hollow pageantry, a calm routine Miera now recognized as a form of strategic warfare. The fortress hummed with a restrained energy, its courtiers drifting through the gilded halls like pieces on a chessboard, moved by unseen hands. She joined them, her expression was one of serene curiosity, the veilstone resting like a cold, polished lie against her throat.

She had become a master of listening, of collecting fragments of conversation. A remark on trade deficits, a veiled complaint about the Avenali delegation, a mention of Corthen spoken with the casual disdain of a rival. She fitted them all into the vast, intricate pattern that was re-forming in her mind. The clarity was intoxicating, a precision long denied returning to her like breath after drowning.

At midday, she made her move. She sought permission from a court steward, a man whose brow was permanently furrowed from the weight of minor crises. Her request to assist the archivists was a study in calculated innocence, a task so innocuous, so perfectly aligned with the quiet, scholarly persona she had cultivated, that it invited no questions. It was granted with a dismissive wave.

The archives' cool, dry air greeted her like an old accomplice. The scent of Vertharian preservation oils, sharp and mineral-rich, mingled with the fragrance of aging parchment and leather, a perfume that settled her thoughts. She moved carefully among the towering shelves, her hands steady as she reviewed faded bindings and cracked wax seals. The act of creating order was a counterpoint to the chaos churning within her. The calm she projected was no longer a gift from the pendant. It was a remembered discipline, a weapon she was re-learning how to wield.

Her search was not random. The vision from the other night, the map room and her own voice giving commands, had provided a key. The Redmere Accords. She had been studying the political fallout of that treaty. It was a starting point, a thread to pull. She located the section, a shadowed alcove far from the main reading room where the light from the high arched windows barely reached.

The archive's organization revealed its purpose. This room was not merely a repository of Vertharian records, but a trophy room. Captured documents from a dozen conquered territories lined the shelves, seized correspondence and stolen treaties displayed like hunting kills mounted on a wall.

Of course. Halric would keep evidence of his enemies' secrets here, under his son's nose, a constant reminder of Verthar's reach and Corthen's humiliation. If any record of Corthen's royal correspondence existed in this fortress, it would be here on display.

A conqueror's pride. The realization was both useful and enraging. Her kingdom's secrets, her own handwriting perhaps, preserved not for their intelligence value but as trophies of subjugation.

The Vertharian archival system was obsessively organized by the reign of each king, a catalog of conquests and decrees. Any foreign document would be an anomaly. She began her work. Her fingers, light and sure, traced the faded gold leaf on the heavy leather bindings. Her heart beat a slow, steady rhythm against her ribs, the cadence of a soldier before a battle, not a victim facing her past.

Her breath stilled when her fingers brushed against it. The ledger was thicker than the others, its binding a darker, unfamiliar hide. It was not the stamped Vertharian leather but a finer grain, a Cortheni shadow-hide that was smoother and cooler to the touch.

A cascade of memory, sharp and overwhelming, broke against the walls of her mind. A negotiation table of polished blackwood. The low murmur of voices speaking in the fluid, lyrical cadence of her mother tongue. The distinct weight of a heavy silk gown on her shoulders, the scent of Moonlace woven into her hair.

She pulled the ledger from the shelf. Its weight was a solid, grounding reality. She carried it to a secluded reading nook where a thin beam of sunlight cut through the gloom, illuminating motes of floating particulate. Her hands were steady as she opened the cover. The pages were filled with records of diplomatic correspondence, trade concessions, and border demarcations related to the treaty, all in the precise, angular script of a Vertharian scribe.

Then she found it, tucked between two pages of tariff schedules like a pressed flower. A letter. The parchment was finer, a creamy vellum distinct from the rougher Vertharian stock. The handwriting was not the script of the archivists.

It was a fluid, elegant cursive that she knew, with a bone-deep certainty, to be her own. The ink, a deep shade of Cortheni blue, had a faint metallic sheen unique to the mineral pigments used by the royal scribes of Mirenweald.

As her eyes scanned the familiar loops and flourishes, a low hum started in her ears. The vibration traveled up from the pendant at her throat. The veilstone. It had sensed her transgression. The hum deepened, becoming a physical thrum against her skin, and the air around her seemed to thicken, to shimmer with a faint, oily distortion.

The words on the page began to blur. The ink seemed to bleed and waver as if submerged in water. A wave of vertigo washed over her, a nauseating lurch that threatened to pull her under a current of placid ignorance. The pendant was not just suppressing memory. It was actively fighting her, a magical jailer determined to keep her locked in this cage of forgetting.

She gasped, her fingers whitening as she gripped the

edge of the heavy oak table. No. The word was a silent snarl in her mind, a rebellion that tightened every muscle in her body. She would not be pulled under. She would not be erased.

Planting her hand flat on the cool wood, she anchored herself, forcing her will against the disorienting magic. The hum intensified, a piercing whine in her skull that made her teeth ache, but she held fast. It was a battle of attrition, her own awakening identity against the enchantment that sought to smother it.

Her vision swam, the dark wood grain of the table wavering before her. She was a fortress under siege, and the enemy was a part of her own adornment.

She forced her focus onto a single line near the bottom of the page, a closing signature beneath a formal valediction. The letters broke apart and reformed into meaningless shapes. She held her breath tight in her chest, pouring every ounce of her concentration into that one single act of seeing. She would break the spell or it would break her. The world narrowed to the small patch of vellum, the space between her and the truth.

And then, for a heart-stopping second, the magic faltered. The oily shimmer in the air dissipated. The whine in her skull ceased. The words snapped into perfect, terrifying focus.

Your servant in this, and all thing,
Seraya, Crown Princess of Corthen.
Seraya.

The name detonated in the quiet of her mind. It shattered the last vestiges of the woman called Miera. She was Seraya.

She was the woman in the vision, the commander, the strategist. Mor than just a woman, she was a princess. The truth was so immense, so absolute, it left no room for anything else. The forgery of Miera crumbled into ash.

The hum from the veilstone ceased abruptly. Its magic retreated as if in defeat, leaving a void of profound silence. But the silence was broken by a new, more immediate threat.

Footsteps. A slow, rhythmic scrape of leather on stone, echoing from the main corridor. They were drawing closer.

The archivist.

Panic, cold and sharp, seized her. To be found here with this ledger, with this proof, would be a death sentence. But then another instinct, older and far more powerful, rose to meet the fear. Composure.

It was a familiar cloak, a practiced stillness she had worn in other courts, before other enemies. It was the muscle memory of a stateswoman, a spymistress, who knew that the most dangerous thing one could ever show an opponent was fear.

With a hand that did not tremble, she gently closed the heavy ledger. The sound was a soft, definitive thud in the silent room. She slid it back into its exact place on the shelf, her movements fluid and unhurried, leaving no sign of its disturbance.

Seraya took a slow, deliberate breath, smoothing the front of her gown. She composed her face into a mask of placid inquiry, the Miera mask, and turned to face the threat.

The shadow of the archivist, the young, earnest Elian, fell across the entrance to the alcove. He peered into the gloom, his brow furrowed with a mild, proprietary concern. He was newly appointed to this post, eager to prove his diligence to his masters. Such men were often the most dangerous.

"My lady? Are you finding what you need?"

She turned fully toward him, a faint, polite smile gracing her lips. The Miera smile. Gentle. Harmless. A weapon of misdirection. "I was just admiring the binding on this volume," she said, her voice soft and even.

She indicated a book of Vertharian poetry on an adjacent shelf, one she had noticed earlier. "It is remarkable work. But I fear the verses within are a bit too martial for my tastes today. All steel and conquest, with very little nuance."

Elian's face cleared. Her disarming calm, her gentle critique, dissolved his suspicion. He was looking at Miera, the quiet guest, the harmless scholar whose fragility was a known quantity in the fortress. He had no idea he was standing before the Grand Spymistress of Corthen, a woman who had just armed herself with the truth. He saw a dove, not the hawk whose sigil now burned behind her eyes.

"As you say, my lady," he mumbled, already backing away, his duty performed and his curiosity satisfied. He was eager to return to his ledgers and his quiet, ordered world.

She gave a small, graceful nod and moved past him, stepping out of the shadows and back into the main hall of the archive. The light seemed brighter here, the air thinner. She felt the cold, familiar weight of the veilstone against her skin, a constant reminder of the cage she inhabited. It was inert now, a defeated sentinel.

Everything had changed. The arena was the same, but she finally knew her place in it. The man who had presented himself as her savior was her jailer. The peace he had offered her was a meticulously crafted prison.

She walked with measured grace toward the corridor, her expression a perfect mask of serenity, but her mind was a blade being sharpened on the stone of his betrayal.

The question was no longer who she was. She knew who she was. The question, now, was what he was so terrified of her remembering.

CHAPTER

TWENTY-SIX

The day unfolded with the mechanical precision of a clockwork deception. Jareth attended the morning briefings, his posture an exercise in princely authority, his face a mask of placid command. He signed decrees with a steady hand.

Silven Drael's probing questions had ceased. The subtle provocations, the elegant verbal traps laid at every meal, had vanished. This absence was more threatening than any open confrontation.

It was the stillness of a predator gathering itself to strike, the profound quiet of a forest just before the wolf lunges from the trees. Every polite nod from the Avenali delegation now seemed a mockery, every moment of peace a carefully measured pause in a game of anni-hilation.

He spent the afternoon weaving a web of clandestine orders, each instruction a silken thread layered over the next until the pattern became invisible. He moved through intermediaries, his commands fractured and encoded using a book cipher keyed to *The Book of Virtue*, a text so common in the hold as to be beneath notice.

Even Rilen, his most trusted confidant, received only fragments of the whole design. Monitor every move. Restrict all access for coastal couriers. Report any attempt by the Avenali delegation to leave the hold without authorization. He was building a cage of information, convinced that absolute control was the only path to safety.

Yet the harder he worked to impose his will, the more the fortress itself seemed to resist him. A palpable tension had taken root in Durevin Hold, a subtle poison in the air. The servants moved with a new and unsettling caution. Their steps were too quick on the stone floors, their eyes too careful, never quite meeting his.

Whispers died in the corridors as he approached, leaving a wake of watchful silence that felt more damning than any accusation. He was the prince, the heir, the center of power in this fortress of stone and steel, and yet he felt like a ghost haunting his own halls. He was being watched. The certainty that his control was a fragile architecture of lies grew stronger with every passing hour.

This spiraling disquiet sharpened to a fine point at the royal supper. The Great Hall was a familiar tapestry of gilt and torchlight, the banners of his house hanging like silent sentinels between carved pillars. The air hung heavy with the scents of roasted quail and spiced wine. He took his seat at the high table, a long, imposing slab carved from a single petrified ironwood trunk. His movements were measured, his gaze sweeping the room as a general surveys a battlefield.

And then he saw her. Miera.

She sat among the ladies of the court, a picture of serene composure. Her posture was flawless. Her hands rested quietly in her lap. She did not glance his way, her attention seemingly fixed on the court musician plucking a soft, melancholic melody from a harp. It was the *Lament for the Lost*, a traditional Vertharian piece about a love severed by war. But her calm was wrong. It was too absolute, too perfect.

It was not the soft, pliant peace induced by the veilstone, a state he had come to know with an unsettling intimacy. That was a buffered quiet, an emotional landscape muted and gently blurred. This was something else entirely.

This was the disciplined stillness of a soldier on watch, the placid surface of a frozen lake concealing unknown depths and dangerous currents. It was a performance. A disguise. And for the first time, he could not see what lay beneath it.

The realization was a shard of ice lodging in his gut. He had lost his primary means of control, his anchor for her mind. The tranquility she felt was no longer his to give or to take. It was her own.

After the meal, he could not bring himself to seek her out. The thought of facing that unreadable calm was more terrifying than a confrontation with his father. He retreated to his study, the one place where he still felt a semblance of command.

He waved away the servants, refusing the offer of candles, and let the darkness settle around him like a shroud. In the shadows, he could pretend he was still the master of this game. He could pretend the most dangerous element in his careful arrangement had begun moving of its own accord.

He knew what he should do. He knew what a prudent ruler would do. He should distance himself from her. He should create a space between them that would starve the court's suspicions and render her less of a target. It was the correct, selfless action, the move a king would make to protect a valuable asset, even at personal cost.

But the thought of it was a physical agony, a betrayal of an oath he had only ever made to himself. His protective instincts had curdled into something darker, something possessive and consuming. She was his secret, his vulnerability, his to guard. The idea of letting her drift even an inch from his influence was intolerable.

He pulled a heavy, leather-bound ledger toward him, a dry report on Verthar's agricultural policy he had been meant to review. He had not read a word of it during the council meeting. He had been too consumed with her, with watching her, with dissecting the quiet armor of her composure.

He dipped his quill in ink, the scratch on the parchment unnaturally loud in the silent room. He should have been making notes on grain tithes and borderland tariffs.

Instead, his hand moved with a will of its own in the margins. He sketched a crude, hurried map. It was a map of the stone corridors and hidden stairwells that connected his study to her chambers. The lines were sharp, obsessive, the ink a dark stain on the page. It was the work of a jailer, not a prince.

He slammed the ledger shut, the sound a dull thud in the oppressive dark. A wave of self-loathing washed over him, cold and bitter. He was becoming his father, seeing people only as pieces to be controlled, vulnerabilities to be exploited. But the thought no longer held its familiar horror. It felt, instead, like a grim capitulation. A surrender to the inevitable.

He pushed the ledger aside and drew a fresh sheet of parchment. He would not surrender to this weakness. He would master it. He would master her. He would double down, intensify his efforts, and regain control of the board.

He began to draft a new set of coded orders for Rilen's agents, the men he called his Iron Watch. His script was sharp, aggressive, the quill digging into the paper. They would not just monitor the Avenali. They would infiltrate their delegation.

He worked for hours in the suffocating darkness, his world shrinking to the scratch of his quill and the frantic, looping maze of his own thoughts. The fortress was silent around him, a sleeping beast that held his entire world in its stone belly. He had built a prison of lies to keep her safe, and now he found himself trapped within its walls, his every move watched, his authority a hollow echo against the stone.

He finished the last order and reached for the stick of black wax. As he held it to the candle flame, watching it melt and drip like thick, dark blood onto the parchment, a chilling certainty rooted itself in his mind.

The critical shift, the source of this suffocating tension, was not external. It was not Silven's games. It was not his father's threats. It was her. The disguise of tranquility she wore was not a mask to fool the court. It was a wall built against him.

The change was not in his enemies. It was in her. Miera was remembering. And the silence he had so carefully engineered to save her was about to become their tomb.

TWENTY-SEVEN

The morning dawned clear and bitterly cold. It was a Vertharian cold, one that seeped into the iron-veined granite of the fortress and clung to the air like a shroud. To Miera, it had once felt like a fact of the climate. To Seraya, it felt like a strategic asset, a natural defense that bred a certain hardness in its people.

She now moved through Durevin Hold with a purpose that was entirely her own, a ghost wearing a familiar face. The fortress hummed with a restrained, nervous energy. Its courtiers drifted through the high arched corridors like chess pieces moved by an unsteady hand. She joined their silent game, her expression a mask of serene curiosity, the veilstone resting like a polished, cold lie against her throat.

She was no longer a guest. She was an operative. Her mind, once a foggy landscape of confusion, was now a finely tuned instrument of analysis. She listened not with the gentle interest of a recuperating ward but with the sharp, discerning ear of a spymistress.

She collected fragments of conversation, slivers of data dropped like coins in the cavernous halls. Two lords from the eastern provinces spoke of tariffs on ironwood, their voices low, their postures defensive. They feared King Halric's new levies were a precursor to appropriation.

A lady in waiting whispered to her companion about the Avenali delegation, her words laced with the cloying scent of a cheap perfume meant to mimic a Cortheni original. The imitation was as clumsy as her gossip.

The information flowed into her, where it was sorted, cross referenced, and filed away in the neat, ordered compartments of her reawoken mind. The clarity was intoxicating. It was a precision long denied, returning to her like breath after drowning.

But her preternatural calm, once a source of comfort to the court, had become a source of scrutiny. Her silence was no longer seen as the gentle reserve of a fragile guest. It was now perceived as something else, something watchful.

She saw it in the way eyes tracked her and then darted away, in the way conversations would pause for a breath when she entered a room. She was no longer just Miera, the prince's mysterious ward. She was an unknown variable in a fortress on the edge of a blade.

The test came in the grand gallery, beneath a tapestry depicting a Vertharian victory over a forgotten border skirmish. The Vertharian falcons were rendered in bold, triumphant crimson, while the defeated Cortheni sigils were small, almost an afterthought in muted silver thread.

Lady Elara, a woman whose quiet demeanor belied her position as a known confidante of the king's war council, approached her. Her gown was a severe cut of dark velvet. Her expression was one of polite, probing interest.

"Lady Miera," she began, her voice smooth. "You have become a regular fixture in the public archives. It is admirable to see such a devotion to our kingdom's history."

The question was a dart wrapped in velvet but aimed at a vital organ. Seraya's heart gave a single, hard thump against her ribs, a traitorous signal no one else could perceive. Her expression did not waver.

The smile she offered was gentle. "I find the old stories help quiet my thoughts, my lady. A welcome distraction."

"Indeed," Lady Elara pressed, her eyes sharp, missing nothing. "And what part of our history have you found so distracting? The trade ledgers? The border treaties?"

The lie came to her lips with a speed and ease that was frightening. It was not a fumbled deception born of panic. It was a seamless execution, a tool she remembered how to wield. This was a classic Cortheni deflection, a technique known as the 'Hollow Lure,' offering an opponent something so perfectly in character that they would not think to look beneath it.

"Oh, nothing so dry, I assure you," Seraya said, her tone light, almost apologetic. She gave a small, self-deprecating laugh. "I was only seeking poetry. The ballads of the First Dynasty. I find their romanticism a comfort, though I confess I spend more time searching than reading."

The lie was perfect. It played on the court's perception of her as a gentle, slightly melancholic soul, a woman who would naturally seek solace in art, not intelligence. She saw the tension in Lady Elara's shoulders ease, the sharp glint in her eyes softening to mere curiosity. The woman had been fishing, and Seraya had offered her a beautiful, empty shell.

"Of course," Lady Elara said, a dismissive note entering her voice. She had lost interest. Poetry was of no strategic value. "A noble pursuit." She gave a curt nod and moved on, her dark velvet gown whispering over the polished stone floor.

Seraya stood for a moment, the echo of her own voice in her ears. The skill had returned so naturally, so completely, that it terrified her. This was who she was. Not just a princess. Not just a strategist.

She was a weapon forged in the elegant, brutal courts of Corthen, a place where a lie was a key, a shield, and sometimes, a blade. Alone, with the weight of her successful deception settling upon her, she refined the mental map of her prison.

Silven Drael, the elegant Avenali, was the provocateur, a man sent to light a fire and watch what scurried from the smoke. King Halric was the predator, circling, waiting for any sign of weakness to justify a killing blow. And Jareth.

The thought of him was a physical ache, a deep, wounding throb beneath her ribs. He was the man in the middle, the complicit keeper of secrets. He was not merely her protector. He was her jailer. He had built her cage, furnished it with kindness, and locked the door with a kiss. He stood between her and the other predators, not to save her, but to keep her as his own.

She saw him now as he truly was, a man guarding a secret he could not confess. The knowledge that she had loved him, that some broken part of her still did, was a pain sharper than any blade. The peace of ignorance was gone, replaced by the cold, clear agony of betrayal.

As dusk settled over the fortress, casting long, geometric shadows across the courtyards, she sought the high ramparts. The wind was a physical force here, cold and relentless, whipping strands of dark hair across her face. It smelled of snow from the high peaks and the faint, mineral scent of the stone itself.

From this height, she could see the fortress's strategic layout, the kill zones below the walls, the sightlines from the towers. Her mind cataloged it all without command. Below, the fortress glittered with torchlight, a perfect pattern of order masking the chaos that seethed within.

Recovery was not enough. Remembering was not enough. She had to act.

She would use the court's own curiosity as her cover. She would investigate Jareth himself. She would discover precisely what he was hiding, what he was so afraid of her remembering, and she would use that truth to reclaim her life.

She turned back toward the dark maw of the stairwell, her decision a solid weight within her. As she moved, she felt a faint, unstable pulse against her skin. The veilstone. Its gentle, rhythmic glow was gone, replaced by a fitful, inconstant light, like a heartbeat caught between obedience and awakening.

The magic was fighting her, but it was a battle it was now losing. She was no longer a prisoner of its calm. She was the mistress of her own mind, and she was preparing for war.

TWENTY-EIGHT

The morning unfolded in a pageant of managed tension. Courtiers moved through the halls with the subdued grace of shadows, their voices a low current that never rose above a murmur. Servants hurried through their duties, their gazes fixed on the stone floors, their movements too sharp, their efficiency brittle.

Every conversation seemed to halt when Jareth entered a room, the ensuing silence a heavier thing than any word spoken. Durevin Hold, his fortress, his inheritance, had become a sealed chamber of secrets, and he was the hollow man at its center, projecting a calm he did not possess.

His day was a meticulous performance. He began by inspecting the guard posts along the inner wall, his expression a mask of impassive authority. The men wore Verthar's black armor, the polished steel gorgets bearing the embossed sigil of the falcon. He spoke to the captain in a tone of cool command, his questions about patrol rotations and watchwords precise, routine.

Yet his mind was not on the answers. It was on the gaps between them, the tiny hesitations, the flicker of an eye that might betray a lie. He was testing the integrity of his own walls, consumed by a suspicion that felt like a slow poison in his blood.

Later, in the king's council, he endured his father's open impatience. Halric's temper was a sharp, cold instrument, and he made no secret of his displeasure. The lingering Avenali delegation, the unrest they seemed to seed with their very presence, grated on the king's nerves. He demanded visible progress, a resolution Jareth could not deliver. Halric sat at the head of the table, his heavy dragon signet ring tapping a sharp, predatory rhythm against the wood, a sound like a headsman testing his block.

Jareth deflected with rehearsed ease. His words were a polished shield of diplomacy and strategic patience, speaking of ongoing negotiations and the need for restraint. He concealed how much ground he had already lost, how Silven played him with smiles and courtesies while his own agents worked in the shadows.

He felt his father's eyes on him, cold and calculating, a predator testing the strength of its kin before deciding whether to support it or devour it. The entire council watched, their faces unreadable stone. Jareth knew he was being judged not merely as a prince, but as a future king. He held his ground, the very picture of a leader in unshakable command.

His intelligence network, however, told a different story. The web of agents he had deployed through Durevin Hold was proving porous. Reports arrived throughout the afternoon on thin scrolls of rice paper sealed with grey wax, the mark of his private network. Each was a small, sharp failure.

They had intercepted another of Silven's communiqués to the coast, a mundane message about grain shipments. Yet two other messages, dispatched at the same time, had slipped through their net. Their absence was a screaming void. He knew the Avenali doctrine. Their emissaries were not mere diplomats. They were gardeners tending to seeds of treason planted a generation ago, and Silven Drael, the Gilded Viper, was here for the harvest. The emissary had increased his contact with lesser ministers, using the unimpeachable cover of diplomatic courtesy to conduct his work in plain sight. Jareth's plan to contain the man had only partially succeeded. He was holding back a tide with a sieve.

The facade finally shattered in the late afternoon, not with a roar, but with the quiet arrival of his cousin. Rilen entered the study, his usual composure fractured. His polished officer's uniform seemed to hang on him, its weight suddenly too much. He closed the door, his movements stiff.

"The reports are confirmed," Rilen said, his voice low. He held out a folded parchment. The contents were a death knell to Jareth's fragile sense of control. "It is not just rumor. Three scullery maids from the lower kitchens.

A stable hand. Two attendants from the guest wing. They have vanished."

Jareth took the report, but he did not need to read the neat script. He knew what it would say. Vanished without authorization, without a word, their few belongings left behind. This was not the desertion of disgruntled servants. This was an extraction. It was a physical infiltration of the fortress, a violation of his innermost sanctum.

The news was a shard of ice in his gut. His paranoia had been focused outward, on Silven, on his father, on the enemy at the gates. He had been so consumed with watching them that he had failed to watch his own house. A breach of this nature could only happen with assistance from within, from someone inside his own security structure. A traitor.

"It is tied to her, is it not?" Rilen's voice was barely a whisper, a question that was also an accusation.

Jareth's gaze snapped up, his control splintering. "Do not say her name." The words were sharper than he intended, a guttural command born of pure terror. In that instant, his fear was not for the kingdom, not for his own power, but for her. He saw it all in a sickening, blinding flash.

The servants were not random. The guest wing. The kitchens she sometimes visited to escape the confines of her chamber. The stable hand who cared for the placid mare she liked to watch in the yard. These were not just missing workers. They were potential witnesses.

People who had seen the mysterious Lady Miera, who might have heard her speak, who could describe her face to the wrong ears. Someone was not just probing his secrets. They were methodically erasing any trace of her existence.

This was Silven's work. He was certain of it. The Avenali spymaster was not just gathering intelligence. He was clearing the board.

The guilt that had been a constant, smoldering coal in his gut did not vanish. It was forged into something new. A cold, grim certainty of purpose. The shame of his lies evaporated, leaving only the hard calculus of duty. A weapon.

He had hoped to be a better man than his father, a ruler who led with something other than fear. He saw now what a fool's errand that had been. Mercy was a currency for peacetime. In this world, control was the only scepter that kept you alive.

He walked past Rilen, his stride measured, his purpose now horribly clear. He would find the leak. He would find the traitor. And he would purge them from his fortress with a ruthlessness that would make his father proud.

By evening, Durevin Hold felt like a sealed tomb. Jareth walked through the great hall, his presence a cold weight that silenced all who saw him. He moved with the composure of a commander in absolute control, though internally he felt the slow, terrifying fracture of all certainty. He was a king in a kingdom of whispers, a warden in a prison whose walls were turning to smoke.

He paused near the central hearth, the firelight painting his impassive face in hues of orange and deep shadow. In the oppressive quiet, a sound echoed from high overhead. A sharp, violent report, as if a massive stone in the vaulted ceiling had split under an unbearable weight.

Every head in the hall turned upward. A collective gasp was swallowed by a silence so profound, so absolute, it felt as if the very fortress had held its breath. Specks of mortar drifted down through the torchlight from the high, dark rafters. The sound passed. Nothing fell. But the unnatural hush that followed was worse than the noise. It was the silence of listening.

Jareth's gaze did not waver from the shadows pooling at the far end of the hall. He had built his fortress of lies to protect her, but the walls were now compromised. The enemy was inside.

He turned and strode toward his study, the echo of his boots on the polished black marble the only sound in the cavernous space. He would review every report, every guard rotation, every name. He would trust no one. Rilen's loyalty, his father's authority, the court's obedience, all of it was now suspect.

He closed the heavy oak door of his study behind him, the suffocating silence pressing in. He stood in the darkness, surrounded by his maps of a fortress he no longer trusted, of a kingdom he was failing to hold.

The true threat was not Silven's cunning or his father's wrath. It was not the enemy at the gates. It was the one who had opened the door for them. The one who had stood beside him, who had taken his orders, who had offered counsel. The real danger was the one wearing the face of a friend.

TWENTY-NINE

The tension within Durevin Hold had ceased to be a rumor whispered in shadowed alcoves. It had acquired a physical weight, a pressure that settled in the cold, still air of the fortress. Guards now stood posted at every junction of the stone corridors, their movements stiff, their purpose absolute.

Their patrols were doubled, and their silence was the profound quiet of a secret being contained, the discipline of a court disguising its own rot.

Miera sensed the shift not with the vague anxiety of a sheltered guest but with the sharp, analytical precision of a predator. The fear was a tapestry of carefully woven threads, and she recognized the loom. She had seen this before. In another life, she had managed this exact strain of unease.

She moved through the brittle atmosphere, her own composure a flawless reflection of the court's pretense.

The formal niceties exchanged in the galleries had turned sharp, their edges honed enough to draw blood.

A courtier's smile, once merely a polite gesture, was now a strained performance that never reached the eyes. The Avenali envoy, Silven Drael, still moved through the court with his practiced grace, but the mirth in his gaze was gone. It was replaced by the flat, empty watchfulness of a player who knows the game has entered its final, bloody stage.

The servants' murmurs were a constant, low hum beneath the fortress's formal life. They spoke of missing workers, of scullery maids and stable hands who had vanished without a trace. They spoke of the western gates being sealed after dusk, of a sudden curfew they called the Crimson Gate, a protocol she felt she should know. That brand of fear felt intimately familiar.

In another palace, she had wielded such rumors herself, containing them with silence, enforcing order with a discipline disguised as calm. The recognition was not abstract knowledge from a book. It was instinct. It was muscle memory.

That night, in the profound, waiting quiet of her chamber, she made a choice. For days she had treated the veilstone as an experiment, a thing to be tested and observed. Now, she saw it for what it truly was. It was a leash.

The false safety of ignorance was a cage, and she would no longer be its willing prisoner. She intended to reclaim her identity, not in the fragments she had been granted, but as a whole.

She walked to the narrow ebonized writing desk, its polished surface reflecting the low firelight like a dark, still pool. The air in the room felt heavy, charged, as if waiting for a command. She raised her hands to her throat and removed the veilstone.

The fine silver chain was cold against her fingers, the pendant itself colder still, its metallic scent sharp in the contained air. She did not set it down. She held it, a deliberate invitation to the chaos she knew would come. She was unbinding her own mind.

The effect was not a gentle tide but a deluge. The first crash was a flood of sensation, a disorienting rush of sounds and scents that had no place in this stone room.

The lilting cadence of the Cortheni court tongue, her own voice a current among the whispers. The mineral smell of wet stone after a rainstorm on the coast. The crisp, papery scent of ciphered letters, their ink still fresh on near-translucent rice paper.

Then came the images, a storm of them, sharp and overwhelming. A hidden compartment in a wall, its mechanism released by a sequence of pressure points her fingers still knew by heart. Her own hands, gloved in soft, sound-proofed leather, marking a map with coded symbols.

A line of loyal agents, their faces a blur of dedication, swearing an oath not to a king, but to her. The weight of her station, her duty, her secrets, crashed down upon her. She was the Grand Spymistress of Corthen. She was the shadow behind the Veiled Council.

The flood of memory did not bring instant clarity. It brought chaos. A decade of training, of secrets, of carefully constructed networks and contingency plans, all crashed into the woman who had been Miera. For a long moment, she could not move. Could not think. The two identities warred within her, the trusting woman who had loved a prince and the ruthless spymistress who had commanded shadows, each demanding primacy.

Miera recoiled from the cold calculations now filling her mind—the tactical assessment of exits, the cataloging of potential weapons, the immediate suspicion of everyone she had trusted. Seraya dismissed the softness as weakness, a vulnerability that had nearly destroyed her. Then, slowly, the self buried deep inside her asserted dominance. Not because it was stronger, but because it had been built for exactly this—for surviving the unsurvivable.

The Night Veil had trained her to function through shock, through pain, through betrayal. Miera had never learned such armor. And so Miera retreated into some quiet corner of her consciousness, and the Spymistress rose from the ashes of her own making. Her name. Seraya. It was not a whisper this time. It was a shout, a command, a truth that could no longer be denied. She gripped the edge of the desk, her knuckles white, her body trembling as the aftershocks of memory rolled through her.

When the maelstrom subsided, it left her breathless and shaken on the cold floor. Her first instinct was not fear or panic. It was caution. This was the psychological conditioning of her training, reasserting itself with absolute authority.

Her calm, she now understood with perfect clarity, had never been a gift from the veilstone. It was a skill. It was her own conditioning, a habit of composure forged under pressures far greater than this. The pendant had only enforced a state of unnatural, placid forgetfulness. It had not given her peace. It had stolen her mind.

Slowly, she rose to her feet. Her movements were steady, deliberate. She opened the top drawer of the writing desk, the scent of old wood and dried ink a comforting anchor in the storm of her thoughts. As her fingers brushed the interior, they traced a nearly invisible seam along the bottom panel.

An instinct, sharp and certain, told her that a precise pressure near the back corner would release a false bottom. The knowledge was another piece of herself slotting back into place. She looked at the veilstone one last time. It lay inert in her palm, its light extinguished. It was a beautiful, dangerous lie.

She placed it inside the drawer, next to the small stack of ciphered notes she had been compiling, and closed it. The click of the drawer settling into its frame was a sound of finality. A threshold had been crossed.

The air in the chamber felt lighter, the oppressive weight of the magic finally lifted. But beneath that newfound relief, a hollow emptiness hummed, a pulse waiting for a purpose to return. She was free, but she was also exposed.

She stood in the center of the room and took a slow, calming breath. Her mind was already shifting from victim to strategist. Jareth. His protection had been a prison. His kindness, a tool of suppression.

The spymistress in her had already begun cataloging assets, her training asserting itself with cold, mechanical precision. The servant passages she had mapped during her months of apparent docility—those would serve her now. The guard rotation she had unconsciously memorized, the patrol gaps she had noted without understanding why.

Seraya realized that every observation had been preparation for exactly this moment. She would need provisions: the kitchens kept hard cheese and dried meat in the cold larder, accessible through the servants' corridor behind the great hall. She would need a weapon: the dinner service included small paring knives, easily palmed by someone trained in sleight of hand.

She would need an exit: the eastern postern gate, the one used for refuse removal, was guarded by only two men during the dinner hour when the garrison ate in shifts. And she would need a distraction—something to draw attention inward while she slipped outward. The chaos in the council chamber had provided that, greater than anything she could have conjured herself. The fortress was in disarray, guards rushing to secure the king, courtiers fleeing in panic. Now she simply had to move before order reasserted itself.

The trust she had placed in Jareth, the intimacy they

had shared, it had all been built upon lies. The knowledge should have ignited a fire of rage, but instead it left a cold, hollow ache. The fracture of her trust was not a jagged tear but a clean, deep wound, and she knew it would never fully heal.

She would not confront him. Not yet. A direct accusation was a clumsy tool, a cudgel for a tavern brawler. She was a woman of precision. She would gather proof.

She would uncover the full scope of her mission, the reason for the ambush, the identity of the traitors within her own network. She would operate from within the heart of the enemy fortress, using their perception of her as the fragile, amnesiac Miera as her shield. The court was a stage, and she would play her part to perfection.

A sound in the corridor broke through her thoughts. It was not the heavy, rhythmic tread of a guard patrol, the sound of studded boots on stone. This was a softer sound, a lighter tread, something altogether furtive.

Her body went still. Every sense sharpened to a razor's edge. She did not move toward the door. She did not breathe. She simply listened, her training a second skin. The footsteps paused directly outside her chamber.

A moment of absolute, listening silence followed. She imagined someone on the other side, their head tilted, their ear perhaps pressed against the thick oak. She could not tell if it was chance or a deliberate, chilling observation.

Then, as quietly as they had come, the footsteps faded, moving away down the hall.

She let out the breath she had been holding. Her awakening had not gone unnoticed. She was being watched. The knowledge did make her fearful. Instead, it ignited a bright flame of focus. Her enemies thought she was a pawn, a broken piece to be manipulated on their board. They had no idea she had just remembered all the rules of the game. And she was a master.

CHAPTER

THIRTY

The day began under a shroud of strained ceremony. A brittle, formal calm had settled over Durevin Hold, the sort of quiet that follows a scream. Jareth moved through it as a player moves across a board, each action a calculated performance of command. He knew he was being watched.

He felt the weight of his father's scrutiny, the analytical gaze of the Avenali envoy, and the collective stare of the entire court. They saw a prince, a commander, a bastion of Vertharian certainty. They did not see the man whose foundations were fracturing, whose fortress of lies was poised to be swept away by a tide he could no longer command.

The air in his study was thick with the scent of old parchment and the metallic tang of his own fear. Rilen stood before him, the report held loosely in his hand, a confirmation of the disaster Jareth had tried so desperately to prevent. The fortress had been breached.

Servants had vanished, witnesses methodically erased. It was an act of infiltration so clean, so precise, it could only be the work of a master. The quiet efficiency of it mocked Jareth's own strategy of containment, revealing it as the hollow fortress it had always been.

"The names have been noted," Rilen said, his voice stripped of the warmth Jareth usually relied upon. "The families..."

Jareth cut him off, his gaze fixed on the frost that feathered the windowpane. "And their families?" he asked. The question was quiet, almost lost in the oppressive stillness of the room. "See they are provided for. Without question and without record." It was a flash of the ruler he had once hoped to be, a man who remembered that the small folk paid the highest price for the games of kings. A brief, useless gesture of compassion in a world rapidly running out of it.

Rilen gave a single, sharp nod. "Of course, my prince."

The midday audience was a pageant of ghosts. Courtiers assembled in the great hall, their faces pale masks of deference, their whispers dying the moment Jareth entered. The floor of polished Obsidian Vein marble, gleaming with beeswax, reflected their strained, hollow formality.

Jareth took his place at the foot of his father's throne, his posture rigid, his gaze sweeping over the silent assembly. He noted every glance, every half-whisper, each one more cautious than the last. The absence of the lower attendants was a palpable void, a question no one dared to ask aloud.

He had tightened the guard rotations, masking the order as routine protocol for the audience. He had even posted sentries from his own Wolfguard at the minor entrances to the hall, an uncommon precaution. Yet the effort felt like holding back a flood with his hands. He felt Silven Drael's presence before he saw him.

The Avenali envoy entered the hall not with the arrogance of a conqueror, but with the serene, unassailable confidence of a man who had already won. His smile was impeccably courteous, his words to the king flawless gems of diplomacy. Beneath them, however, hummed a quiet, triumphant power.

Jareth's strategy had been a fool's errand. Silven had never intended to be contained. He had used Jareth's caution as a smokescreen, gathering his intelligence, activating his network, and preparing for this very moment.

The envoy's questions in the past had not been attempts to learn. They had been provocations, tests to measure the depth of Jareth's deception. And now, the final move was on the board.

Silven concluded his formal address to the throne with a slight bow. Then, with a theatrical slowness that drew every eye in the hall, he produced a document. It was a single sheet of stark white Avenali parchment, folded and sealed with an unbroken stamp of crimson wax that bore the mark of the Gilded Ring. It was not a formal communiqué. It was a weapon.

"A small matter of correspondence, Your Majesty," Silven said, his voice carrying easily through the cavernous, silent hall. "A point of confusion I felt was best clarified by you directly."

The silent act of defiance was masterful. It bypassed Jareth's authority completely, dismissing him as an irrelevant obstacle. It forced the crisis into the open, directly at the feet of the one man Jareth could not control. King Halric's gaze, cold and sharp as a shard of obsidian, moved to his son for a single, terrible second.

Jareth stood trapped, a prisoner of his own making, as his father extended a hand gloved in black wyvern hide. The sound of the king breaking the crimson wax seal was a sharp, violent crack that echoed in the profound stillness. The entire court held its breath. Jareth watched his father's eyes scan the letter, the muscles in his jaw tightening into ridges of stone.

In that deafening silence, Jareth felt it.

It began as a vibration, a deep, low-frequency pulse that traveled up through the soles of his boots. It was a thrum, rhythmic and unnatural, a beat that seemed to emanate from the very heart of the fortress.

The political threat from Silven, his father's cold fury, and this inexplicable, rising magical disturbance were all twisting together. They were forming a single, unstoppable catastrophe.

King Halric folded the letter, his movements precise and deliberate. The silence that followed was heavy, deliberate, and terrifying. When he finally spoke, his voice was a blade of ice, carrying no trace of emotion, only the unassailable weight of decree.

"Prince Jareth."

Jareth stepped forward, his heart a hammer against his ribs. "Father."

"You will meet with the envoy Drael. Privately," the king commanded. "And you will resolve this... matter of correspondence. Before nightfall."

It felt like a loyalty test, delivered on a public stage for the entire court to witness. He was being ordered to clean up a mess his father now knew he had made. Jareth bowed, the movement stiff, his mind racing. "It will be done."

As the courtiers dispersed, their relief a palpable rush of sound and movement, Jareth felt the fortress itself tighten around him. Walls, eyes, whispers, all amplified, all accusing. He left the great hall, the hum of voices fading behind him, but the unnatural pulse in the stone remained, a low, rhythmic counterpoint to the pounding of his own blood.

He strode toward the council wing, his composure a mask carved from pure necessity. He had to confront Silven. He had to uncover what was written in that damning letter, and he had to protect Miera from the truth the envoy intended to expose. One wrong word, one misstep, and he would not only lose his father's faith. He would ignite a war.

As he walked down the long, echoing stone corridor, his mind a maelstrom of failing strategies and desperate plans, the unnatural thrumming beneath his feet intensified. It was no longer a vague vibration in the floor. It was a distinct, rhythmic beat that seemed to match the pace of his own heart.

For a horrifying, soul-splintering second, he felt it not just in the stone, but in the back of his own mind. A silent, pulsing, insistent presence. It felt like a word, a name, being beaten like a drum against the inside of his skull. A word he could not understand, but knew, with a certainty that stole the breath from his lungs, was not his own.

CHAPTER

THIRTY-ONE

Afternoon light, pale and cold, slanted through the tall windows of her chamber, carving long, distorted shapes from the shadows. The stillness was a lie.

Beneath the distant, muffled murmur of fortress life, a sound ran too steady to be wind, a vibration too rhythmic to be chance. It was a low hum that seemed to rise not from the corridors, but from the very stones of Durevin Hold, a pulse that resonated in the bones of her feet and in the hollow of her chest.

She closed her eyes, standing motionless in the center of the room. The pulse from the mountain's heart matched her own for a moment, a steady thrum against her ribs, and then it overtook her, a deep, resonant beat that was both alien and intimately familiar. It was the echo of her own unmaking.

The fortress, whose magical stability had been unknowingly tethered to the suppression of her identity, now resonated with her unbinding. She had cut the thread, and the very foundation of Durevin Hold, a fortress carved from the Ironridge Bluffs, was screaming its dissent. The realization sent a chill through her, colder than any draft from the window.

The sensation, insistent and unnerving, drew her to the narrow ebonized writing desk where she had hidden the evidence of her former life. Her fingers, acting on an instinct she did not question, first traced the underside of the main drawer, searching for the telltale catch of a hidden compartment she could not consciously recall. Finding none, she slid the drawer open.

The ciphered notes lay where she had left them. Beside them, the veilstone rested on the dark wood, its silver setting catching a sliver of the weak light. The pendant itself was a void, its crystalline surface dark and absorbing, yet the hum in the chamber intensified the closer she came.

The air around the stone seemed to resist her, shimmering with a faint distortion as if space itself warped in its presence. The metallic scent of ozone, of charged and angry air, pricked at her senses. She reached out, her fingers hesitating an inch from the stone. A strange, palpable energy pushed back against her skin, a physical pressure that warned her away. This was the source of the malady shaking the hold. Of that, she had no doubt.

Before she could retreat, a commotion in the corridor shattered the charged quiet. The sound was a discordant clash of hurried footsteps and panicked, whispering voices that rose and fell like frightened birds. Her training as a spymistress took over. She moved without a sound to the door, pressing her ear against the cold, heavy oak.

A voice, tight with a courtier's practiced fear, hissed, "...the king has summoned them. The prince and the Avenali envoy. To the council wing. Now."

"Is it the tremors?" another voice asked, thin with alarm. "The lights in the lower vaults..."

"It is more than that," the first voice cut in, sharp and certain. "The envoy. They say he forced the king's hand."

The voices faded as the men scurried away, their fear a lingering stain in the air. Miera pulled back from the door. Her mind, suddenly sharp and clear, assembled the pieces with cold, irrefutable logic. It was not two separate storms breaking at once. It was a single, perfectly orchestrated tempest. Silven had made his move, provoking a confrontation with the king. And her own act of reclamation, the discarding of the veilstone, had unleashed a power that was now shaking the fortress to its core.

Her first instinct was a deeply ingrained command to vanish. To fade into the shadows, to protect herself, to observe and to wait. It was the cautious, pragmatic response of a spy caught behind enemy lines, a piece on a board suddenly illuminated by a hostile light.

But as the rhythmic pulse in the floor grew stronger, resonating through her bones as if urging her toward the conflict, she understood that passivity was no longer an option. Her silence, her hiding, was a greater danger now than any action. It was her awakening that was causing this chaos. She had a responsibility to it, and to the innocents caught in the path of its unfolding.

She had to unlearn the instinct to retreat. Composure, she reminded herself, was armor. She had worn it her entire life, a shield of elegant calm that disguised the mind of a spymistress. She would wear it now. She smoothed the fabric of her borrowed Vertharian gown, a garment that felt like a costume for a part she was no longer playing, and wrapped that ingrained stillness around herself like a familiar cloak.

When she stepped into the corridor, the fortress seemed alive with a malevolent energy. Shadows in the corners deepened and stretched as if reaching for her. The oil-fed sconces on the walls guttered wildly, their flames bending and twisting with each low, gut-wrenching tremor that rolled through the stone. Servants huddled in alcoves, their faces white with terror, whispering of curses, of ghosts, of magic long thought dead. They saw an earthquake. Miera knew it was an unbinding.

She navigated the escalating chaos with a calm that felt both natural and utterly false, a lifetime of practice made manifest. She kept to the less-traveled service corridors where she could, her movements fluid and silent, a ghost in a fortress that was beginning to remember her name. The hum that had begun as a whisper in her chamber now roared in her skull, a deafening, insistent beat that was the sound of a cage breaking apart from within.

By the time she reached the upper level of the council wing, she felt the vibration in her teeth. The air was thick and heavy, pressing in on her like a physical weight. She found the narrow, arching doorway to the gallery that overlooked the council chamber. It was a place for unseen observation, a relic of a more paranoid architectural style, and it was blessedly empty.

She slipped inside, the darkness a welcome shroud. Creeping forward to the polished wood of the balustrade, her fingers gripped it as another tremor shook the walls. Below her, the stage was set. The great ironwood table was a dark, forbidding line dividing the room. King Halric sat at its head, a figure of granite and fury, his face a thunderous mask of royal displeasure. Jareth stood slightly behind him, his posture rigid, his princely attire a poor disguise for the desperate tension in his shoulders. On the opposite side stood Silven Drael, his expression a study in composed, triumphant satisfaction. He had played his hand, and the board was now his.

The voices from below were sharp, indistinct, the words lost to the distance but the venom clear. It was a confrontation of kings and princes, of spies and manipulators. As she watched, the low, rhythmic hum that had followed her through the fortress built to a crescendo. It filled the gallery, the air, her very bones, a vibration so powerful it seemed the world was about to tear itself apart.

Then, it peaked. And collapsed.

The roaring hum vanished, plunging the world into a profound, suffocating silence. The vibration in the stone ceased. The argumentative voices from below were cut off mid-word. The wild dance of the torchlight stabilized into an unnatural stillness. Everything stopped. It was a silence so absolute, so void of life, that its presence was more terrifying than any sound. The entire fortress, from its deepest dungeons to its highest spires, seemed to be holding a single, indrawn breath, waiting. Miera stood frozen in the gallery, her own heart a silent drum in the terrifying, bone-deep stillness, staring down at the confrontation that had just been swallowed by a quiet more dangerous than any storm.

THIRTY-TWO

The council chamber was oppressively still, a sealed tomb where the air itself was a relic. Light slanted through the high windows, falling in pale, indifferent bars across the long, polished surface of the ironwood table. A faint, persistent hum vibrated up from the very stone of the fortress, a low, dissonant chord Jareth felt more in his bones than his ears. It was the only stirring thing in a room carved from silence and royal will.

His father, King Halric, sat at the head of the table, a figure of granite authority. His expression was a void, a mask of cold composure that concealed the simmering rage Jareth knew lay just beneath. Silven stood opposite him. His posture was a study in relaxed patience, his smile as composed and elegant as it was predatory. He was a man who enjoyed the slow, methodical dissection of his rivals, and Jareth was the specimen on the table.

Jareth stood slightly behind his father's chair, his

posture rigid. He clasped his hands behind his back, forcing a stillness his blood refused to obey. The fine wool of his princely attire felt abrasive against his skin. Every nerve was tuned to the envoy's next word, every instinct screaming that this was the final move in a game he had already lost.

Silven began with a masterpiece of diplomatic cruelty. He offered courteous apologies for the unavoidable confusion that had gripped Durevin Hold. His voice was silk over steel, a soft, melodic tone that made the veiled threats all the sharper.

He spoke of misplaced trade records, of inconsistencies in royal correspondence, of the unfortunate and unsettling tremors that had disturbed the court's peace. Each phrase was a careful, deliberate circle, spiraling ever closer to the one truth Jareth could not allow him to speak.

Then, he spoke it.

"And, of course," Silven murmured, his gaze flicking to the assembled advisors before settling on the king, "the matter of the woman. The one of Cortheni bearing."

The chamber, already silent, somehow stilled further. The hum from the stone seemed to deepen, its dissonance sharpening. Jareth's own pulse thundered in his ears, a frantic, trapped drumbeat. This was the precipice.

His father's gaze, sharp and cold as a blade, shot to him. It was a silent, brutal command. Deny it. Fix it.

Jareth stepped forward, his movements measured, his face a mask of practiced calm. "The envoy's information is speculative, at best," he said. His voice was steady, betraying none of the chaos churning within him. "We have no evidence to support such a claim."

The words were cinders on his tongue, a worthless defense he was sworn to mount. He knew, as did every man in the room, that it was a parry both weak and desperate.

Silven's smile widened, a slow, satisfying curve of his lips. He had anticipated the denial. He had counted on it. "Evidence," he mused softly, as if the word itself were a curious trinket. "Of course."

With a grace that was almost contemptuous, he produced a scroll. This was not the formal Avenali document he had presented earlier. This was older, the parchment aged to the color of bone, a Cortheni vellum far finer than Verthar's coarse sheepskin. He broke the wax seal with a delicate, deliberate snap and unfurled the scroll upon the table.

A collective, sharp intake of breath rippled through the gathered advisors. There, embossed in faded gold leaf, was the unmistakable royal crest of Corthen. The coiled hawk, proud and regal. It was proof, stolen from their own archives. Proof Jareth could not refute.

As if in response, the hum vibrating through the fortress intensified. On a nearby sideboard of petrified ironwood, a set of hammered silver goblets began to tremble. They were spoils from a conquered northern province, a testament to Verthar's might, now shivering at an unseen power. Their faint, high-pitched ringing became a counterpoint to the deep, resonant groan from the stone.

Jareth's gaze shot upward. In the high rafters, a

strange, thin light wavered, shifting like heat distortion above a flame. The air grew thick, heavy with the metallic scent of ozone and fear. The magic was unraveling. The fortress was breaking.

He saw it with horrifying clarity. The lie he had constructed to protect Miera was now physically shattering the world around him. The deception he had believed was a shield had become the very weapon that would destroy them all. The fortress, a monument to the stone and secrets of his kingdom, was cracking under the weight of his own falsehoods.

"Jareth."

His father's voice was not a shout. It was worse. It was a low, lethally quiet command that cut through the rising tension like a shard of ice. Halric's face was a mask of cold, absolute fury. He demanded an explanation, a reason for the treachery that now sat exposed on his council table.

Jareth's composure, the carefully constructed armor he had worn his entire life, finally fractured. He hesitated, his mouth opening without sound, his mind a void. The denial was dead. The truth was unspeakable.

Before he could find a single word, a violent, gut-wrenching tremor rolled through the floor, a deep, groaning roar erupted from the very foundations of the hold, and one of the tall, arched windows across the chamber exploded inward. A crystalline spiderweb of cracks erupted into a shower of glass and freezing air.

A fine rain of dust and mortar drifted from the ceiling, coating the polished table and the damning Cortheni scroll in a layer of gray grit. The royal guards moved instinctively, their hands dropping to the pommels of their longswords, their oaths warring with the shock on their pale faces as they searched for a threat that came from everywhere and nowhere at once.

In that suspended moment of chaos, as the fortress groaned around them, something inside Jareth snapped. It was a bond, a magical tether he had never consciously known was there, a faint, psychic connection forged by the veilstone's enchantment. It broke with a silent, visceral recoil. In its place, a new awareness flooded him. He could feel her. Miera. Seraya. She was near. Not as a thought or a worry, but as a tangible presence, a beacon of raw, untethered power pulsing within the fortress walls.

His entire world narrowed to a single, desperate point. The political ruin, his father's wrath, the court's judgment, it all faded into meaningless noise. Silven's look of quiet, triumphant victory was irrelevant. The only thing that mattered was her.

The king rose to his feet, his voice booming over the chaos. "Clear this chamber! Now!"

Jareth obeyed, his movements stiff and automatic. As he strode from the shattered council chamber, leaving the ruin of his own making behind, he knew his only goal was to reach her. He had to find her before his father's guards or Silven's agents could. He had to protect her not from the truth, but from the consequences of it.

As he stepped into the corridor, the resonant hum that had plagued him for days was no longer a vague vibration in the stone. It followed him, a clear, magnetic thread of magic pulling him forward. It was a direction. A supernatural beacon calling him toward the heart of the storm. Toward her.

He was not the only one moving. Behind him, he could hear his father's fury finally unleashed, a torrent of orders to his personal guard. Ahead, the triumphant Silven was now free to act. The race had begun.

CHAPTER

THIRTY-THREE

The first tremor struck from a depth of profound, unnatural stillness. The quiet that had swallowed Durevin Hold did not break. It shattered. A violent vibration ripped through the stone beneath her feet, a low, guttural snarl from the bones of the fortress. She was thrown against the polished wood of the gallery's balustrade, the impact a sharp protest in her ribs.

Below, the council chamber became a tableau of frantic motion, courtiers lurching from their seats, their shouts a distant, inconsequential sound. The true storm was not in the room. It was inside her.

The vibration was a key turning in a lock that had been rusted shut for months. It thrummed with a pulse she recognized with a terrible, blinding certainty, a rhythm that matched the frantic beat of her own heart, now magnified and echoed by the foundational stone of the keep. In the corridor behind her, the torches in their iron sconces did not simply waver.

Their flames bent and writhed, drawn toward her as if by a sudden, violent inhalation. A raw, untethered power, her own, was surging through the very arteries of the fortress.

She had to move. The instinct was an imperative, a command from a self she did not know. Pushing away from the balustrade, she ran. The corridor pitched like the deck of a ship caught in a gale, the flagstones heaving in sickening waves that threatened to throw her from her feet.

Servants scattered before her, their panicked cries about a quake, about curses, about some long-dead god's displeasure, were meaningless against the roaring hum that had taken root in her skull. It was the sound of her own mind tearing itself open.

Memory did not return. It invaded. It was no gentle tide but a brutal, agonizing flood that scoured the empty spaces of her mind. Faces materialized behind her eyes, sharp and clear as cut glass. The calculating smiles of diplomats in the gilded, treacherous halls of Avenal.

Her own hand, steady and sure, pressing a warm wax seal onto a decree, the scent of melting beeswax and parchment filling the air. She felt the cool, misty caress of Corthen's forests on her skin and tasted the air of the Vale of Tears, heavy with the phantom scent of ozone and wet stone.

A name tolled within her, a sound that was also a memory, a physical weight that settled into her bones. *Seraya.*

She stumbled, her hand lashing out to brace herself

against a heavy tapestry. It depicted a Vertharian king from a harsher age, a ruler famed for solidifying the kingdom's creed of *Rule by Steel and Sovereignty*. The image of a crown, cold and heavy, blazed in her mind.

And with it came understanding, sharp and absolute. The veilstone Jareth had given her was never a charm to quiet her thoughts. It was a leash on her memories, meticulously crafted by a court mage with a flexible conscience. It had reinforced the veil already upon her, the herbal suppression she had read about in that folklore book had been no myth. Someone had dosed her long before he found her in the forest, and Jareth's pendant had simply maintained the prison another had built.

It was designed to contain not just her memories, but the inherent, sovereign power she carried in her blood, a power the very stones of this fortress now seemed to recognize. The unbinding had set that power loose, and the keep itself was convulsing in response to the presence of its equal.

She reached the gallery overlooking the council chamber just as the great doors below burst open. Guards spilled into the corridor, half dragging, half supporting stunned courtiers who fled from a storm of noise and falling debris. A thick pall of fine grit rained from the ceiling, obscuring the scene in a choking haze.

Through the chaos, she saw Jareth. His princely coat was torn at the shoulder, his face a mask of pale, stark disbelief as he shouted orders to clear the room, his voice strained and thin. Behind him, King Halric's voice boomed, a thunderous, impotent rage that no one obeyed.

Near a shattered window, his elegant envoy's attire filmed with grit, stood Silven of Avenal. His face showed no fear. It was alight with a terrible, triumphant comprehension. He had orchestrated this.

He had played his game of whispers and provocations, prodding and probing at the foundations of her fragile reality until the lie broke. He was reveling in the destruction he had wrought. His gaze lifted, a predator's sharp focus, and found hers across the churning chaos.

That silent, victorious stare was the final key. The last dam in her mind did not break. It was obliterated.

The truth crashed through her, a wave of such immense, soul-crushing weight it drove her to her knees. She was not Miera, the ghost Jareth had named her. She was Seraya, Crown Princess of Corthen, regent-in-waiting, and her kingdom's Grand Spymistress. She remembered her coronation, the weight of the silver circlet on her brow, her father's hand a steady warmth on her shoulder.

She remembered the secret negotiations, the exhausting nights spent drafting the Accord of Kinsholm, a fragile pact signed on neutral ground, designed to prevent the very war Jareth's father had been planning all along. Halric had broken it. He had ordered her ambush in the Forest of Hollow Echoes, the overwhelming assault of veilmancy that had shattered her mind and stolen her life.

And Jareth. He had found her in that forest, a broken thing with no name. And he had let it happen. He had bound her in ignorance, cloaked her in the beautiful lie of Miera, and held her captive with his gentle, devastating kindness. Every soft word had been a bar on her cage. Every moment of shared quiet, a turn of the lock.

The only sound that filled the world was the resonance of her own name, a name whispered by every straining stone and groaning timber in Durevin Hold. The fortress, a place built on the brutal strength of Vertharian sovereignty, seemed to feel the presence of another, older claim to power.

The very stones, hewn from the Ironridge Bluffs, were rejecting the lie of Halric's rule in the face of her own. The pressure built, an agonizing pain splitting through her temples as the last of her power, her memory, her very identity, surged free. She gripped the balustrade, gasping as the world dissolved into light.

A blinding, silent flash of white light burst from her, carrying a force that felt final and undeniable. Whatever falsehood had been anchored at the fortress's core shattered in its wake. The roaring hum in her skull vanished. The tremors stopped.

When her vision cleared, she was still on her knees in the gallery. The fortress trembled with faint aftershocks, settling around her like a great beast sighing after a fever. Below, the council chamber was a ruin.

The great ironwood table, a massive thing carved from the petrified trunk of a single colossal tree, was split down the middle. It lay buried under a thick shroud of pulverized stone and fractured glass from the high, shattered windows. The stolen Cortheni scroll, unrolled by Silven as his final gambit, lay half buried in the debris, its proud crest mocking the devastation.

Through the haze of settling grit, Jareth looked up. His eyes, those pale Vertharian eyes, found hers. For a single, eternal heartbeat, everything between them was laid bare. The truth. The guilt. The sickening realization that every tender moment between them had been built on a lie. And above it all, the profound, unforgiveable betrayal.

She saw it then, in the utter devastation on his face. It was not the malice of a captor, not the cold calculation of an enemy. It was something worse. The arrogance of a man who had decided what she was allowed to know about her own life. Who had looked at her every day and chosen the lie.

The knowledge hit like a blade between her ribs—and then the fire came. Not grief. Not sorrow. Rage. Cold at first, then building, a fury so vast it threatened to tear her apart from the inside. Every gentle word he had ever spoken was a lie. Every touch, every reassurance, every moment she had trusted him, and all of it was built on the foundation of her stolen life.

She needed to decide what to do. Seraya of Corthen, was not a merciful woman. She would have used this moment, this shattered chamber, as a weapon. Miera was a ghost, a fiction built on stolen memories and lies.

That woman's tenderness had been a cage. Her tentative affection for Jareth had been cultivated like a crop, and he had been the farmer, tending her ignorance, harvesting her gratitude. No more. The bars of her cage were visible now, and so was the man who had forged them. She saw him for what he really was: her enemy. The Night Veil did not forgive. The Princess of Corthen did not forget. And the woman who contained them both would make him understand exactly what he had taken from her.

Her eyes burned, but she would not weep. Would not give him that. If tears came, they would come later, alone, in some dark place where no enemy could witness. Here, in this ruined chamber with his pale eyes fixed on her face, she would show him nothing but the steel he had forged by breaking her.

The heavy sound of armored boots echoed from the corridor below. The first of the king's guards rushed into the ruined chamber, their swords drawn. Halric's voice thundered again, demanding order, demanding answers.

Seraya rose to her feet. Her limbs felt steady, imbued with a cold and killing purpose. She looked down one last time at Jareth's upturned, guilt-stricken face. Let him see what lived behind her eyes now—not the bewildered gratitude of the woman he had caged, but the patient fury of the one he had set free.

She would remember this moment. She would remember the shape of his remorse. And when the time came to repay him for what he had done, she would make certain he remembered it too.

The fortress was in chaos. It was the perfect cover. She moved through corridors choked with panicked servants and shouting guards, all of them rushing toward the council wing. None of them paid attention to the woman walking calmly in the opposite direction. Before she fled entirely, she made three stops, each executed with the precision of a lifetime's training.

She went to the kitchens first, where she slipped

through the chaos of cooks preparing remedies for the injured. She filled a leather satchel with hard cheese, dried meat, and a waterskin—provisions for three days if she rationed carefully. Next, she went to the stables, where she did not take a horse. It would have been too conspicuous, and made her too easy to track. But she did take a farrier's hoof pick that would serve as a lockpick in desperate circumstances, and a coiled length of rope from a groom's kit.

Finally, she hurried to the west tower's abandoned guardroom. She had noticed weeks ago that someone had left an oiled travel cloak hanging on a peg, forgotten and unclaimed. She donned it now, its dark wool swallowing her silhouette. The eastern postern gate was unmanned, both guards had been pulled to reinforce the council wing.

She slipped through the narrow opening, pressed herself into the shadow of the outer wall, and was gone before anyone thought to look. Preparation. Observation. Patience. Miera had gathered the intelligence without knowing why. Seraya used it to vanish into the night.

THIRTY-FOUR

Smoke, acrid and bitter, still fouled the stone corridors hours after the silent detonation of light. It was the ghost of a power for which Verthar had no name, a lingering stain of scorched magic and shattered deceit. The council chamber had been sealed, its great ironwood doors barred, its fractured windows crudely boarded against the biting wind. Behind that barrier lay a tomb of ash, glass, and the tattered remnants of Jareth's authority.

He walked through the ruin of his own making, his boot heels sharp and solitary in the oppressive quiet. Guards, their faces pale beneath their helms, moved like specters through the upper halls, their movements stiff and uncertain.

They collected fragments of burnt parchment and bagged shards of stained glass, sealing evidence behind wax and silence. But the truth was not a thing to be swept into a sack and burned. It was in the very air. It was in the unnatural stillness of a fortress that had, only yesterday, thrummed with life.

The pulse was gone. The vibrant, rhythmic hum that had grown from a whisper to a roar had vanished completely, leaving a profound and unnerving emptiness. Jareth felt the loss not as an absence of sound but as an absence of life. Her life. The very stones seemed to mourn her departure. He passed a long tapestry depicting the Vertharian conquest of the Sunstone Coast; the black falcon of his house now seemed a vulgar predator, its victory rendered meaningless in the profound silence.

Lord Rilen followed at a distance, his captain's armor gleaming even in the dim, smoky light. His usual composure was shaken, his face a mask of grim duty as he issued Jareth's orders in his stead. Close the outer gates. Double the patrols on the ramparts. Question every servant, every courtier. Contain the chaos. But the chaos was not in the corridors. It was in the cold, dead air.

The report came an hour after the detonation: the eastern postern gate had been found unguarded, both sentries having abandoned their post to respond to the crisis. A travel cloak was missing from the west tower guardroom. Food had been taken from the kitchens. She had not fled in panic. She had executed a tactical withdrawal with the precision of a trained operative.

The official explanation they gave the locals, that a localized tremor, a structural failure in the ancient stone foundations, satisfied no one who had been in that chamber. They had all felt the pulse of power, had seen the light erupt from the gallery where she stood. The court mages were already whispering of sovereign magic, of bloodline abilities that had not manifested in generations. Archmage Lyren had examined the blast pattern and gone pale, refusing to commit his findings to writing.

Royal resonance, he had muttered, the words barely audible. *The stones recognized her.* Jareth had silenced him with a look that promised consequences. His father demanded answers Jareth could not give without revealing everything—that the woman they had kept captive was not merely a Corthen noblewoman but royalty, that her awakening had been felt by the very foundations of Durevin Hold.

So he deflected, obfuscated, buried the truth beneath layers of plausible denial. Declared the wing structurally unsound and sealed it for repairs. But the questions would not stop. The fortress itself seemed to remember what had happened, its stones humming with a residual charge that made the hair stand up on passing servants' arms. The truth was written in the cracks that now webbed the council chamber walls, and no amount of mortar could hide it forever.

Jareth found himself standing in her abandoned chamber in the west tower, though he could not recall giving the order for his feet to carry him there. The room was cold, the hearth long dead, her scent already fading from the linens. He searched without knowing what he sought, some trace of her, some proof she had been real and not a fever dream that had burned through his life and left only ash. It was in her old chamber, when he returned there later, that he found it.

Beneath a loose floorboard near the washstand, his fingers closed around a small, leather-bound journal. Its pages were filled with her careful script, dreams recorded in trembling detail, observations about the fortress and its rhythms, questions she had been too afraid to ask aloud. He read her words by candlelight, each entry a dagger to his conscience. She had fought against the cage he built for her mind, even when she did not understand what she was fighting.

The veilstone had dulled her memories, but it had not stopped her mind from trying to force the memories to the surface. That spirit had been scratching at the walls of her prison long before she remembered why she needed to escape.

His father found him in the corridor overlooking the ruined wing. King Halric was not a man given to overt displays of fury. His rage was a cold, compressed thing, a killing pressure that warped the space around him. The silver embroidery on his high-collared coat caught the weak light, glinting like shards of ice. He did not shout. He did not need to.

"You have brought shame and weakness into my house," Halric said, his voice a low, gravelly rumble more terrifying than any scream. He gestured with a dismissive flick of his wrist toward the sealed chamber. "An Avenali viper makes a mockery of our security, and a foreign witch tears down my walls. All while my heir stands by and watches."

Jareth listened, his gaze fixed on the boarded windows of the council chamber. The accusations washed over him.

Negligence. Treason. Sentiment. He had heard the words before, but they now carried the weight of irrefutable truth. He did not offer a defense. What defense was there? He had set every piece on the board and then watched as she had swept them all aside.

"The reports from the gate captains confirm it," Halric continued, his eyes like chips of flint. "There was a coordinated distraction at the southern postern. A supply cart, a fire. In the confusion, a small, cloaked party slipped out. She had help. Your precious, unidentified woman was a spy with a network already in place, waiting for her."

Jareth's blood ran cold. He had imagined a desperate, solitary flight into the wilderness. But an organized extraction meant allies. It meant a strategic withdrawal. She was not simply a princess who had remembered herself. She was a spymistress returning to her command, her purpose sharpened by his betrayal. The game had not ended; it had merely moved to a new, larger board where he was no longer a player but a target.

"Find who helped her," Halric commanded, his voice dropping to a near whisper, a sound more dangerous than his rage. "Find the leak in our walls. Find a scapegoat. I want a head on a spike by week's end. The court needs to see that weakness is purged with steel. Erase this failure, Jareth. Erase her."

The command tatum so devoid of humanity, that it broke something deep within him. For his entire life, Jareth had tried to be the son his father wanted, a prince of iron and calculation. He had lied, manipulated, and caged an innocent woman in pursuit of that ideal.

Now, standing in the wreckage of that ambition, he felt a profound, soul-deep revulsion. His father was not asking for justice. He was ordering another murder to cover the first. The role of the ruthless prince, a costume he had worn for so long it had nearly fused to his skin, suddenly felt like a stranger's clothes.

When Halric finally stormed away, leaving Jareth with the suffocating weight of his command, the fortress's silence pressed in. Erase her. The words echoed in the empty hall, a final, damning instruction for the man he was supposed to become.

He turned away. The instinct for control that had guided his every action had been scoured away by fire and light, leaving only a hollow, aching guilt. He had to understand. He had to face the full scope of what he had done.

He walked to her chambers. The journey was a pilgrimage of shame, each step a confirmation of his crime. The guards posted at her door stood aside without a word, their eyes averted as if his disgrace were a contagion.

The room was just as she had left it. A book, *A History of Vertharian Court and Culture*, lay on the bedside table, a silent accusation. A dress of dark wool was folded neatly on a chair. The air was still, holding the faint, spectral scent of her, of soap and ink and a quiet, stubborn resilience.

The emptiness was a physical presence, a palpable ache in the center of his chest. Tucked between the pages of the book, he saw the deep red petals of a pressed Emberrose, a flower he had once given her in the gardens.

A symbol of enduring love, he had told her. The lie was a bitter acid in his throat.

His gaze fell on the narrow ebonized writing desk. The top drawer was slightly ajar. He moved toward it, pulled it open. Inside, nestled among a few pages of ciphered notes she must have written in her final days of remembering, rested the veilstone.

It was dim. The brilliant light that had once pulsed within it was now a faint, milky glow, like the last ember of a dying fire. Its magic was broken, expended. But it was not dead. He lifted it carefully. The silver was cold against his skin, but the stone itself held a faint, residual warmth. The moment his fingers closed around the pendant, a weak, rhythmic hum returned, not to the fortress, but directly into his hand, a heartbeat fading after a long and terrible battle.

And with it came the echoes of feelings and emotions. A confusing, overwhelming flood of sensation and emotion that was not his own poured into him. The pure terror of waking in a strange land, surrounded by enemies posing as saviors.

The suffocating weight of a kindness that was also a cage. The sharp, disorienting ache of a memory trying to break through a psychic wall. The chilling realization of being observed, tested, and manipulated by the one person offering safety.

He felt the cold triumph in Silven's gaze as the emissary played his final card. He felt the crushing return of her own name, Seraya, a key turning in a lock that opened not a door but a wound. He felt the agony of a trust so completely betrayed.

He saw, through her eyes, his own face. His own gentle lies. His own calculated reassurances. He felt her grief, her rage, her profound, shattering disillusionment. He had told himself the lies were a mercy.

He had convinced himself that ignorance would keep her safe, a shield he had forged for her protection. But standing in the hollow ruin of her stolen life, holding the very tool of her imprisonment, he finally knew the truth.

He had not protected her. He had caged her. The mercy he had offered was a poison, a slow, gentle erosion of her very self. The realization did not come as a thought. It came as a physical recoil, a pain so profound it stole the air from his lungs and sent him stumbling back from the desk.

Guilt was too small a word. This was a wound, deep and septic, a corruption of his own soul. He clutched the veilstone in his fist, his breath coming in ragged, shallow gasps. The polished floor seemed to tilt beneath his feet.

Rilen entered the chamber, his expression carefully neutral. He took in the scene at a glance. Jareth's stricken face, the open drawer, the faint light of the pendant clutched in his prince's hand.

"My prince?" he asked quietly, his voice a steady anchor in the swirling chaos of Jareth's mind.

Jareth held out the veilstone, his hand trembling. "Take this," he said, his voice raw, scraped clean of all artifice. "Secure it. Under lock and seal. It is evidence."

Rilen's eyes widened slightly, the only break in his

soldier's composure, but he did not question the order. He took the pendant with a gloved hand and carefully placed it into a sturdy oilcloth pouch at his belt. "It will be done."

As his cousin left, Jareth walked to the window. He stared out at the snow-dusted peaks of the Shardspine Mountains, a jagged knife-edge against the bruised twilight sky. Somewhere beyond them lay Corthen.

Somewhere beyond them was Seraya. No longer hidden, no longer his to protect. The woman he had wronged was now his enemy, and he had personally handed her every reason to burn his kingdom to the ground.

Later that night, he stood on the highest rampart of Durevin Hold. The cold night wind whipped at his somber, unadorned coat, a brutal, cleansing force. The sky was a vast sheet of black velvet, mercilessly clear and studded with stars like chips of ice.

He had defied his father, not with words, but with inaction. There would be no scapegoat. There would be no purge. The failure was his, and he would bear it.

He closed his eyes, the scent of snow and smoke filling his senses. He whispered a vow, not to the gods he did not believe in, not to the kingdom he had failed, but to the woman he had lost. A vow only the wind would hear.

He would find her. Not to reclaim her. Not to explain or to justify. He would stand before her, offer her the unvarnished truth, and accept whatever judgment she saw fit to deliver. Even if that judgment was his own death.

As he stood there, a solitary figure against the cold expanse of the night, a faint tremor vibrated through the stones beneath his feet. This was a soft, rhythmic pulse, no longer erratic but deliberate, a cadence impossibly old. It was not an echo of Seraya's pain, nor the fortress's collapse. It was something new. Something a part of the world, woken from a long slumber. And it felt as if it were waiting.

~

Six Days Later

The safehouse was a shepherd's cottage in the Thornwood, so unremarkable that

Vertharian patrols had passed it twice without a second glance. Seraya had found it not through memory—the Night Veil's network had never extended this far north—but through the old signs. A chalk mark on a boundary stone. A particular arrangement of rocks at a crossroads. The signals that Corthen's loyalists used to guide their own home.

The woman who opened the door was gray-haired and sharp-eyed, a farmer's widow to any casual observer. She had taken one look at Seraya's face and burst into tears.

"Your Highness," she had whispered. "We thought—everyone thought—"

"I know." Seraya had allowed herself to be drawn inside, to accept the thin soup and rough bread that were all the widow could offer. "I need to send a message to Mirenweald. To whoever remains of my mother's council."

"It will take time. The networks are scattered, the routes watched."

"Then we begin now."

She did not let herself think of Jareth. Of the look on his face when the truth had shattered the lie between them. Of the part of her—Miera's part, the part that had loved him—that still ached with his absence.

There would be time for grief later. For now, there was only the mission.

Far to the north, in a fortress gone cold with her absence, a prince stared at a hidden journal and made a decision that would damn him in his father's eyes forever.

The game was no longer about survival. It was about redemption—and the only path to redemption led through treason.

THE STORY CONTINUES

The story continues in book three, *THE CROWN BETWEEN US,* coming to Amazon soon.

She betrayed him. He lied to her. Now fate forces them back into the same dangerous game.

Seraya returns to Verthar Palace wearing a servant's disguise and carrying enough guilt to sink a ship. Months ago, she fled after Prince Jareth discovered the woman in his bed was a spy stealing his secrets. She used him. He deceived her about who she really was. They destroyed each other with equal precision.

Coming back is reckless. Coming back is necessary. And coming back means risking everything—including her heart.

Jareth haunts every corridor, his presence a constant

threat to her cover and her composure. The man who once held her through the night now rules a kingdom on the brink of war, unaware his greatest enemy is three doors down scrubbing floors. She tells herself the ache in her chest is just guilt. The way her pulse races when she hears his voice is just fear of discovery.

She's lying again. She's always been better at lying to him than to herself.

The palace remembers traitors. Her heart remembers everything else.

Can love survive when built on lies? Or will the truth destroy what betrayal couldn't?

OTHER FLORID ROMANCE BOOKS

To be notified of new releases and special promotions from Florid Romance, please join our email list:

https://floridromance.lmbpn.com/about/sign-up-for-our-newsletter/

For a complete list of books published by Florid Romance please visit our website:

https://floridromance.lmbpn.com/

BOOKS BY RIVER TATUM

The Dating Diary

One is too Many BF's (Book 1)

Two Many Choices (Book 2)

Three is a Crowd (Book 3)

Four is a Disaster (Book 4)

The Dreamweaver's Pact

Whispering Dreams (Book 1)

Shattered Nightmares (Book 2)

Dawn Awakening (Book 3)

The Elemental Chronicles

Fire and Water (Book 1)

Earth and Sky (Book 2)

Chaos and Harmony (Book 3)

The Cursed Worm Court

The Healer and The Dragon (Book 1)

The Dragon's Bargain (Book 2)

Vows and Wings of Flame (Book 3)

Marked By Magic

Spellcasters (Book 1)

Tides of Fate (Book 2)

Final Spell (Book 3)

Crown of Lies

Princess with No Name (Book 1)

Prince of Shadows (Book 2)

The Crown Between Us (Book 3)

BOOKS BY MICHAEL ANDERLE

Sign up for the LMBPN email list to be notified of new releases and special deals!

https://lmbpn.com/email/

For a complete list of books by Michael Anderle, please visit:

www.lmbpn.com/ma-books/

CONNECT WITH MICHAEL ANDERLE

Website: lmbpn.com

Email List: michael.beehiiv.com/

Facebook: Facebook.com/LMBPNPublishing

Twitter/X: Twitter.com/MichaelAnderle

Instagram: Instagram.com/lmbpn_publishing/

Bookbub: Bookbub.com/authors/michael-anderle